ALLURE

A Watcher Series Prequel

ROBIN WOODS

Second Edition

Epic Books Publishing

Lead Editor: Beth Braithwaite
Additional Editing: Alexis S. and James Stewart

Copyright First Edition © 2013 Robin Woods
Edition 1.5 © 2022

Cover Design by Vera Walker

Summary: As America tries to forget the horrors of the Great War by embracing jazz, flappers, and the speakeasy, the Watchers remain vigilant by protecting the innocent and maintaining order among the Immortals—including a powerful line of Seers who are all but extinct. But the real horror is just beginning. When George Yates is ordered to escort the beautiful Rosemond Le Clair to safety, he finds himself in the middle of an ancient feud that demands her blood. Without the Watchers' help, he must struggle to protect the last remaining daughter of the Le Clair family from these dark powers, even as he defies fate itself.

[Fiction-Fantasy, Fiction-Young Adult, Fiction-New Adult, Fiction-Paranormal, Fiction-Vampires]

Paperback ISBN-10: 0985454288
Paperback ISBN-13: 978-0-9854542-8-9
Hardback with Dustcover ISBN: 9781941077245
Hardback Laminated Case ISBN: 9781941077344

To my "Sweathearts"

Mic & Kris

Thanks for always being there to back me up.

"Storms make oaks take deeper root."

—George Herbert

CHAPTER 1
OWE ME

October 5ᵗʰ, 1928

ROSEMOND

Everything inside me screamed out against her simple request. Perhaps because there was nothing simple about it. "No, Mother. I won't. I won't do it!"

"You are no longer safe with me, my darling." She looked at me pleadingly, her pale blue eyes threatening to pierce my protestations. She pushed back the dark bangs from my forehead.

Refusing to meet her eyes, I sat abruptly on the edge of my bed and worried the ends of my shawl. The yarn perfectly matched the small blue flecks in the fine wool of my dress. I crossed my feet at the ankles and the new shoes she had given me squeaked on the slick hardwood floor. I was working through each argument I could muster, but defeating them before uttering a sound.

Feeling her eyes on me, I finally whimpered. "I don't want to leave you, Mother."

She was all I had left since my sister had been slain and my father had disappeared. He was dead. I knew it in my heart. Before the Watchers had sent out search parties I knew there was no hope and told my mother as much. She had slapped me in response.

I'd deserved it, not always being as delicate as I should be. Cringing back the memory of that dreadful night, I finally relented and returned her gaze.

"They are sending someone to collect you," she informed me.

"I won't go with whomever it is," I replied, but the ire I had been feeling the moment before was waning.

She sighed. There was a knifelike edge to her voice. "You will, and you will do as he says. I may have a tolerance for your spiritedness, but the Concilium will not. We need them to keep you safe. There is a price on my head and I will not allow you to be found out."

My shoulders sagged. "There is something you are not telling me, mother."

She turned her back to me and started busying herself pulling clothing from the bureau. "We must get you packed. Your escort arrives tonight."

I glared at the back of her head. "Tonight! Who is it? One of those cold-hearted Slayers or some stuffy old Watcher with hair growing out his ears?"

"Rosemond, please. You must be civil. I don't know who exactly, but I heard Parsons say something about Yates's son. If that is the case, he couldn't possibly be more than ten years your senior."

"Then you are acquainted with his father, Mr. Yates?"

"Many years ago. He was an honorable man." Light sparked in her eyes and she grinned. "Surely his son will have a perfectly respectable mole growing in the middle of his face, probably hairy. I'm sure he's much too young for it to be sprouting from his ears."

I grinned back at her, unable to maintain my scowl. "So what are you not telling me, mother?"

All the levity of the moment before drained away. She leaned forward, supporting herself with her hands braced on my dresser. She exhaled a long, steady breath, keeping her back to me. When she responded there was a faint quiver in her always-steady voice. "When you depart, you will never see me again."

GEORGE

I strode into the room a little more dramatically than necessary and flopped down onto the captain's chair directly in front of my father's desk.

"How much longer must we stay in this infernal place?" I blew out my breath through my teeth, fluttering the papers in front of me.

Father took longer than necessary to look up at me from the pile of papers that resembled the Leaning Tower of Pisa. He was trying to teach me patience. Though, he seemed to be the only person capable of causing my unbridled impatience.

He cocked his head to the side and chewed on the side of his mouth. "I am leaving on a steamer in two days. You, my son, have been tasked to help with relocating a person of interest."

It took every ounce of my will not to roll my eyes. He hated that. "Father, you can't be serious. Hand holding isn't in my purview."

"This girl needs our protection."

"A girl? As in freckles and pig-tails?"

He raised an eyebrow. "No, a young woman. A Seer."

"You wish me to remain here to escort a fortune teller?" I asked incredulously.

He stood and circled the desk and sat in the chair opposite me. "Son, she is the genuine article. This doesn't leave this room." He paused and shifted in his seat, "She is a member of the Lux Casta."

"I thought they were ancient history, the last of them lost to Madame Guillotine in the 1790s, only to become a fairy tale in Watcher lore."

He gave me a tight lipped smile.

"So. Not just a girl. A royal—a *French* royal!" I let out a single laugh, though there was no humor in it. I narrowed my eyes. "Evans is trying to kill me isn't he?"

He sighed. "She's an American and quite unaware of her heritage. She knows *what* she is and has been trained, but has been given no details."

"These Americans are almost as bad as the French," I grumbled.

"George," he said in warning. "*I* am tasking you—not the Concilium."

I blinked at him for a moment. There was a strain in his voice I hadn't picked up on previously. "I'll do it, but this bloody well better be worth it. If this takes too long, you know what I will be giving up. You will owe me one, Father. More than one."

My father clapped me on the shoulder and stood. He handed me a file. "Of that I am sure. Everything you need will be in the file. Only tell her what is absolutely necessary. Burn it when the details are memorized," he commented with an odd amusement in his tone.

I hate her already.

CHAPTER 2

OH

ROSEMOND

My hand started to ache, and I realized it had been squeezing my father's pocket watch in a closed fist for who knows how long. Releasing my grip, I slid the treasure into the front pocket of my dress hidden underneath the heavy velvet band encircling my hips.

I glanced at my packed bags near the front door, and then at my mother staring out the front window through the lace curtains. The weather had already grown bitterly cold in the evenings. The dry, leafless branches unnerved me as they scraped across the window pane upstairs.

"How much longer?" I asked.

My mother jolted infinitesimally and turned to look at me. The edges of her eyes were red. "Anytime now," she replied, her voice thick.

I wanted to comfort her but was so overwhelmingly angry

that she was sending me away. We'd never been apart for longer than two days during my eighteen years.

"Why 'never,' Mother?" I finally asked, releasing enough of my hurt to speak of something other than the time.

She appeared utterly lost as she gazed at me. "If you are ever able to settle permanently, my contacting you could destroy that. Everything I have done is for a reason. Maybe it was a mistake keeping your heritage from you. But I don't believe so. Rosemond, your birth was at home *for a reason*. We had private tutors for you *for a reason*. All of it was to hide your existence. We tried with your sister, but when the delivery went wrong and your father, he..." She shook her head. "Sometimes a single sheet of paper is all it takes. You need to vanish. *Forever*."

"But—"

She walked over and took my face in her hands. "My dearest one, I do this because I love you. Although, it mustn't feel that way." She paused, "You will forgive me someday."

"Mother, why—"

The squeak of automobile brakes drew our attention. My mother walked through the room and into the entry to the front door. She waited a moment and glanced through the window without disturbing the curtains, dipping her hand into the umbrella holder by the door. Her hand emerged with a gleaming pistol.

I gasped in shock, not knowing if it was caused by the sight of seeing a weapon in my mother's hand or how comfortable she was with it. Her eyes didn't waver from the window. I pressed myself against the far wall, trying to be invisible.

Then, the tense pose she wore leaked from her as she dropped her guard. She didn't turn to look at me. "He really does look like his father." There was a wistfulness to her voice. She must have known this Watcher's father more than she had acknowledged before.

I remained hidden and didn't move from my place against the wall around the corner.

A second later, there was a polite knock at the door, then the wafting sound of the door opening, followed by light foot-steps. He spoke softly to my mother, but I couldn't hear the words, just the base tones of his voice. She must have been closer to the doorway, because I could hear her much more clearly.

"Yes, she is ready," Mother said in response to something my soon-to-be-escort had said.

He spoke again.

"Your father is well?" she asked.

More answering low rumbles.

My mother let out a rather girlish giggle; this irritated me for some reason. I heard a few more words exchanged, and then my name was called.

Unclenching my fists and smoothing down the front of my grey dress, I joined them in the entryway where stood a gentleman bent close enough to whisper to my mother. He was younger than I'd expected, which brought me up short. He couldn't have been more than three or four years older than me.

As he straightened up, the little bit of humor that was on his face drained away, and his expression became unreadable. I suddenly felt self-conscious, which was rare. Averting my eyes, I examined the scuffs on my black Mary Jane shoes to center myself again. And, after a long moment, met his gaze.

There was a stillness about him that was immediately

comforting, yet the penetrating look in his eyes made me feel as if he could see beneath my skin, like he knew my secrets, though I could think of nothing I would ever have need of hiding from a fellow Watcher.

The edge of my lip curled up into an ironic smile. *I suppose this is what people feel like when I look at them, the girl with the piercing, lavender eyes.*

The mist from outside clung to the gentle waves in his medium brown hair. It was cropped short in back, but the front was long enough for tendrils to be hanging into his eyes. For some reason, he hadn't worn his hat to the door; his hair was far too damp to have used it. He was curling the brim of it in his hands.

His face was an odd mixture of features: sharp cheekbones, soft rounded nose, flared jawline, rosy cheeks, and a dimpled chin. A small scar cut through his right eyebrow and abruptly stopped, then picked up again diagonally on the left side of his bottom lip for another inch, just skirting his chin. It caused a small pucker in his generous lower lip. I looked back up at his eyes again, large and hazel with annoyingly thick lashes, realizing I'd been staring at him for far too long without speaking. He looked at me expectantly, but I wasn't sure what I was supposed to say.

My mother finally broke the silence. "Rosemond, this is Mr. Yates. He will be your escort."

He stoically moved forward with his hand extended. "Miss Le Clair, pleased to meet you."

I shook his hand and blurted, "You're British," not knowing why this was shocking. In the network of Watchers we had always been surrounded by people from all over the world.

He raised his eyebrows and parted his lips, as if to speak,

but stopped and looked at me blankly. He turned his head toward my mother. "Zach and Sariel should arrive at any moment."

"A Slayer," I stated, my tone a little sour. All Slayers had angelic names.

Mr. Yates looked at me again, with a smooth expression. "They are both Slayers." When my expression didn't change, he added, "Zachriel."

"Ah," I nodded—an angel name.

Instantly feeling sick, I turned towards the window, hoping that he didn't see the blood drain from my face. If the Concilium was dispatching two Slayers, my mother had seriously downplayed the danger we were in. It was immediate.

Movement outside caught my attention, a dark colored Studebaker parked behind the Model A in which Mr. Yates must have arrived. I turned back to Mr. Yates just as my mother was pointing out my bags. He picked them up and strode outside with them. He was stronger than I would have thought. I watched from the window as he stopped in the middle of the walkway, still holding my bags, and spoke with both of the Slayers who had emerged from the newly arrived motorcar.

One of them was an enormous man with jet-black hair and broad shoulders, large packs of muscles evident, even under his navy blue pea coat. Next to him was a statuesque blonde woman who carried herself with unadulterated confidence. They looked the part of efficient killers, the standard for Slayers.

My negativity towards their kind was unwarranted; these protectors had devoted their lives to guarding humans from malevolent immortals. I knew Slayers had saved the life of my mother more than once.

Maybe I was bitter because they hadn't saved my father or my sister. *Maybe it was simply because they lacked any sort of empathy. As if they were made of metal and clockwork instead of blood and bone.*

THE SLAM OF THE CAR TRUNK AS MR. YATES SQUARED AWAY my belongings broke into my reverie.

I turned towards my mother; she had been watching me. It seemed difficult to press my lips together in some semblance of a smile. Rushing to me, she wrapped me tightly in her arms. She pressed her mouth to my ear and whispered fervently, "Please know I love you and sending you away is as hard for me as it was to lose your father and your sister. Be brave and live a wonderful life, my precious, precious girl." She held me for a long while.

I tried to speak more than once, but the lump in my throat prevented it. Only upon hearing the clearing of a throat in the doorway did she release me. Mr. Yates was standing there awkwardly. "My apologies, but we really need to be leaving. The sun has already set."

"Mother," I whispered, and squeezed her hands.

She shook her head to silence me. "I know, sweetheart." Her eyes were all the forgiveness I needed for being cross and angry with her. "Now *go*."

Mother walked towards the front door and I followed. The twilight landscape was settling into shades of blue. She reached out and took Mr. Yates' hand as if she were going to give him some parting wisdom, but instead she froze in place, her expression strained; she searched his face for a moment then turned her gaze on me.

She gave me a warning look when I opened my mouth again. It was evident that she had seen something, a vision perhaps. She glanced at me once more, then at the door, and turned the rest of the way towards him. "Mr. Yates, this assignment is going to take longer than you think." She sighed.

Before I could beg her not to send me away, I forced myself to move around her towards the door. I stepped outside, but strained to listen. "You take care of her. You have a good heart. I see that, please..." and then the door shut, muffling the rest of the conversation.

I stood awkwardly between the house and the Slayers. They were quite aware of me but did not turn immediately to acknowledge my presence. They were discussing locations on a map. Finally the female addressed me. "Miss, I will accompany you and Mr. Yates for a day or two, until you are clear."

"That will be nice," I said politely. "You are Sariel?"

"Yes, but you may call me Sara." Her eyes were a warm brown, soft in their expression. This was the first time any Slayer had given me permission to use a nickname of any sort. A ghost of a smile crept onto my face.

Bobbing my head slightly, "I would like that." *Maybe it is possible to like a Slayer.*

They stepped aside, allowing me to approach the motorcar without having to walk on the muddy grass.

On the walkway a few yards from the vehicle, I peeped back at the house around Sara and Zach. I could see through the window in the door that my mother was still holding Mr. Yates' hand and speaking fervently to him.

He looked as if she was stacking books on his shoulders,

the weight of them increasing with each item she shared. She had seen something about his future, or perhaps mine, or both. I could see it in the way she held her body.

My impulse was to ask her to stop burdening him. It seemed such an odd urge to protect him. I didn't know him, and he seemed quite capable of taking care of himself.

Feeling uneasy, I glanced at the damp ground and noticed the buckle on my shoes had almost come undone.

Bending to fix it, I felt someone brush past me but didn't bother to look. I assumed it was either Zach or Sariel. The buckle had somehow become twisted and was being stubborn. I took a steadying breath and stood, peering at the house one last time. The blue light of evening had given way to darker tones, and the only illumination spilled from the living room window.

The door was shut, and Zach was making his way to the steps. Sara, who stood watching him, turned slightly towards me.

At that moment, gunshots shattered the still night, and my eyes flew to the muzzle flashes just inside the front door. Immediately, Zach was up the steps, hand reaching for the door. There was another series of shots, and Zach fell to his knees, hand still on the knob. I stood in horrified silence as Zach's chest heaved over and over again. He pulled a dagger from inside his jacket and struggled to stand.

I started to make a break for the house; I opened my mouth to scream, but a smothered "M—" was all that escaped before a hand clamped over my mouth.

An arm went round my waist, pulling me backwards. I stomped my heel on the foot of my captor and elbowed him in the ribs with crushing accuracy.

"It's me," Mr. Yates groaned in my ear, obviously in pain. I stopped fighting but tried to move towards the house again.

He spun me around, pulled me to his side, and held me. His expression was fierce. My eyes went back at the house. Zach had disappeared inside, leaving a trail of blood behind.

Sara was almost inside, but just before she entered, she pointed at us and then at the car. She mouthed the word, "Go!"

Mr. Yates grabbed my hand and didn't let go. He threw open the passenger door and got in, pulling me behind him as he slid across the bench seat into the driver's seat. He let go of my hand and reached over me, pulling the door shut before my brain had caught up with what was happening.

All I could think about was that my mother was in that house. Mr. Yates had fired up the engine, before I could process anymore, and raced into the blackening night.

He pushed the car to its limit for what seemed like an eternity. When the city lights became sparse, he slowed slightly, and when they had long disappeared from the horizon, he pulled into a service station.

Tilting my father's pocket watch towards the window, I noted that it had been a little over an hour since we fled. We sat in silence while a grubby-looking attendant ambled out from an office sandwiched next to a small garage. Mr. Yates rolled down his window. The unpleasant aroma of a hot engine wafted inside.

The attendant placed his hand on the door. His nails were black half-moons, visible even in the dim light. "Yuh like me tuh...fill 'er up?" He scratched his head questioningly, like he wasn't sure why we were there.

"Yes, please."

The attendant nodded and went to work filling the car with gasoline and motor fluids.

I examined Mr. Yates. He was still holding the steering wheel in a vice-like grip, his eyes focused somewhere in the distance. A light sheen of sweat glossed his brow, and his breathing was a little labored. The shoulder of his jacket appeared to be wet, so I cautiously reached out breezing the fabric. He remained unmoved, as if he hadn't been touched. I pulled my hand back and examined the scarlet stains at the tips.

"Mr. Yates?" I kept my voice low so the attendant wouldn't hear.

He broke his stare, turning his head to look at me as if he had forgotten my presence. Everything in his expression was blank, save his eyes. "I'm sorry. We will break protocol soon and inquire about your mother."

"No, it's not that. I mean, yes. Thank you, but...." I shook my head. "You are bleeding." I held up my fingers.

He blinked at me a few times, then studied his shoulder. "Oh. I believe I was shot," he said matter-of-factly, as if he were reading from a grocery list. He was so calm it was unsettling.

Sliding closer to him, I reached out again and prompted him. "Lean forward."

He complied. Blood had run down and soaked his coat clear to the waist. "It came in the front and went straight through," he murmured.

"You are losing a fair amount of blood. We need to get you to a hospital."

"No. Too public. We can't risk it. I'm not sure if they knew we were out there. If we are lucky, they will think it was only Zach and Sariel. But, I don't know."

He obviously wasn't worried about himself for his own sake, so I tried another tactic. "If you are to help me, I need you alive."

"No hospitals."

I bit my lip. "There is no bullet to remove, yes? Do you have any supplies? Something to sterilize the wound, some thread, a needle, something to dull the pain?"

"I have a standard medical kit for field dressings."

The attendant appeared back in the window. "Was seven gallons at twenty-one cents. Thad'll be $1.47, please, sir."

Mr. Yates gingerly reached inside his coat pocket and handed him two dollars. The attendant returned a few moments later with change jingling in his hand. Yates gave him a tip and then dropped the change into his pocket.

He started to reach for the gearshift and winced. "Can you drive?"

I let out a weary laugh. "Lucky for you, my father wanted me to be ready for anything." He started to open his door. "Stop. I'll go around. You slide across. Save your strength."

Quickly moving on our way, I glanced over at him. He was definitely in shock of some sort, though he managed to give me clear directions.

It took a half hour to get to a small apartment stashed away in a bad neighborhood in the next town. I was thankful that it was dark and that I couldn't see the area clearly. He had me retrieve a key from a hidden compartment in the paneling of the house. I grabbed only what was necessary from the car and followed him inside.

He slid heavily into a chair at the tiny café table in what

was supposed to be a kitchen in the one room apartment. Mr. Yates saw the disapproval on my face. "Slayer hideout. Sorry if it isn't up to your standards."

I chose to think that the condescending comment was the pain and shock. "Just relax while I prep the supplies." I unloaded the medical kit and lined up the implements carefully on the table next to him. As quickly as possible I rummaged through the tiny kitchen and set some water to boil.

While I waited on the water, I found some linens in the hall cabinet that could be used to help clean the wound. Picking up the bootleg pint of gin from his bag, I loosed the lid. Sniffing at it, my eyes immediately watered. I thrust it at him. "Drink this."

He grit his teeth as if he was about to protest.

"You don't have a choice."

He glared at me a moment longer, then tipped the bottle to his lips. "Then by your royal decree, let it be so." His body seemed to relax after he had taken several long swigs.

The truth was, I longed to take a swallow to settle my nerves. Somehow, a bullet wound seemed much different than the bone-deep gash my father had once made me sew up on his arm.

I stood next to Mr. Yates' side and examined the wound. Remarkably, most of the bleeding seemed to have stopped, but the moment we peeled his clothing away, it was going to gush. He had been wounded too long ago to soak the shirt off; he needed to be stitched up now. I took a deep breath. "Let's start with your jacket."

He swallowed and looked up at me, his face a mask of control once again. The surliness of a moment ago vanished. I helped ease his jacket off and hung it over a chair, then helped him off with his shirt. It was completely crusted to his body. As I tore it away, a fresh surge of blood flowed from the wound from both the front and back. The metallic smell of it stung my nose. The bullet couldn't have gone through a more perfect place: the right shoulder, beneath the collar bone, missing everything of importance.

I cleaned the area with the hot water and the gin, then went to work. He never made a sound. He trembled a bit, but that was from the shock and quite involuntary. Surely he would have controlled that if he could have. I finished and went to the kitchen sink to scrub the blood from my hands. Afterwards, I sat down in the chair next to him, happy to be sitting.

"Thank you," he said hoarsely. "My apologies. I shouldn't have been unkind to you."

"You saved my life, getting shot in the process. I can afford to give you a little grace."

He focused on me again with that penetrating look of his, and suddenly I felt uncomfortable. I had never before been alone in a room without a chaperone with a boy so close to my age. A good-looking boy. A good-looking boy without his shirt on. I quietly let out a breath and tried not to notice how nice he looked without said shirt. I suddenly felt shamed thinking such things while not knowing if my mother was alive or dead.

I stood abruptly. "What can I get for you? Would you like help putting on a clean shirt?" I offered, wanting to cover him up before I noticed the elegant curve of his collarbone again.

"Burning up. Afraid the davenport is all I require." He stood on unsteady legs.

"Well, hero, you get the bed."

"I can't—"

"You need to be whole and thinking straight tomorrow. I promise as soon as you are well, the bed is mine." I winked at him, then immediately flushed, realizing how that might have sounded flirtatious.

He nodded and weaved his way to the other side of the flat unfazed. I beat him there and pulled the covers of the bed back for him. He eased himself down. I observed the fresh veneer of sweat across his chest from the effort of walking across the room.

I prayed that it was the trauma and not some sort of infection setting in. He watched me as I covered him up with a sheet; his eyes seemed cautious. I gave him a thin smile and made my way to the couch. His lids grew heavy after a short while, and his breath evened out as he drifted off to sleep.

I stared down at my lap. My dress was ruined from blood. My thoughts went to my mother. I realized nothing would ever be the same again.

CHAPTER 3
NEW PLAN

GEORGE

I wanted to jump out of my skin, but instead stilled myself and waited and listened. Cool fingers tentatively touched my forehead and then my cheek, followed by a relieved exhale. At hearing this, the events of the night before came flooding back. I didn't move, didn't open my eyes. "Still alive," I whispered.

Two quick steps backwards. Her voice came out breathy. "Glad to hear it, Mr. Yates," she paused. "Are you in much pain?"

I moved my left arm and fingered the dressing on my right shoulder. "Should be fine," I replied reassuringly, but remained still.

"I would like to look at the wound," she said with a small shake in her voice.

A little humor crept into my voice. "No, you wouldn't."

Her voice was no longer tentative. "No, you are correct. I

don't, but I need you, Mr. Yates. Please sit up so I can check your injury."

Feeling remorse for having upset her, I opened my eyes. She wasn't looking at me; in fact her gaze was studiously away. But her expression wasn't that of being upset, but rather uncomfortable.

Dark, brown hair fell in long waves over slender shoulders, the tips brushing the bend of her elbow of her crossed arms. Her face appeared to be freshly scrubbed—cheeks rosy, and lashes damp. She had changed out of the attire stained with my blood.

I struggled to sit up without vexing my shoulder. When finally seated in an upright position, she returned to my side and pulled up a chair alongside me. She carefully pulled away the layers of cloth with which she had padded the wound.

Again, not looking at me, her eyes were fastened only on the bandages. I could feel her shallow breaths spill over my skin, raising gooseflesh. Her fingers were confident and not at all cautious like I had previously thought. She stood to her feet and returned with some type of poultice or herbal pack on a damp cloth and placed it against both the entrance and exit wounds.

"Where did you get that?" My voice more reproachful than I had meant it to, but she was not to leave the safe house unprotected.

She met my eyes for the first time, her expression offended. "From my bag. I always keep some medicinals with me. My mother—" She stopped short and shook her head, not explaining any further.

I wanted to say something sympathetic, or at least encouraging, about not knowing what had happened to her mother.

But then I realized, she had to have returned to the vehicle alone to fetch her bag. "Don't leave the flat without me." Again, anxiety made me sound like a cad.

She quietly finished wrapping my shoulder, her lips in a hard line, anger marking her movements. When she finally broke the silence, it startled me. "Are we to remain here until you are well?"

"No," I said too harshly. I cringed and softened my voice, "No, another night at most. We will...I..." I didn't know exactly what we were to do. This was not the easy escort which I had been planning. I sighed. "I will devise a new plan. One that avoids getting either of us shot."

She gave me a small smile and retreated to the davenport a couple of meters away, picking up a novel lying down, open-faced on the cushions. My mind was racing. I didn't know if the attack at the house meant that everything in our plan had been compromised. *Is it safe to retrieve the package with her new identities? Should we avoid Boston all together?*

I glanced at Rosemond again. She still looked uncomfortable and a little too interested in her novel. I debated for some long moments whether to ask her the question that had been plaguing me since the previous night. I twisted and untwisted the sheets in my hand until the wrinkles in them were probably permanent.

Clearing my throat, I asked. "Is your mother always right?"

Her shoulders sagged a little. She met my gaze and then dropped her eyes to her lap. "Always." She paused. "Unless one intentionally intervenes, she is invariably correct."

I reached for something peaceful inside me, groping around like one both lost and blind, and kept my face carefully expressionless. If her mother was correct, then she was no more, and this girl sitting before me was the last of her kind.

On my left, she had laid out a clean shirt on the bed for me. Then I noticed there was food on the kitchen table, some biscuits, an apple, and what looked to be figs.

She started speaking in a rush, still not looking at me. "There is a small market a few doors down. I'm sorry. I couldn't find any food, and you need to keep up your strength. And I didn't go through all your things. I presumed you would have a weapon somewhere in your bags. I took your revolver with me. I know how to use it. It's daylight. I believed the risk would be low. I—"

"Please, you mistake my silence for anger. It's not..." My voice trailed off. I wasn't sure how to finish the sentence I had started. Slowly, I stood to my feet and shrugged into my shirt.

Once dressed, she looked up at me, suddenly appearing more at ease. I felt a small smile quirk the corners of my mouth with my epiphany. Her discomfort had been the product of having a half-clothed man in the room, not with my anger.

I pushed down the thought of her innocence being pleasing, her mother's words still echoing in my head as quietly as an air raid siren.

"Have you eaten?" I asked.

"I'm fine." She twisted her legs under her, checked to make sure her knee-length skirt was covering her legs properly, and stuck her nose back in her book.

I wasn't sure if that meant she had eaten or not. I didn't know her well enough to know if she would go hungry to make sure I had enough. She may have not had much money, and even seasonal fruit would be expensive this far from transport lines. I sat at the minuscule table and ate the biscuits. Sliding a knife from the block on the counter, I carefully cut the apple in half, avoiding stress on my injured shoulder.

I walked the few steps to where she was perched and handed it to her. She looked up at me with her wide lavender eyes and took the apple from my outstretched hand. Juice dripped from my fingers, and I put them to my lips. "You haven't eaten anything."

She didn't answer; she shrugged slightly and held up the apple a little. "Thank you."

Clenching my teeth, I crossed back to the table.

I don't hate her.

I sighed, feeling the full weight of my realization. If her mother was always correct...

I closed my eyes.

I need a new plan.

CHAPTER 4

METTLE

ROSEMOND

"Are you sure you are comfortable with driving?" he asked, his tone measured and neutral.

"I prefer, Mr. Yates, that you do not pull the sutures I placed in your shoulder. And yes, I am quite capable of driving."

His face remained blank, but his eyes were amused with me.

I couldn't decide what to think of him. He barked commands sometimes, making me bristle, which always left me in want of stomping on his foot. Then, on other occasions, I caught him watching me in tranquil moments, looking absolutely lost. I tried to stave off judgment; he had been shot. Anyone is liable to be out of sorts for a while, though he was remarkably composed ninety-five percent of the time.

We were packed and off before noon, heading to a new town, to a location where he said he had a drop box with money and at least a new identity for him. We were to assume all other avenues were compromised. For our security, he wouldn't contact the Concilium until the end of the week.

"I want you to teach me," I pronounced as we rumbled down the road.

"And what am I to teach you?" he asked quizzically.

"I don't want you to provide me with new identities; I want you to teach me how to create them. I don't want to be reliant on others if I can do it myself. It is a terrible thing to feel helpless."

"I had already come to the same conclusion. I will teach you."

"Oh," I uttered in surprise. My expectation was that he would put up some sort of fight. Apparently, I had wasted my time coming up with a list of reasons. It made me forgive him a little more for the times he had been cross.

With gentleness, he added, "I have a difficult time believing you ever feel helpless."

"Mr. Yates, you hardly know me."

"True, but I am a very good judge of character." He took a shallow breath. "Please, call me George."

"Your name is George?"

"What type of question is that?"

"I'm sorry. I suppose I pictured you as Nigel or Basil or some other strictly British-sounding name that requires you to be proper all the time."

"And I thought you hardly knew me," he replied, a hint hurt in his tone.

"Mr. Ya—George. I am sorry. It is a perfectly respectable name. I did not mean to offend you. I have a horrible habit of blurting out whatever crosses my thoughts when I am comfortable around someone." *As long as you are clothed.*

I felt a rush of heat to my cheeks and wondered why I told him that I was comfortable around him. I bit my lip and hoped that his eyes were somewhere on the landscape beyond the rain-stained windshield. If he looked at me, he would surely see my mortification.

He remained quiet.

Several minutes later, I broke the silence. My voice came out softer than I had intended; he must have had to strain to hear me. "I hope you can forgive me. I truly wasn't trying to disparage your name."

His head swiveled in my direction. It seemed as if I had pulled him from some faraway place. "We need money."

"So what may I ask is the next order of business?" A little surprised he had moved on so quickly.

I risked taking my eyes from the road and glanced at him. He sat with his mouth tugged downward in the corners and his thumb and forefinger pinching the bridge of his nose. "Sell the motorcar and take the train to Philadelphia."

"Sell it? Are we not safer in this?"

His tone became more relaxed, "Not if they are looking for it. They produced six hundred and twenty-nine of this model last year for the whole of the U.S. No more than half of those are on the East Coast. I don't like the odds, however remote, that we might be recognized." I must have looked worried. He quickly added, "Hopefully, they are not looking for us at all."

"Six hundred and twenty-nine," I repeated.

"I remember things," he said, as way of an explanation.

"As in all things?"

"Most anything I read."

I nodded, but didn't take my eyes from the road.

~

WE REMAINED SILENT FOR THE BALANCE OF THE TRIP. AFTER arriving at our destination, we found a place to sell the motor-car, and the buyer telephoned for a cab to deposit us at the train station.

George acquired tickets for a private compartment in one of the passenger cars. Night had fallen, and the chilled air seemed to slither its fingers through my clothing. I couldn't wait to board the train and feel less exposed.

We stood on the platform and watched as the mist occasionally raced across the empty tracks. I shivered and tried not to let my lips quiver.

"Are you cold?" George asked as he stood there perfectly still, save the wind ruffling his brown locks.

"I'm fine." I managed a smile, sure that my lips were a nice shade of purple. I always seemed to battle a chill whenever I became tired. And I was truly exhausted.

He frowned and bent to his brown leather bag, careful to keep his right arm wrapped around his torso for protection. He unlatched his luggage and pulled out a meticulously folded overcoat and gracefully swung it around my back with one hand before I could protest. As I stood there peering up at him, his warm hazel eyes seemed bottomless for a moment.

"Thank you," I spoke just loud enough to overcome the deafening huffs from the approaching train.

Then his control set in, and his eyes became distant. He gave me a curt nod just as the train screeched to a halt.

I stepped back a little to put space back between us. We

watched as haggard travelers disembarked from the passenger cars. Drivers whistled and called out to get the attention of their charges. Railway employees bustled on and off the cars seeing to their various duties.

Squeals from reunited families and lovers reverberated in the night air. The wind kept swallowing up all the sound as it decided to gust and make its presence known with growing force. I was thankful for George's coat and tried not to enjoy the fact that it smelled faintly of his cologne.

An odd sensation hit the pit of my stomach.

Desire.

It was the only word I could associate with the feeling, but it wasn't quite right.

Spying up at George again, I wasn't sure what to make of it. It was almost palpable. I began to turn away from him, but he grabbed me and pulled me to his chest, tucking my head into the small of his neck. My cloche hat protested as the narrow brim flattened against him. I was too shocked to exclaim or struggle or do anything but to allow the closeness.

GEORGE

My eyes were tirelessly sweeping the crowd every few moments; I felt exposed with her out on the platform in this threatening weather. There simply wasn't anywhere to discreetly wait for the locomotive. All the open space had me on edge—we were vulnerable. I stilled myself, desperate not to let her distract me from my mission.

I glanced down at her, and she suddenly became alert in a way I had not seen her before. She pressed her lips together, pushed her shoulders back slightly, and tilted her head to the side. Her eyes closed as if she was listening to something. Then upon opening them, she peered up at me for a fleeting moment as she started to turn away from me.

At that instant, a line of text from her file came screaming to the surface of my mind. It was almost as if the words were before my eyes. It had seemed like nonsense, on my initial read. Some fragment from a prophecy now thought moot due to the demise of the Lux. Ten lines or so had been translated, un-poetically, and kept with her file.

> *"She will be drawn to what will protect and destroy her, and it to her."*

I surveyed the direction in which she was starting to gaze and watched as Gareth exited the train. His hulking figure and yellow eyes were instantly recognizable. I spun her towards me and crushed her to my person.

His attention was focused the other way, but his body was turning in our direction. I tipped my hat to shade my eyes, pressed my lips to her ear, and whispered as quietly as I could. Praying the surrounding noise would prevent even a vampire from hearing me, "Keep your face hidden."

She nodded and clutched handfuls of fabric from my coat in her fists, her lip trembling slightly. I wondered if it was from the cold or if she was as terrified as she should be.

I wondered why Gareth was here.; and more importantly if his brother would be close. They were both legends throughout France—more than France. A chauffeur scuttled up to Gareth just a few meters away. They had a brief conversation, and the chauffeur dashed off.

Still holding Rosemond, my shoulder was screaming, but I

couldn't seem to ease my grip on her. Gareth stood, an unmoving monument in the wind, not six meters from us. He appeared as if he had lost something and was trying to remember what it was. His eyes lazily wandered over the throng of people around him.

When his eyes were close to us, I dipped my head down, letting the brim of my hat hide my face, and ran my hands affectionately over Rosemond's back. I tried to send the thought: *Just two lovers greeting one another, nothing more.*

Gareth walked closer; he was larger than he had seemed in the illustrations. My Durateus dagger was in my bag, and it would have been painfully obvious if I'd reached for my pistol. Not that it would do much good for long. Gareth took few steps toward us; he now stood only a meter away, between us and the train.

I didn't dare raise my head to see where he was looking. Slowly, I felt Rosemond release her grip on my overcoat. She ran her hands over my chest and then inside my suit jacket. I stiffened for a moment, wondering what she was up to, and then I felt her fingers find the handle of my pistol. I sighed. *Clever girl.*

A few solitary flakes of snow drifted, hovering and swirling in the air, making it appear as if all life had slowed. We stood in that posture for what seemed an eternity.

Rosemond turned her head and pressed it to my chest as she silently withdrew the revolver from the holster and stood at the ready. I lowered my chin to the top of her head and prayed she wouldn't have to use it. I could feel her breath as it heated the fabric of my shirt, sending a shiver down my spine. Somehow I knew, without a doubt, that she would have the mettle to pull the trigger.

Two men joined Gareth briefly, all of them silent. After another excruciating minute, they slowly moved away. I watched their shoes as they soundlessly walked across the platform, leaving patchy footprints in the thin layer snow.

I lifted my gaze, still trying to hide my eyes under the brim of my hat. When they reached the end of the dais, they seemed to shrug off whatever they were sensing and began to talk. I didn't recognize either of Gareth's companions. They could have been vampires, servants, or familiars. All I knew was that I wanted off this platform immediately.

The conductor announced boarding.I stared at the end of the platform one last time, trying to discern whether we were truly in the clear or not. "I believe they have gone," I whispered into her hair.

She nodded against my chest and holstered the weapon. When she withdrew her hands from my overcoat, she asked. "You knew them?"

"*Of* one of them."

She blinked once, picked up her bags, and waited expectantly for me to lead the way. With a nod, I grabbed my bags with my good arm and forged ahead toward our compartment.

I had the dismal feeling that the next seven hours were going to be very, very long.

CHAPTER 5

BEST TO REMEMBER THAT

ROSEMOND

We stepped inside the compartment, and I watched as George locked the door behind us. Before I could set my bags down, pain shot through my temples, and I felt as if my eyesight was being obscured by water flowing over my eyes.

Feeling like I wasn't in my own body, I heard myself gasp and sensed the weightlessness of falling forward as the darkness closed in around me.

GEORGE

When I turned after throwing the bolt on the door, Rosemond was focused on me. Fear seized me as I observed the colour drain from her cheeks. She pitched forward, and her eyes rolled back as her body went slack.

She was having a vision; somehow I knew it as the cause.

I dropped the bags and lunged for her, catching her before

she cracked her skull, not caring about the pain in my shoulder. Easing onto the floor, I pulled her onto my lap and held her. The feeling of utter helplessness was overwhelming. A sheen of sweat blossomed on her brow. She looked as pale as moonlight, and her eyes darted beneath her lids restlessly.

Slowly, I cupped the side of her face and cradled it in my hand. I hadn't expected her to be so beautiful, so strong.

I oughtn't think her beautiful.

I cringed away from the connection I already felt. My father warned me of the Lux Casta's allure; I now understood his amusement.

In jest he had always called me "Iron George" because of my single-mindedness and unwavering nature when I had set my mind to a task. He warned me to keep focused on my duty. I had laughed at him.

His words now echoed in my head, "She may be a Siren's call, though her heart will be pure. Any distraction on your part could cost both of you dearly. Son, I ask you to do this because I trust you implicitly, and I am hoping you will be impervious to her."

I had asked him if all men fell in love with the Lux. He had given me an odd smile. "No, but enough of them do." He paused, and his face became grave. "And not just human men."

I refocused on her again. Duty—I had never thought it a foul word before. I was to set her up in a new life and leave her alone. There were no other options.

She started to stir. I pulled my hand from her face like a child about to be caught. Her lips parted, and tears spilled from her eyes. Her lids fluttered open. I expected her to be disoriented, but she looked at me with such clarity it sent a shiver down my spine. I had a sick feeling swell in the pit of my stomach.

"Are you well?" I asked. My voice was rough, even to my own ears.

The fact that she was lying on the floor in my lap seemed to register. Roses bloomed on her cheeks as she sat up abruptly and leaned against the bench opposite me, carefully checking her knee-length skirt for modesty.

She took a small breath and wiped the tears from her cheeks before meeting my eyes again. "I apologize, Mr. Yates." She paused and bit her bottom lip. "George, I'm sorry. The visions are new to me. I don't always feel them coming. I...I have always had dreams, but..." She didn't finish. She simply stared at me with the same clear expression she had when she woke.

"What did you see?" I finally asked.

She pursed her lips and looked at her lap, rubbing at the lace on the edge of her blouse for a moment before meeting my eyes again. "Something that I must... *intentionally* alter."

A ghost of a smile flickered over her face before being replaced by that same look again. I finally identified the look. She looked lost, *knowingly* lost.

ROSEMOND

We settled in. It was nice to rest for a while. I curled onto my side on the bench seat opposite George. He was examining papers in a worn-looking folder. It seemed as if he were finding the secrets to the universe in there, he was so engrossed with it.

Closing my eyes, I still felt exhausted from the vision. My

mother had told me that it would become easier, but I had my doubts. It seemed like trying to control a wild beast or the weather. I nodded off.

I woke to hunger. Horrible, horrible hunger. There had been only one proper meal in two days, besides the little bit of fruit. I glanced over at George. His head was leaned back and his eyes shut. He looked younger. The worry line between his brows was nearly invisible. He stirred and rubbed at his closed eyes, then his shoulder. He was still awake.

I propped myself up on one elbow. "Do you think the dining car is open this late?"

His expression was blank for a moment. "I believe so." He nodded and then seemed to collect himself. He stood keeping his knees soft to account for the swaying of the train. We started for the door, but then I came to a halt, remembering my vision.

"Wait." I opened a piece of my luggage and pulled out a beaded handbag and a wide garter for my thigh. "Do you have a weapon that would fit in here?" I asked holding up my purse.

His expression didn't change, but he paused for a long moment. "Yes." He popped the latch on his suitcase and pulled out a small, snub-nosed revolver. I pressed the release, flicked out the barrel, spun it, and pushed the cylinder back into place before sticking the loaded gun in my handbag.

"And a small knife?"

He rummaged again and placed it on my open palm, raising his brow questioningly. I motioned for him to turn his back to me, and he complied. As I slid the garter into position and lodged the knife in place.

"My mother never agreed with my father. He was the one who insisted I be trained to defend myself." I paused, upset for allowing her to convince me not to bring anything with me. She had told me the Slayer arriving with my escort would have more weapons than necessary.

"You may turn back around." I said, almost breathless, trying not to conjure up images of the flashes from the barrel of a pistol in the darkened entry of my home. We exited our compartment and moved towards the dining car.

As we walked, I thought about my vision. What happened was clear enough, but the location I could not make out. I saw rushing mist as a backdrop behind George. I would have said we were on something moving, but I had seen his entire body as the cloudy background moved briskly by. Maybe we were on a hilltop of some sort. Frustrated, I tried to dig at the edges of the vision.

My distraction was so complete that I walked into a man with a yellow scarf draped around his neck. I sputtered an apology. The man grumbled something to me in an irritated tone and moved off.

George, seeing my inability to focus, looped his arm through mine. I allowed him to guide me through three cars, barely seeing what was before me as I was so lost in my thoughts.

The first two of the cars were identical to ours, and the other had a wide walkway with a huge sliding door on our left, so we could actually walk side-by-side. There were compartments on our right marked with plaques like "Storage" and "Personnel Only." After a couple of more passenger cars, we arrived in the dining area.

A short time later, my thoughts returned to the present; I gazed at him, not really remembering sitting or ordering food. He sat twisted to the side, precisely positioning himself so that he could see both entrances to the dining car. It was at this point he noticed that I was watching him.

Keeping his voice low, he asked, "Do you mind telling me where you've been off to?"

I frowned. "I'm sorry."

"You apologize far too much," he replied, a hint of teasing in his tone. His lightened attitude seemed juxtaposed to the heaviness I felt. Releasing a slow steady breath, I allowed myself to gaze at him. The dim lamplight cast odd shadows on his face. When he blinked, the movement of his lashes seemed as if the shadow was caressing his cheek.

I realized I hadn't answered him and shook my head in disagreement to the comment that I apologize too much. "When I see things, they are often pieces or snippets. I have to connect the dots. I have been trying to search for additional information."

"You can't simply let it play out?"

I felt a pinch in my chest. "I don't think either of us would be happy with that scenario."

"Do you not want to tell me what happened in it?"

"Not really."

"Is your vision why you asked for the weapons?"

He wasn't going to let it be. I sighed, and held his gaze, willing my voice to stay even. "George, I watched you die."

His expression didn't change. "I can see your reluctance in wanting to tell me."

"This was meant to be changed, George."

He lifted his teacup to his lips and made no further comment. I think he was more rattled than he appeared; there was an infinitesimal tremor in his hand.

It felt as if the train were slowing. My attention turned to

George who seemed captivated by his now cold tea. "Is the train making many stops?"

He tore his eyes away from his beverage. "Just one..." He pulled out a pocket watch. "And that won't be for another..." He stopped short and looked at me. I could see that he had caught up to the reason I had asked before he spoke again. "We *are* slowing."

He cupped his hands around his eyes and peered out the window, then bolted from his seat, still favoring his shoulder, and did the same on the other side. "There is no reason to be slowing right now. We are on straight track in a flat area. A road runs parallel on your side; it makes us vulnerable. Let us get out of sight, back to the cabin."

I nodded and wrapped the remainder of my scone in a white linen napkin.

We began to travel through the train, and as we entered the third car, the one with the wider walkway, I realized the man with the yellow scarf was at the far end, coming towards us, with another man in tow. He still looked grumpy, and his eyes were dead-locked on me.

At that same moment, we heard the door behind us. George tightened his grip on my arm. As we paused mid-car, a slider on the right side of the train opened. A blast of cool air whooshed inside, and it was then that I perceived there was a truck driving alongside the train on the parallel road. A large man swung himself into the train car—he must have been the one that had opened the side-door.

George immediately opened the door to a compartment marked "Personnel Only" and started shoving me inside, ordering me to bolt the door. I glared at him in protest, and my heart crystalized as I noticed the mist speeding by behind him. It was now—*now*—now. I knew where the shooter had to be standing.

As George backed away from me to engage the men, I pulled the knife from my garter and stepped forward towards the passageway with the blade end in my palm, arm raised to throw it. I prayed my aim would be true; the gunman was going to be close.

Two men came into my line of sight, and one was raising his lanky arm to fire his Colt at George. His body was turned entirely in my direction, but he was looking to his right. He wasn't even aware of my standing there—that is until my blade penetrated his arm. He jerked and fired the gun into the ceiling as he plummeted backwards out the open door into nothingness.

The hulking man who had pitched himself into the train moved. He'd been next to the shooter. I turned to dive back into the compartment, but I only made it a couple of steps before his fingers clawed at my ribcage, knocking me into the wall in his attempt to seize me. I dove to the floor for my handbag and narrowly managed to loop a finger through the strap as he hoisted me to my feet.

Instantly, I jammed my heel into his foot and elbowed him with all my might. He scarcely moved at all until a gunshot rang out a few feet from us. Taking advantage of the split-second distraction, I managed to slip from his grip and pull the pistol from my handbag. I spun around and targeted him.

He raised his hands slightly and took two steps back so he was in the hallway again. He glanced to his right and then back at me. Coolly, with a sneering grin on his lips, he reached into his coat.

I hesitated, and in that moment, he yanked out a gun. But

he didn't aim it at me, he aimed it to his right. He took another step back and urged me forward with his chin. I timidly inched towards the passageway again.

There was a man who looked to be mortally wounded, writhing on the ground. He moaned and pleaded for help. Standing above him was the man with the yellow scarf wielding a knife—and he had George.

The thick-handed oaf directly in front of me had his revolver aimed at George. He growled, "Come with me, little lady, or I drop him here."

I kept my pistol trained on him and glanced at George. He shook his head almost infinitesimally. They were going to kill George regardless. I knew it, and so did he.

"You have exactly three seconds before I drill a hole in him." He started to cock the weapon. "One—tw—"

I fired.

He had just enough time for shock to register on his face as he fell from the train. In the few seconds it took the man to fall, George had broken free from Yellow Scarf. I started to aim at him, but Yellow Scarf winked at me and jumped.

Lunging forward two steps, I watched as he landed agilely in the bed of a truck driving parallel to the train. Yellow Scarf banged on the roof of the truck and the driver hit the brakes. Within a minute, the vehicle had vanished from view completely.

Upon the floor, was one dead body, two revolvers, one linen napkin, and one trampled scone. Looking at the scone, I realized there would be no normal for me, no simple future that I could plan on. I stood frozen for a moment and then retrieved my handbag from the vacant compartment.

When I emerged, George had rolled the body from the

train and was sliding the door closed. We each picked up a gun, and then he grabbed my hand and started leading me away. "We need to get our baggage and find a new compartment. No one responded to the gunfire. That doesn't sit well with me."

As we hurried to our compartment, we could hear the muffled sounds of fear in some of the passenger compartments, but not a single employee from the railway investigated.

Once inside our room, I asked, "Did you see the driver?"

"Yes, it was Gareth. The vampire from the platform."

I frowned. Now he was after us, and I still didn't know what he looked like. "Do they know about me?"

"Doubtful. Vampires figure anything a Watcher would protect is something they want."

"That was a high price for an unknown."

"Humans mean nothing to them, Rosemond. They are a commodity to be used and eaten. It is best to remember that."

I nodded, a lump in my throat. We finished packing up the few items we had removed from our bags. My mind wandered to the ambush at my home. I couldn't help but wonder if this was connected—if there were actual vampires inside my home.

George handed me another knife. He stopped when he saw my expression and gazed at me expectantly.

"I killed two people today, George," I whispered, my voice betraying me with a shake.

"Thank you." His voice was a little huskier than normal.

I nodded again. "Do you have a plan?"

"Yes. Not to be on this train when it stops."

CHAPTER 6

NEW HAVEN

ROSEMOND

"What are the chances that neither of us breaks anything...or dies?"

"I'm an optimist by nature," he said, looking out at the tracks spilling behind the train being swallowed up by the darkness. George's face was smooth without a trace of worry. I wondered how he did that.

A small nervous laugh gurgled out of me and he met my gaze. His dark hair was whipping around in the chilled night air. "You, sir, are not an optimist. You are a realist, who is trying to ease my fears."

He didn't argue, but his eyes seemed to soften for a moment before he looked out at the tracks again. "It is starting to slow."

After a moment of concentration, the reduction in speed was discernible. Taking an inventory of myself, I had on a pair of George's pants under my dress to protect my legs and his spare coat over the top of everything. I felt ridiculous but thankful. A few long minutes passed as the wind continued battering us.

"It is almost time," he said, without taking his eyes from the tracks.

I nodded in acknowledgement, though he wasn't looking at me. I was jealous of how calm he appeared. I was too frightened to utter a word but tried to be more like him and to fix my face with something that might resemble words like 'brave' or 'fearless' or at the very least, 'plucky.' But it probably resembled something more like 'has-horrible-food-poisoning' or 'about-to-tame-a-lion-whilst-covered-in-meat.'

Perhaps he sensed my bubbling anxiety, or I may have made a sound, because he turned towards me and gave me a most comforting half-smile. His eyes looked almost black against the night landscape.

He raised his hands and buttoned the top button of his coat that I wore. Strangely, this small gesture made me feel so safe, as if I could fly from the train and not be harmed.

Taking a steadying breath I said, "You are a good man, George Yates." I felt a little embarrassed that I had said it but at the same time, knew it was true.

The smile faded from his face. It appeared as if he wanted to say something. He cleared his throat, "Almost slow enough. The luggage, then us. Remember everything I told you...roll when you hit the ground."

"Roll when landing, avoid large rocks and trees and also dying. Was that all?" I managed to quip.

"Farm animals should also be avoided," he replied, deadpan.

The train had slowed to a little faster than a man could run. I had asked him why we couldn't unhitch the caboose, but he said if someone was looking for us at the next stop, it would be immediately obvious. He wanted to allow for the possibility that we slipped by them at the station—to spread their forces thin.

It made sense, and jumping was probably the better option. But I didn't care for pain, especially if it involved large amounts of it. I groaned internally.

"It is time," he said, giving my arm a squeeze before he quickly tossed the bags off with one arm. And then it was my turn.

I leaped without thinking about it anymore. Then there was the wind being knocked my from lungs, the stinging of scrapes through my clothing, the clinging of muddy earth to me as I rolled, and the smell of freshly crushed weeds. I came to an abrupt halt when my body hit what felt like a wall of rain-softened dirt.

My eyes were clamped shut as I rolled onto my side, pulling my face out of a puddle of water—lungs bursting as they starved for air. As soon as I managed a breath, I coughed up some of the muddy water. The metallic twang of blood over-whelmed me. I ran my tongue over the inside of my cheek and found a small fissure. I must have bitten it while landing.

Regaining my senses, I sat up and grasped that I was in a ditch of some sort. It hadn't been visible from the train. Panic welled up in me—George was nowhere in sight. I had felt him jump a split-second after me; *he couldn't have landed far from me.* I listened. Nothing. Scrambling up towards the tracks, still staying low, it was difficult to see in the darkness. Barely detectable, there was a lump in a large clump of weeds not far.

Keeping bent, I limped my way over as my heart threat-ened to hammer out of my chest. George lay unmoving; I dropped onto my knees next to him. He opened his eyes, and a ghostly smile flickered across his features.

"Still alive," he whispered.

I let out a relived half-sob-half-laugh-half-thank-you-for-not-dying-noise, probably sounding like a lunatic.

"Are you injured?" he asked, his brows pinned together.

"Minor scrapes and probably a bruise or two." I wiped my nose with the coat sleeve and realized that all that had been accomplished was to smear more mud on my face. "Are you able to move?" I asked, he still hadn't stirred.

"I think I was supposed to be the gallant hero and find you first," he frowned. "Must have lost consciousness for a moment, but all my bits and pieces seem to be intact." He struggled into a sitting position, keeping his right shoulder stiff. He looked as if he were suppressing a scream with a wince-like smile.

The sound of the train whistle in the distance sliced through the misty night air. It would be stopping soon. George stood on shaky legs. Walking as quickly as possible to retrieve our bags, we disappeared into the trees. We traversed what must have been a mile and decided to find a landmark large enough to find later. Then we stashed all but one bag and headed towards the outskirts of civilization just as the sky opened up and made its best effort to drown us.

I grit my teeth, determined to keep my attitude in check. It was dark and cold. This, combined with being wet and in pain, made it all too easy to feel hopeless or to despair.

George came to a halt and looked up into the sky, opening his mouth to drink in the rain. "At least one thing is working for us," he commented after he swallowed.

I looked at him confused. "The rain?"

He nodded, the hint of a smile on what little of his face I could make out. "Washing away our tracks. If they *are* after us, they will have no idea which direction we traveled."

I let out a relieved breath, not realizing how incredibly fraught with worry I'd been.

We were so soaked it didn't matter that I was standing in the downpour. Liquid kept collecting on my lashes until it became too heavy and dripped into my eyes, temporarily blurring my vision. I didn't bother wiping it away as it would have been fruitless since it simply collected there again in moments.

We maneuvered through the last of the trees and came in behind a row of businesses. Rain-soaked boxes had given way under the weight of water, and wooden crates had swelled and become useless.

We found a small alleyway, little more than a gap, between two of the businesses and stumbled through the space, black as pitch, tentatively emerging onto a street. Every window was shuttered and door bolted, as to be expected in the wee hours of the night.

"Where do you think we are?" I whispered.

"No clue," he uttered. George walked slightly ahead of me and started reading the signage in the windows. Then he began to look fixedly at a sign.

"Does it say the name of the town?"

George pinched the bridge of his nose with his left hand and laughed. It was low, throaty, and ironic sounding. "Ethan."

"We are in *Ethan?*"

He let out a single laugh, "No. I may have a friend here—a mate from school. This is New Haven."

I surveyed the main street—the entire block of it. "Really? In this town. In the middle of nowhere."

"Let us just pray he still lives here." He pressed his palm to his forehead and thought for a moment. When he dropped his hand, splotches of dark rainwater dripped down his face. He looked in each direction. "There must be a petrol station, we may be able to find directions there. Even if they are closed, many of them have a rudimentary map in the window." I trailed behind him, praying he did indeed still have a friend here.

GEORGE

As we walked, five years of boarding school memories tumbled through my mind. *Ethan, of all people. He was the one who had been in turmoil, yet he may have helped me more than I ever did him. He was wholly my friend, though it must have been difficult.*

I found myself smiling and feeling thirteen again. It had also been raining the night Ethan had arrived at the boarding school.

Eventually, we found a petrol station. One small light shone on the porcelain sign on the front of the building. It was just enough illumination to make out the map that I had prayed would be in the window.

"Is there enough detail in the map?" she asked. Her voice excruciatingly tired, yet she had not complained a single time.

I pivoted, to regard her. Her dark hair had come out of the twists she always kept them in. It flowed in rivulets over her shoulders with the rain. It was rare to see a girl with such long hair. They had all cut it short in flapper rebellion or to emulate stars like Louise Brookes or even the Queen of Belgium.

Her bottom lip was trembling, and there was nothing to provide her with any warmth. In an effort to reassure her, I offered, "Yes, he lives just off of the main street and down a few blocks. We will be there straight away."

She reached up to pat my arm, and I stiffened. She caught the shift in my posture and pinned me with her eyes. "You reopened your shoulder. That's why you didn't get up right away."

I looked away from her all-knowing stare. "Let us see if Ethan still lives here."

"If you go septic on me and die, I will be very cross with you."

I couldn't help but grin crookedly, knowing the expression she wore on her face without looking, and that fact alarmed me. Turning to see her wide disapproving eyes, furrowed brow, and pouted lips, I could not hold her gaze for long.

"Taken under advisement," I replied while keeping my tone as neutral as possible, then turned and headed to what would hopefully be a place of safety.

We covered the distance in about ten minutes' time and arrived at the address I had recalled from posting a few letters.

The house stood dark, gothic, and spidery amongst the other homes on the street. It was on a rather large parcel of land, and the grounds teaming with chimes and odd-looking sculptures. But my sense was of relief looking at the ominous home that appeared as if the mad Usher twins from Poe's story could be skulking about inside. Ethan had said his aunt's home was "both a place of wonder and terror." Somehow his description had stuck with me.

Rosemond sidled close behind me and touched my left elbow tentatively. The heavy rain had abated, and there were only fat drops that splatted on the ground few and far between, reminding us that the clouds were ready at any time to reopen their deluge and sink us. "Is this it?"

"Yes."

"And you want to go *in* there? I may want to take my chances with the vampires."

"Why, Rosemond, are you actually afraid of something?" My tone was teasing.

She uttered a frustrated sound, set her jaw, and stomped off towards the door. Before I could catch up, she had loudly knocked on the wood that framed a rather melancholy-looking stained glass inlay. Dim light was emanating from deep inside the house, and I could make out a darkened shape moving slowly towards us.

With a loud creak, the door opened and Ethan's towering form stood before us, running his hand through his always disheveled hair. He turned on the porch lamp and stood blinking at me, then at Rosemond, and then at me again. Finally, a look of recognition warmed his face, and he seemed to come alive.

"Georgie!" He exclaimed and leapt out the door and picked me up off the ground in an energetic embrace. I tried not to shout from the pain. "Georgie!" he said again as he plopped me down and held me by the shoulders, leaning back to look at me. "What on earth are you doing here? In the middle of the night? In America! I had given you up for dead." He grinned, knowing full well I hadn't died, but was simply a terrible friend who had let him slip away—for his own good really.

"Long story, old sport. We were hoping to find lodging and a place to clean up. We fell into a spot of trouble."

"Always one for understatement, my friend. Of course, come in...come in," he said, ushering us through the door. We followed him inside and shut the door behind us. The house was filled with boxes—everywhere. Sheets were draped over the furniture in what must have been a drawing room. "Are you hungry? There's food." He didn't turn to look at us, but simply strode farther inside the house.

"I apologize if we woke you," I began, but Ethan cut me off, waving his hands.

"I was up. Working on a project. Sorry about the boxes. This way."

We entered a luxurious kitchen dressed in black and white with accents of green. Ornate white cabinetry solidified the lavishness. It appeared to have every modern appliance available. He turned on a burner and set the kettle on before turning around to look at us.

He was taller than I remembered, but perhaps he had grown. I had last seen him three years ago, and he had then only recently turned eighteen. Now in his twenties, he seemed to have aged more than he should have, but his dark blond hair still stood up in waves like a mad-scientist. The bright light of the kitchen illuminated his vivid blue eyes. They had the same clear quality as Rosemond's.

"Ethan, this is Rosemond Le Clair. She is—"

"Stunning," he finished and closed the space between them, swept up her hand, and kissed it.

I almost rolled my eyes, but part of me marveled at his ability to do such things yet always come across as charming and never overly forward. It was perhaps his heart. It was impossible for him to hide his goodness, although his pretty-boy looks never seemed to hurt him.

He shot a devilish look at me. "And what are you doing

with stuffy old George?" He grinned, turning back to Rosemond.

If she was disconcerted by any of this, she didn't let on. "Pleased to meet you, Ethan..." her voice trailed, indicating she would like to know his last name.

"Ethan Kendrick."

She looked confused for a moment. "You are American," she stated. I could see this was more surprising to her than Ethan's considerable personality.

"Do you normally label everyone you meet?" he asked, with a humorous tone.

"No, it's just that George said you were school mates. I had expected..." She didn't complete the thought.

"Actually, you did label me at our meeting," I commented dryly.

A nervous giggle bubbled from her. "I suppose I did." She looked at me with a very endearing guilty expression.

Ethan cleared his throat, and his words came out in a rush. "So George, are you going to tell me why you are here, in the middle of the night with this ravishing creature, both bleeding and muddied?"

"*Both* bleeding?" she asked.

"Your head." Ethan pointed to Rosemond, and my eyes shot to her. I hadn't noticed the cut behind her temple just inside her hairline. It made me feel sick. Then he indicated the ground beneath me. "And George, something is not right under that coat."

I leaned my head forward and looked at the black and white tile. Drips of diluted blood were plummeting from the edge of my right sleeve and from the bottom of the coat. I turned back to Rosemond, who was staring at blood on her fingertips; she must have probed the wound on her head.

Ethan became a little more serious. "I will see what sort of supplies I can dig up." The teapot started to whistle. "Pour some tea and take a seat." He started to leave and then turned back towards me in the doorway. "George, too bad you are only the useless sort of doctor." He chuckled to himself and disappeared.

Rosemond looked at me confused. "Doctor?"

I frowned and poured us some tea, spreading more red droplets all over Ethan's once clean floor. "I have a doctorate in classical literature."

She held the hot cup in her hands and closed her eyes while she absorbed the heat. Her lips had finally stopped the subtle tremble from the cold. She cocked her head to the side and gazed at me.

"That is an amazing accomplishment. I...I guess I thought you were younger."

I hadn't realized Ethan was back. "He is young," he interrupted. She looked at Ethan. "It's just that giant brain of his leaves the rest of us behind. He stayed in the dorm at our school, even after his early graduation, and attended classes at the university. He was finishing his Master's when I left. We were eighteen."

She gave me a small smile. "You remember things." She repeated my words back to me.

"Speaking of age, I know it is impolite to ask a lady's age," he hinted, raising an eyebrow.

"Eighteen. I'm eighteen," she said softly.

"And your parents allow you to run about with the likes of him without a chaperone?"

I watched the little color she had drain from her face.

Ethan realized immediately. "Apologies. I shouldn't be so free with my questioning. Are you all right?"

"Yes, I think it is simply the wet clothes and the lack of sleep." She fingered the collar of my soggy coat she was still wearing.

"I am drawing a bath. It should be almost ready. My aunt's clothes will be a little large on you. But they are clean and dry. I placed them with some towels on the counter." He offered his hand to Rosemond and escorted her out of the room.

Watching my friend as he exited, I felt blessed. For all his quirks and occasional oversteps, he was the kindest person I had ever known.

CHAPTER 7

CRY OUT

ROSEMOND

The sound of Ethan humming guided me back to the kitchen after my long bath.

The wind was howling outside as rain pelted the windows at the rear of the house. I stood in the doorway; Ethan was stirring something savory that smelled like heaven—heaven being anything with meat and potatoes and the scent of rosemary. A moment later, I entered in the borrowed sleeping clothes that hung on me like overly colorful drapes.

I couldn't decide if the tune Ethan was humming was happy or sad. It made me feel nostalgic and in want of being home. But somehow his abode felt like the best place I could be, since my home no longer existed. There was something about George's friend that immediately made me feel more at ease.

Gazing at him while he cooked, he bobbed his head to the tune he half-mumbled, half-hummed. He had to be a couple of inches over six feet tall, with broad shoulders, but the rest of his frame was narrow, the sort of wiry build that was slender, but innately strong. His creamy, olive complexion and the sun-streaked dark blond hair made him seem even sunnier.

Bowls clattered as he pulled them from a cabinet to his right. He spun on his heel and was so startled to see me standing there that he almost dropped them. He laughed, a short burst of a chuckle.

"If I had known you were there, I may have hummed something a little more romantic." He wagged his brows and placed the bowls on the table. Ethan was warm—the type of person who could make you feel like the center of the universe when he looked at you. He glanced at me again. "You look much improved."

"Yes, thank you. A bath is just what I needed. And thank you for the loan." I ran my hands over the collar of the flamboyant nightdress with matching housecoat.

His sky blue eyes twinkled as he admired the frock hanging off of me. "Yes. Well, my aunt had interesting tastes. She wore her art as much as she created it, even in her sleep. Sorry about that." He shrugged his shoulders and returned to the stove to retrieve a saucepan.

"Had?" I felt awful the moment it had slipped from my lips.

When he turned again, with the steaming saucepan in his grip, sadness flickered on his face. Yet, his expression remained open. He didn't try to hide his feelings.

He let out a sigh. "Please take a seat. George said you two hadn't eaten in a long while. It's not much—leftovers, a meager stew, but it's warm." He pulled a chair out with his free hand and entreated me over to it.

The moment I was seated, he ladled half the contents of

the pot into my bowl until it was brimming. He returned the pan to the stove and reduced the heat. I wanted to say something, feeling horrible for causing him pain.

He picked up a cloth napkin from the table as he sat across from me, crossing his long legs and resting his knee on the edge of the table. He kept his eyes downcast as he fussed with the napkin, shaping it into something resembling a rose. "She passed, two weeks ago. Hence..." He pointed at the boxes in the hallway and in the corner of the kitchen. "I'm not sure what to do with everything. I'm afraid you have stumbled upon me in a state of flux."

"I am so sorry for your loss."

"He said you do that a lot," he replied with a faint smile.

"What?"

"Apologize for things you shouldn't."

"So you were speaking about me when I didn't have a chance to defend myself?" I raised an eyebrow and grinned at him.

"Yes, terrible things were said," he answered conspiratorially in a raised whisper.

I knew he was joking, but part of me wondered what George might have said. "Where is George?"

"Cleaning up in the other bathroom. I thought it better to wash the mud away before patching both of you up." He paused, then answered as if he had read my mind. "All George said about you was that you impressed him and that he owes you a great debt. And trust me—to impress George is indeed a feat in itself."

I looked down at the stew, feeling warmth spread across my cheeks.

Ethan chuckled, suddenly lighter in spirit. "And she

blushes. Now you threaten to steal my heart. I'll check on George, make sure he didn't pass out on the floor somewhere. He wasn't quite looking himself." He stood, the chair scraping on the tile. "Why was he bleeding anyway? I know this must be shocking, but he didn't tell me why."

I bit my lip and met his eyes, not sure what to say. But then again, he would know the moment he saw the wound. "He was shot...saving me."

A slow smile spread across his face. "And he owes *you* a great debt. Sounds like Georgie has a yarn to tell." Then he vanished into the hallway. I heard the creak of stairs and footsteps above. Testing the stew to make sure it was cool enough, I shoveled it down like I hadn't seen food in a month.

GEORGE

The knock at the door told me it was Ethan. Everything in my bag had been thoroughly soaked. So there I sat, beleaguered, next to the tub, in another man's pajamas, in the middle of the night, unable to stop the bleeding in my shoulder. It would require stitches again. I cringed, knowing that it would have to be Rosemond, unless Ethan had overcome his aversion to blood in the last three years. I took a deep breath. "Enter."

The door creaked open, but Ethan simply leaned on the doorway instead of entering. "Just making sure you weren't bleeding on the floor in here too. Trying to keep my cleaning to a minimum. The maid is on sabbatical."

"So, I shouldn't be alarmed then, if I see you in a black dress and pinafores," I jested.

"My legs are quite nice," he replied, but he wasn't smiling.

He was looking at the towel I had pressed to my shoulder. "Bullet wound," he stated.

Rosemond must have told him. "Just keeping things interesting." I pressed the towel to my shoulder a little harder. "Afraid my stitches were pulled."

"Interesting, indeed."

"I don't want to bring you any trouble, my friend. Once we get a few hours of sleep, we will be on our way."

Ethan smiled, the type of smile I knew meant he was going to try to convince me of something. "No, you are going to stay a few days until that shoulder is healing properly and you are rested. No one could possibly know you're here."

Staying was what I wanted more than anything. "One more night, then we will see. How are your sewing abilities?"

Ethan swallowed hard. "Hmmmm. Well, I...I no longer lose consciousness at the sight of blood. I'm stellar with bandages and bedpans, but...."

"It's perfectly all right. Rosemond is fairly skilled. I just didn't want to ask her unless necessary."

"You like her then?" he asked.

I tried to keep my face as neutral as possible. "I am to help her settle safely in a new life. My feelings are irrelevant. She is my charge."

"And a very pretty one at that," he replied suspiciously. Under his breath, he murmured, "Always so mysterious." It was apparent that he wanted more answers than I was willing to give. "Let's get you downstairs to your nursemaid. The light is better in the kitchen."

I stood, and everything seemed to list to the left like a slowly capsizing ship. Almost instantaneously, I felt Ethan's warm hands on both my elbows. "Brilliant," I muttered.

"How long have you been bleeding?"

I closed my eyes before answering, trying to keep the room steady. "Since we jumped from the train."

"Jumped from the train," he repeated, in a tone so disapproving that I opened my eyes. "Of course. Should have guessed it. That sounds completely reasonable." It was the first time I had seen him actually look worried.

Ethan helped me down the stairs and into the kitchen without asking another question, though I sensed the effort in his silence. Once there, Rosemond's face paled at the sight of me; she was instantly on her feet. "Let's get him on the table. Do you have anything to kill the pain?"

"Like pharmaceuticals?"

"Anything. Drugs...liquor."

Ethan pulled a flask from the back of a cabinet and thrust it into my hand with a guilty sort of shrug—*obviously, he's not a proponent of prohibition.* I sat on the table and spun the cap off of the flask and took a long swig of its stinging contents.

"Are you ready?" she asked me cautiously.

I wasn't as emotionally prepared this time—my usual control gone. Holding up my finger, I guzzled the remaining contents in the flask. My head began to feel woozy. I let out a laugh that came out as more of a morbid girlish giggle.

A curse slid through my lips when Rosemond and Ethan exchanged a concerned look. Grabbing a serviette from the table, I folded the cloth into eighths with one hand, placed it in my mouth, eased back on the table, and bit down. I nodded at Rosemond to start and prayed to God that I wouldn't cry out.

She pressed her hand to my forehead. "George, you are feverish."

My fingers itched to reach up and smooth the worry from her face. My head was swimming, and I realized I had actually lifted my hand, and it was halfway to her face. I dropped my hand onto the table with an ungraceful thud and hoped she hadn't noticed what I had been about to do.

ROSEMOND

Biting my bottom lip, I forced myself to focus. Ethan had neatly laid out supplies while I had bathed. Picking up a clean cloth, I dabbed at his shoulder to clear the fresh blood so I could assess the wound. The damage to his shoulder was much worse than before.

He gazed up at me with glossy eyes, looking so vulnerable. I forced myself to scrutinize the wound and not be distracted by George himself and bit harder on my lip. The hole was no longer circular, but a ragged void over twice the size it was previously. Irrigating the injury, I packed in some of the remaining herbs that managed to survive in George's bag, and started systematically closing the wound.

After a half hour of torturous sewing, it was as repaired as it was going to get. During the procedure, Ethan had moved next to George and allowed him to squeeze his hand. Exhaustion permeated the room like fog on wetlands; it was almost suffocating. Even Ethan looked worn out. After the exertion of surgery, George's fever seemed to be climbing instead of decreasing.

We forced him to eat a small amount of the stew that was now a little dry after sitting on the stove for so long. He would need his strength. George waved me off after only a few bites. His closed his eyes, and within moments, he became very still;

I wasn't sure if he was actually conscious or not. Ethan shook him gently, and the answer was not.

Ethan's voice broke into my spiraling fears. "Let me go set up a bed for him. Are you okay here?" He held my gaze for a moment, maybe making sure I wasn't going to topple over myself. He finally nodded and swept from the kitchen. I washed my hands and then sat resting my head on George's arm, almost drifting off to sleep.

Ethan returned, and I stood. After a few seconds of deliberation, he bent at the knees and lifted up George. As I had suspected, Ethan was thin but strong. He didn't struggle much under George's weight and walked smoothly, George's good arm looped over Ethan's shoulder and dangled with each step.

When they reached the bedroom, the covers were already pulled down. I was impressed with Ethan's attention to detail. Ethan placed George on the bed with a tiny groan under his breath. He stood and rotated his shoulders, re-adjusting his back as he threw the covers over George. I hovered, feeling rather helpless in the doorway.

I examined my hands and realized that even after washing, my fingertips were stained with George's blood, crimson discoloring the cuticles. I eyed the modern-looking fainting couch in the corner. Again, Ethan seemed to read my mind.

"Oh, no. You need to sleep. I can keep an eye on him."

"But..." I started to protest.

He gently placed his hands on my shoulders and turned me towards the hall. He gave me a gentle nudge. "Up the stairs, first door on the right. Shut the curtains and sleep as long as you need."

"Ethan, you must be—"

"I know; I am incredibly charming and good-natured." The

corner of his mouth curled upwards. "Please don't make me show you that I can be equally as stubborn and dastardly." There was humor in his voice, but I obeyed, having no doubt that he could be forceful if need be.

Reluctantly, I made my way up the wooden steps. When I reached the top of the curved staircase and stared down the hall, I realized how immense the house really was. *There must be well over a dozen rooms. How lonely.*

I turned the burnished brass handle on the bedroom door. It didn't creak like all the other doors. The bed had already been turned down, and a lamp with a stained glass shade created odd shapes on the solid panels of the satin coverlet.

Pulling the curtains shut and crawling into the overstuffed bed, I noticed how bruised my knees were and how thin my muscles felt. The oversized nightgown tangled around me as I tried to settle in. It took great effort to stretch and twist the key-like switch on the lamp, plunging myself into utter darkness.

I was barely able to cover myself before sleep overtook me and my dreams threatened to end me.

CHAPTER 8

THREE

ROSEMOND

I woke gasping for air, quivering from the chilled sweat clinging to my body. Half-falling, half-stumbling from the bed, I felt my way to the door in desperation. It whooshed when flung open. Light streamed into the darkened bedroom, and I blinked back the brightness as I dashed towards the staircase, gripping the banister to steady my tremulous legs.

When I reached George's room, I hesitated, with my hand on the knob, and took in a stuttering breath. When I finally swung the door open, I still wasn't able to force myself to peer inside. Half of me was convinced George was dead.

After a moment, I looked up from my bare feet on the bedroom's wooden floor. Ethan had moved the fainting couch from the corner of the bedroom next to the bed. He was sleeping with his long legs crossed at the ankles and feet dangling off the end. He had a blanket on his lap and his right arm draped on the bed, his fingers inches from George.

I stood for several long minutes watching George. He was sleeping deeply, albeit a little fitfully. His cheeks were flushed and his dark hair stuck to his forehead, but he looked better than the deathly pallor of last night.

Tears washed my face without permission. The dream had been so very real. I had really thought George was dead and my last connection to the Watchers severed. Not that George had any long-term obligation, but the thought of his being harmed. I swallowed hard to stop myself from dwelling on it.

When the emotion continued, I pressed the heels of my hands over my eyes in a silly attempt to dam the tears back. My body seemed to be revolting against me.

"Rosemond? Is everything all right?" Ethan whispered almost inaudibly as he sat up.

I dropped my hands and nodded. "A bad dream is all. I thought...I thought." I shook my head, unable to put into words the scene of horror forever etched in my memory.

Sitting up, he patted the couch next to him. He plucked the blanket from his lap and wrapped it around my shoulders as I sunk beside him. Tears started to flow again, and I felt like a fool. But there was no judgment in Ethan's presence. He merely handed me his handkerchief, put his arm around my shoulders, and let me lean on him to cry. He didn't ask why. He didn't give me false comforts. He simply let me be as we watched George in his restless sleep.

When it seemed there were no more tears to shed, I sat up. My temples ached from my silent sobs, but I felt remarkably better. "Are you always so nurturing?" I murmured into the blanket.

"I am well-practiced," he replied warmly.

"Thank you."

"Yes, it is a terrible imposition to let a beautiful girl cry on your shoulder. I'll send you a bill later for my services."

I smiled meekly. "It is your turn to get some rest."

"Sleeping is overrated. Time for some food. Besides, I *am* guilty of some cat naps." He stood and stretched, linking his long, lanky arms above his head and letting out a soft groan. "I'll see what can be scared up." He stepped past me and exited the room, heading for the kitchen.

I slid down to the spot he had been sitting and reached out to run my fingers over George's forehead. Alarm hit me. He was burning up. I racked my brain for what to do. Quickly padding out to the kitchen, I found Ethan with his nose in the icebox rooting around.

"His fever has spiked. Do you have a thermometer?"

Ethan paused for a split-second then turned, rushing from the kitchen without a word; I could hear him as he sped up the stairs. I hurried back to George's room, and less than a minute later Ethan met me there.

Ethan handed me the thermometer, and I placed the glass tube in George's mouth. He started breathing heavily through his nostrils and squeezing a wad of the sheets in his hand. I turned it so I could watch the temperature. Rising faster than it should have, it reached 98 degrees...then 99...then 101. When it hit 102 I gasped as it was still slowly rising. It finally stopped at 103 degrees.

"What does it read?" Ethan prompted when I stood, staring at the thermometer.

"103," I rasped.

He immediately pulled the covers off of George. "I'll get some cool water and wash rags."

I closed my eyes and waited for Ethan to return, unable to

continue looking at George. He was deathly pale with the exception of his overly reddened cheeks. He had perspired so much through the night that there was a ring of moisture on the bedding inches from his body. Besides the thought of wanting him well, I wanted my mother more than anything. She would know what to do. I was much better with sutures and bandages than I was with illness and fever.

Ethan flew back into the room with the supplies. I looked at him helplessly, but he had a determined look on his face. "I put a bowl of water outside to chill. We are out of ice. We can rotate the washrags on and off of him to cool him down. Here." He handed me half the stack of washrags and placed the bowl between George's knees. We each took a side of the bed and sat down.

When we placed the chilled cloths on George, he started murmuring. It was the fever talking. Nothing really made sense. I did make out my name a few times and Ethan's. We kept this up for what must have been hours. If we stopped for long, his temperature crept up again.

"Rosemond, we should really get him to a hospital."

Sitting on the bed, I put my feet flat on the floor, and dropped my head into my hands. The decision was mine. Tears pricked at the back of my eyes, but I willed them away. I knew what George would say.

My thoughts drifted, and I wondered if my father and sister would be alive if her delivery hadn't gone wrong. If my father hadn't taken my mother to the hospital, she would have died. They had narrowly escaped capture, and my sister's birth was documented. I took in a stuttering breath and swiveled around to look at Ethan. "We can't. I'm sorry, Ethan. We simply can't."

"Even if it means he dies?"

My traitorous lower lip trembled a little. "A hospital means death. He has a gunshot wound." Shaking my head, "They would find him...find *us*." I wondered if I was being selfish.

There was aggravation in his tone, but he spoke softly. "Are you going to tell me who is after you? Why you two showed up in the middle of the night both bleeding? I have a hard time believing George is mixed up in something illegal, but he has always been secretive."

I frowned. "It would be safer for you not to know and I don't know if you would believe me if I told you." Biting my lower lip, I looked away from his frustrated eyes, knowing how awful and suspicious it sounded.

George moaned and stirred. We both busied ourselves rotating out the washrags. I stood after a moment. "I'll get the water from outside and put another bowl out."

"It's just outside the door."

I nodded and grabbed the basin and walked slowly from the room, glancing over my shoulder right before crossing into the hall. Ethan sat hunched, with a heartbreaking look on his face, as he watched his friend suffer.

While exchanging bowls from outside, I thought about how Ethan said he was "well-practiced" when asked if he always so nurturing. When re-entering the bedroom I asked, "Did you take care of your aunt in the end? Is that how you know what to do?"

The frustration that had been in his clear blue eyes two minutes ago had already dissipated. "I left England to come back here and take care of my aunt. There was no one else. I'm the last of my family."

"When? Wait—since you were eighteen?"

"Yes, three and a half years ago. That's when I lost touch with George. He'd been my best friend—my lifeline at that school. Outsiders are not exactly welcomed into high British society, even if one of your parents had been from their ranks. Not even when you are thirteen." He smiled, and I could see memories reflected in his expression. "George was always different. Though..." He didn't finish.

"Though, what?" I prompted.

He shook his head. "It was always an odd relationship. He was set apart somehow. In the dorm, he had a room for three to himself, even though the building was overcrowded. I detested my roommates, so I would sneak down and stay in one of the spare beds almost every single night. He never questioned it. We talked until we knew we would regret it the next day. More than once, I ended up in the Dean's Office for falling asleep during a lecture, but George always managed to stay on track. It was just that..." He stopped, but it was obvious he was searching for the right words. He placed a clean washrag in the fresh water and squeezed most of the liquid out. Then he slowly dripped some of the water into George's mouth. Some fluid trailed down George's still overly rosy cheek.

"It was like he was a ghost, even at thirteen. Whenever it was time to go anywhere outside the dorm, he would disappear; we would never walk together. Then he would pop up in the lecture hall or dining commons. Sometimes, he would sit behind me, and we would speak like we were government agents. I thought it was fun at first, and then just grew to accept it as one of George's quirks. I guess part of me wondered if he was ashamed to be my friend." He chuckled, shook his head, and met my eyes. "I have no idea why I just told you that."

"I tend to have that impact on people," I murmured. "Ethan, I..." Pausing, I wondered if it was wise to tell him anything. "George acted that way at school because he cared for you like family. It's the only explanation. He was protecting you."

"From what? I don't understand."

"It is puzzling how he was in school at all. People from our world, at least the inner circle of it, don't attend normal schools and universities."

Ethan laughed in disbelief. "So, you are going to tell me you have never attended school?"

I pinned my brows together, not meaning to answer these types of questions. "Not in the traditional sense, no."

He raised an eyebrow. "You do read don't you? I would hate to think there is an illiterate secret society running about." He was trying to be light, but strain leaked into his tone.

The edge of my lip twitched upwards. "Not everyone has to read to function in society."

He held my gaze and didn't react.

I relented. "I had private tutors. And for the record, I am also fluent in French and Latin. We are a very literate secret society." Cringing inwardly for the last sentence, I knew I shouldn't confirm anything.

"An American knowing more than one language, now that is something."

I smiled, and my shoulders shook twice with a silent laugh. "Ethan, I recognize that you want to know more. But, my desire is to protect you."

He looked at George and then at me again. "Where are your secret society friends now?"

I frowned. "George was reluctant to call for anyone. My

home was attacked when he came to collect me. Either someone picked up on a communication or we have a traitor in our organization. Having always been isolated from most of them, I honestly wouldn't know who to call."

"So, you are on your own?" He asked in an overly neutral tone, which reminded me of George.

Holding up my chin, trying to not seem afraid. "Yes."

"That sounds very lonely."

I dropped my gaze, thinking of the irony in his statement. Despite his sunny nature, I had thought him very alone too.

GEORGE

The sound of soft breath threaded its way into my consciousness. Slowly I came to the realization that I had been asleep for a very long time. My body ached clear to my bones. A lingering heat clawed at my skin, but I found myself shivering. Forcing my lids open, I rolled my head to my left and found Ethan sleeping on a fainting couch far too short for his body. He looked like a giraffe trying to nap on a card table. I smiled inwardly.

A moment later it occurred to me that Ethan's soft snore wasn't the breathing I had heard. Rolling my head in the other direction, I found Rosemond curled on top of the blankets. She had a pillow under her head and another clutched to her chest. Her free hand was resting on the crook of my elbow. Even in sleep she looked worried. I had the impulse to smooth the disquiet from her brow again.

I blinked at the white ceiling, realizing it must have been painted tin. An ornate floral design seemed to glare down at me. While filling my lungs with air, I realized my desperate need to visit the water closet. Removing the damp cloths from my forehead and chest, I tried to stealthily pull my arm from underneath Rosemond's hand, but her eyes snapped open with the movement.

There was relief on her face and tears welling in her eyes as she gasped, "You're awake." I must have been unconscious for a disconcerting amount of time.

I went to use my voice and nothing came out. I cleared my throat, trying not to wake Ethan. "H-How long has it been?"

She was smiling now as she did indeed wipe a tear from her eyes. "Three days."

I gasped. "Three?"

"Three," she confirmed once more. She released the pillow and shoved it to the top of the bed and sat up. Gently, she placed her hand on my forehead and then my cheek.

"Well, it looks like I may pull through. You won't have to be cross with me after all." I commented, recalling her dictum about being angry with me if my wound became infected and I died on her.

"I may be cross with you for making me worry so much. My bedside manner is lacking. You are lucky Ethan's is stellar."

"Would you mind helping me sit up? The loo is calling me."

"Oh, yes, of course." Rosemond shuffled off of the bed and walked around to my side. She offered her arm and slid her free hand behind my back. I pulled myself up while she helped. My head felt a little otherworldly, and my shoulder had a blunted type of ache that made my stomach knot. Managing to stand, my feet pricked with pain as I swayed forward. She quickly righted me. My skin was damp, and I shivered from being out of the warm bed.

"Here."

It took me a second to focus on what she was handing me —a robe. With her help, I looped my arms into the sleeves. She crossed the front closed and tied it for me. It was taking all of my mental faculties to stand and not pitch forward. "I thought you said you didn't have a good bedside manner?"

She let out a huff of air. "You are certainly feeling better. Let's get you to the bathroom."

She walked with me, her arm lightly around my lower back until I was able to totter the rest of the way on my own. She stood two meters away from the loo as I entered.

"I'll wait here. If you need something, yell."

I stole a look at her one last time as the door clicked shut. Dark circles were nested under the pale skin of her eyes; even the lavender seemed too tired to shine. I felt humbled and grateful for what she and Ethan must have done. *Three days.*

Pressing my forehead against the closed door, I tried to get my head together. There was a job to do, and having a schoolboy crush on someone who was to be protected was not going to help.

The distraction could get us both killed.

CHAPTER 9

CAN'T YOU SEE

ROSEMOND

Eight days ago I would have sworn that I would be sitting with my tutor right now, as was the schedule every Friday morning. My life had seemed to be completely made of regiment. Fridays were my favorite, though. Extra time was allowed at the piano, and the literature we studied was always poetry.

It was also the afternoon set aside for physical training. I thrived on this, despite the fact that my instructor was impossible: a Slayer, *of course*. But learning was my foremost desire. I supposed training me had been an insult to a Slayer. Maybe that was why his civility was always kept under a thin skin. Maybe he simply had disliked me personally.

Footsteps in the hall tore me from my wandering thoughts. Ethan emerged through the doorway of the drawing room. I closed the book I had borrowed from the shelf and met his bright blue eyes.

"And what, my lady, are we reading today?" he asked.

I ran my hand over the tawny, leather cover fondly. "Renaissance poetry."

He dramatically dropped to one knee and placed his hand over his heart.

> *"Being your slave, what should I do but tend.*
> *Upon the hours and times of your desire?*
> *I have no precious time at all to spend,*
> *Nor services to do, till you require."*

I looked at him blankly, with an overwhelming urge to giggle. "A poetry fan?"

"Not really."

"Who was that?"

"Shakespeare...Some of *Sonnet 57*."

"Or if you prefer..." He wagged his eyebrows.

> *"My true-love hath my heart, and I have hers,*
> *By just exchange, one for the other giv'n.*
> *I hold her dear, and mine she cannot miss;*
> *There never was a better bargain driv'n."*

"That is *not* how it goes," I interrupted. "I just read that one."

Ethan wriggled his fingers in the air waving off the criticism. "Minor change. It would be odd if I called you a he."

"I thought you said you didn't like poetry."

"I don't, but it works fantastically if you are trying to woo women." He paused, "Are you sufficiently wooed?" Ethan blinked prettily at me.

I rolled my eyes and fanned myself. "Can hardly contain

myself." If I believed there had been any heat behind his flirtations, I might have actually blushed.

He popped back up to his feet and walked over to the chair opposite me, sprawling himself across it. He assessed me with his half-teasing, half-comforting grin. "Lies. All lies. You are not wooed at all. I must be losing my touch."

I did laugh this time.

"I'm actually surprised you and George could wade though all my admirers to get to the door the other night."

Narrowing my eyes at him, "And what would you do with all those lady callers?"

He opened his mouth to answer, but it was George's voice I heard. "Nothing. Ethan here is a living oxymoron."

"Did you just call me a moron?" Ethan asked with faux hurt.

With a straight-face, George explained, "Ethan here could charm the crown off the queen, but he has the morals of a monk—the product of his childhood. Don't let his bohemian nature fool you. He gets that from his aunt, but it was too late for him. His parents had already solidified the bones beneath the façade. Have you ever heard of an artist as reliable as a clock?"

"Afraid I'm exposed. I do love kissing the girls, but I don't bed them—not *all* of them at least." Ethan looked at me wolfishly. "Though exceptions can always be made."

Ethan immediately looked for George's response, so my eyes went to George as well. He seemed to flinch, but it was so brief I wasn't sure if I'd seen it at all. My attention returned to Ethan, and though his posture remained aloof, he was watching George closely.

"George, I'm not rushing you out, but do you know how much longer you would like to stay?"

"You sent the telegram?"

"Yes. Gibberish sent."

"Gibberish?" I asked.

The gravitational force in the room seemed to shift as George peered at me very seriously. "Rosemond." His voice was rough. "I asked for word on your mother. We will listen to the radio tonight. If they received my message, they will play Bix Beiderbecke's *In a Mist* at 8:oo p.m. The song that follows will give us the news. If your mother is unharmed, Gene Austin's *My Blue Heaven* and if..." He didn't say the words. "Bessie Smith's *After You've Gone.* I apologize that there are so many hours between now and then, but it was necessary to give them time to make arrangements. Perhaps I shouldn't have told—"

"Thank you." I clutched the book in my hands. My nerves seemed to painfully prick my entire body, and my heart began to beat at an alarming rate. Feeling short of breath, I stood up but lost my grip on the book, and it thumped loudly on the ground. Sputtering, "Sorry-so-sorry," I reached to pick up the book, but Ethan already had it in hand. He and George wore the same frailly pleasant look on their faces. "Is it safe to walk the grounds, do you think?"

George hesitated. "Yes, I believe so."

"Thank you. I just need some fresh air."

I walked into the hall, still hearing the thrum of my heart more than anything else as I plucked a coat from the hook by the front door. I had no idea whose coat it was that I grabbed, but I wanted outside. Making my way to the back door, the grey day greeted me. It hadn't rained in two days, but patches of the earth were still soft. It squished and gave way as I slowly picked my way across the backyard.

A raven landed on a branch overhead and cawed at me. If I were superstitious, this would seem a bad omen. A few seconds later, a wisp of cigarette smoke scented the air, and I eyed the house. Both Ethan and George were leaning against the porch railing. Ethan was smoking and had his back to me, facing the house, while George leaned on his side with his hip against the wood and had full view of the yard.

The crow cawed at me again. This time, I threw a rock at it. It was ill-tempered of me, but I didn't care.

Dread overwhelmed me with the thought that I would no longer like Bessie Smith's *After You've Gone* later this evening.

GEORGE

In a gentle tone, Ethan said, "You can stay as long as you like, you know."

"We must away in the morning. I'm sure you are ready to be rid of me by now." I knew the smile on my face was bittersweet.

"Are you ever going to tell me what all this is about?"

"Ethan, it is better you not know."

A harsh sort of laugh resonated in his chest. I wasn't used to hearing from him. "That is exactly what your Rosemond said."

"She is not *my* Rosemond."

"You wish her to be," he commented, pushing me to admit something.

I swallowed and felt as though there was a band around my chest preventing me from drawing breath. "I am to return to England as soon as she is sorted. You are mistaken."

"And nothing can alter your course once you set it, eh, George?"

"You seem awfully fond of her, with your flirtations. Though, you have always been *attentive* to the fairer sex." My words sounded more like an accusation than I meant.

He laughed and patted my shoulder as he ground the cigarette butt under his foot. "You have nothing to worry about. I don't intend to steal her away, but you can't fool me, Georgie." Ethan strolled back into the house.

A minute later the clanking of pans emanated from the kitchen. I was going to be sad to leave this place. Sad to lose my friend—again.

SUPPER HAD THE STRAINED UNDERCURRENT OF A DOCTOR'S visit when you are to find out test results. If it hadn't been for Ethan's jovial nature, the sound of forks scraping plates would have been unbearable.

When the meal was coming to a close, I noticed blue splotches on Ethan's wrist bone and pointed at them.

He viewed his wrist absently, his mind elsewhere, apparently not even on what he was speaking about just a moment ago. "Oh, Cerulean Blue." He smudged them away with a serviette.

"You're painting again? That's where you keep disappearing to?"

He smiled, still faraway and leaned back. "I only stopped our senior year. Only sold one piece."

Rosemond turned to Ethan. "I would very much like to see your work."

Ethan smiled at her but didn't really answer. His art was one of the few things he had ever kept private. It was surprising he had sold one.

A short time later we relocated to the drawing room. The grandfather clock at the base of the stairwell began to chime and at the same moment, Bix Beiderbecke's *In a Mist* filled the sudden absence of chimes.

I closed my eyes praying for good news, her pain completely abhorrent to me. Having thought ahead, I specifically requested a short song as to not prolong the agony of waiting. Two minutes and forty-six seconds ticked by. I held my breath in the pause before the next tune. When the melody became clear, Rosemond stood and addressed both of us pleasantly.

"I believe I will turn in early. I wish you both a good night." She made her way towards the hall.

"Rosemond," I rasped. She stopped short, and for an instant, she was unsteady. She quickly grabbed onto the molding around the entryway.

She turned briefly, her eyes despairing. "I will be ready to go at first light, George." She nodded at me, then at Ethan. "Sleep well, gentlemen." And then she was gone.

I wanted to tell her that I was sorry for her loss. I wanted to tell her when she is hurt—I hurt. I wanted to hold her. But she was gone, and all that could be heard was Bessie Smith:

"How can you leave me,

can't you see my tears?
Listen while I say
After you've gone,
and left me crying
After you've gone..."

CHAPTER 10

SIREN

ROSEMOND

Grey-blue, early morning light filtered through the sheers. I hadn't bothered tugging them closed when I fell fully clothed into bed. My numbed-state seemed to dull my senses enough for sleep. The tears had never come, though my eyes felt swollen as if there had been a deluge. I sluggishly kicked back the covers that had managed to twist around me during the fitful night. The effort of it made me feel a breathless.

Struggling to sit up, I stared at my wrinkled dress and was thankful at least to be in my own clothing. It wouldn't have been possible for me to find our luggage again after jumping from the train. George was shockingly good at mapping out directions, and Ethan was able to retrieve our bags without difficulty. Only the books in my shoulder bag were ruined by the rain and mud.

Pulling out the carefully folded clothing and spreading it out on the bed reminded me of my mother's impeccable fashion sense. She had purchased new garments for me in a variety of styles. I shrugged out of my dress and stood staring at the beautiful Nemo-flex undergarments before mechanically putting them on. Then, I stepped into my new misty grey Georgette crepe dress; the velvet collar came to a deep-V in the front, making me feel a little exposed. I picked up my geometric print scarf and tied it around my neck. Sinking onto the stool in front of the dressing table, I fussed my hair into some nice finger waves in the front and two swirling knots at the base of my skull, making sure I had them low enough to wear my matching Cloche hat.

Feeling hollow, I looked at my wan face in the mirror. My mother had always told me to look how I wanted to feel. If you are having a bad day—dress up. I wasn't sure if I agreed. My desire had always been to feel comfortable when feeling ill at ease. But there was a need to draw strength from somewhere, and I didn't want to be a liability—*ever*. I pulled out the make-up bag she had packed and stared at the contents.

My desire was to feel fierce. After covering the bruise on my forehead, I applied charcoal liner around my eyes, powder-puffed pink onto my cheeks, and smoothed a deep rose onto my lips. If not for the lavender eyes staring at me, I looked like a different girl. Satisfied, I tossed the pouch of cosmetics into my suitcase.

Sounds from George and Ethan drifted up from the lower floor. I placed my bags at the top of the staircase, topped with my hat, and descended. Stopping in the hall outside the kitchen, I listened for a moment—not to eavesdrop, but to enjoy hearing them speak to one another.

George was laughing at something Ethan had said; they sounded like schoolboys. I had never felt as if I had missed out

on anything in my upbringing until now. Taking a deep breath,
I stepped into the doorway.

Ethan saw me first. "Wellllll, aren't we looking ravishing
today?"

George didn't comment. He bobbed his head, and the
smile melted from his face. "Morning, Rosemond."

"Good morning, boys." I walked the rest of the way into
the kitchen and took a seat at the table.

"Breakfast?" Ethan asked.

"Yes, please. I can g—"

"Nonsense." He was already halfway to the stove. He
grabbed a plate from the cupboard, and served up what looked
like a ground beef patty, smothered in gravy with eggs on the
side, and placed it in front of me. "My aunt lived in the South
for several years. This was her favorite."

"Looks wonderful." Cautiously, I cut into the meat, a little
leery of it, despite the fact that I shouldn't have been worried;
everything we had eaten here had been wonderful, and this was
no exception.

When I was almost done with my meal, I realized that it
had gotten quiet and looked at both of them. George looked
worried again, the line between his brows strained. Ethan on
the other hand, looked a million miles away, making me
wonder where his thoughts kept drifting.

Ethan pressed the side of his right thumb to his lips and
glanced at me, almost sheepishly before he turned his gaze to
George. "I was working on something the night the two of you
arrived. I think I would like to show it to you...*should* show it
to you."

George raised an eyebrow. "Sounds intriguing."

We trailed behind him up the stairs to a room filled with

morning sun. It seemed as though we should have heard birds chirping outside. More life flourished in this room than in any of the others. It smelled of paint thinner and wood. A canvas was perched on an easel facing the corner. We circled around, and when I took in the image, my breath caught in my throat.

A romanticized portraiture of a mermaid, in amazing detail adorned the canvas. She was hidden behind some rocks, watching a boy...a man. His expression was obscured because he sat with elbows on his knees and hands over his face as if to hide some look of anguish. Sunlight warmed his dark wavy hair. His musculature was evident under the loose white shirt where the wind was pressing it to his body.

Then I focused on the mermaid; her long dark hair hung in a way such that it hid her half nude body. She looked as if she were about to reveal her existence to him. The scales on her lower half looked iridescent in blues and purples and greens. I don't know if I had ever seen anything so beautiful.

"Ethan...it's—" I searched to find the words to express my admiration, but George interrupted.

"It's you."

I was confused and looked at Ethan. He raised his hands as if to surrender. "I have only touched the ocean since you have been here, and it's oil. Look." He dabbed at the mermaid and revealed a dry finger." Puzzled, I bit my bottom lip and turned back to the canvas.

My eyes grew wide with my revelation—the mermaid had lavender eyes, long dark hair, alabaster skin, and Cupid's bow lips. She even had my delicate nose and the few freckles that appear in the summer months. I searched the mermaid's face and had to admit, it was uncanny.

Ethan shook his head and ran his long fingers through his

messy blond hair. "I can't explain it. I saw you in my head over a year ago. Well, not you, but her." He stepped back and looked out the window, the same faraway expression on his face as he turned. "I would like to come with you."

George immediately answered. "It's not possible."

Ethan laughed, "It is, and you know it. This isn't a whim. I have put considerable thought into this."

George interjected, "Ethan, I won't risk your safety. If—"

Ethan pressed his hands together in front of him as if he were about to pray. "I would like you to hear me out. I don't have anything to keep me here and have always hated this house—you know that, George. And now that my aunt has passed, there's no family and no reason to stay.

"That said, I need to say this: First, you obviously have bad people after you. They will be looking for the two of you, not a threesome. Second, you have had me run errands into town, sending telegrams and what not. Wouldn't it be safer for me to continue to do that? Third, I have money, ridiculous amounts of it, and I don't believe you have access to much. You said that you merely had the money from the quick sale of a motor-car. That will last you a while, but..." His voice trailed, and it was apparent that George was still not convinced.

"And you know you can trust me. If you have a traitor in your super-secret organization you won't be calling in many favors. It is one thing to ask for information, but not as safe to ask for direct help. You may need the backup. An extra set of eyes cannot be a bad thing." He paused. "Is there a need to keep going?"

I spoke: "Ethan, people are actively trying to kill us. Actually, kill George and take me. They would think nothing of killing you, too."

"Still sounds like you need help to me." Ethan made a small exasperated sound. "I'll leave you two to confab." He waved his hands in the air as he exited. Heavy clomping steps echoed all the way down the stairwell.

George looked stricken, staring after Ethan for a moment. Then he turned and looked at me with wide eyes.

Hesitantly, I asked, "What do you think, George?"

GEORGE

Standing there, I did not know what to think. Ethan made a reasonable case, but could I allow him in harm's way? I picked up a paintbrush and ran my thumb over the bristles, small bits of dust floated into the air, dancing in the light streaming from the oversized windows. "You think we should leave him here?" I meant it as a statement, but it came out a question.

"I didn't say that." She paused. "But I don't like people hurt on my behalf. Part of me thinks you should turn me loose and go back to England."

"You don't want that." My voice sounded uneven.

She sighed and walked to the window, sitting on the sill. "Not really. I still need to learn a few things before I can truly disappear and survive on my own. Once you teach me to create false identities, you should run far, far away from me."

I grinned at her, saying, "So you are ready to be rid of me then?" Yet cringing internally for asking.

Her cheeks flushed as she looked out the window. "I think we should accept Ethan's offer."

I nodded when she looked at me again but noted she avoided answering my question. I viewed Ethan's painting. It was remarkable. I had thought Rosemond a Siren and here she was in front of me. I wondered what God was trying to tell me. I turned back to her and hesitantly asked, "How are you today?"

There was a small intake of breath, and she gazed at me with those captivating eyes of hers. Somehow she was so vulnerable, and yet so strong, it twisted me inside. A sad smile upturned her lips.

"My impulse is to say, 'Fine.'" She linked her hands in front of her and examined the silver ring she wore on her right hand, spinning it round and round her finger. "I'm not fine, but I am too stubborn to be defeated by the events of late." She paused, and met my gaze again. "Thank you for asking."

I nodded. "Are you ready to tell Ethan our decision?"

"I hadn't realized we had one," she said, cocking her head to the side in confusion.

Starting for the door, I answered, "Yes, he's coming with us." I glanced back to see that she was just steps behind me.

My decision troubled me, but more than anything it made me feel good. It was a sound decision; I knew it in my soul.

ROSEMOND

Ethan locked the front door of his aunt's gothic home and tromped down the steps, joining us at the curb. Before he picked up his two bags, he turned one more time and looked at his home for the last three and a half years. There was a finality in his expression, like he didn't think he would return. George and I loaded the luggage in the backseat and crawled into Ethan's motorcar and waited, giving Ethan a few moments alone.

When Ethan joined us, he asked, "Where to?"

George drew in a breath. "We need a town large enough that the county clerks don't know everyone in the area, but small enough that they trust the intentions of strangers."

Ethan laughed, put the car into gear, and pulled from the curb. A sort-of chortle escaped his lips. "So that's how it's going to be. Nothing like specific-non-specific directions."

"You wanted to help," George dryly responded.

"This is going to be great fun," Ethan said agreeably.

All I could do was pray it would be...

Please, dear Lord, let it be...

CHAPTER 11

RESURRECTION

ROSEMOND

"Well, George. Have to say that I would never have expected to end up here," I commented, taking in the surroundings. I stood on clumpy grass, and the cold from the ground seemed to seep through the soles of my shoes.

"Yes, George, with such attractive travel companions, I would have thought you would pick a more romantic locale. Or you could at least buy me a drink first." Ethan made an overly dramatic sad face.

I giggled, and in the process, snorted. Causing me to blush uncontrollably, and cover my face to hide my mortification. Suddenly, Ethan was directly in front of me.

He pulled my hands from my face and kissed the knuckles of my right hand. "I dare say, are you flirting with me?" He wagged his eyebrows.

Snatching my hands from his, I pushed him away. "Mockery will get you nowhere."

"Mockery? You quite possibly have the cutest snort I've ever heard."

Rolling my eyes, I pointed at George. "Our guide is leaving us behind." Just then he disappeared behind a mausoleum. We trotted a few yards to catch up.

Ethan plopped down on top of a dull-grey tombstone and asked, "So Georgie, you mind letting us in on the reason we are here? As much as I *love* graveyards, it would be nice to know the mission. And by the pinched look on your face, you are up to something."

George's expression opened up, like he'd forgotten we were with him. "Oh, my apologies. We need to find children that have died between the years of 1903 and 1910."

"That is a little morbid, isn't it?" Ethan asked, raising his eyebrows.

"Well, I don't think Rosemond can pass for anyone older than twenty-five."

"Oh," I said, almost involuntarily, realizing what he was doing. I glanced at Ethan, who still seemed baffled.

George stopped. "There are different ways of creating false identities. One of them is to find children who have passed and get a duplicate birth record. The newspaper and clerk's office are in the same building in this town. It would be too suspicious to research old obituaries and then walk across the hall with a sob story about a lost birth certificate. Sometimes it is necessary to do some legwork."

"So we won't be creating fake papers, then?"

"Real papers are always best, but I plan on giving you some forgery lessons, too. We will need to go to New York to get the proper equipment. We aren't ready for that."

Ethan nodded satisfactorily. "So mucking about in graveyards has a purpose," he laughed. He started to search, and then turned back and asked, "Does it matter how long the child lived?"

"Infants are the best. People remember the tragedy but don't always remember the name. Acquaintances haven't had time to bond with the child."

THREE HOURS LATER, WE HAD FOUR POSSIBLE NAMES. I perused the list George had carefully scrawled in his notebook. His handwriting was perfect and well-practiced, but the occasional deviation from the penmanship books had more of an artistic flair than I would have suspected. It made me wonder if George might be more than rules and regulations. I looked back at his list:

> *Stella Taylor*
> *Abigail Newton*
> *Gertrude Kaplan*
> *Vivian Cassidy*

The name Vivian Cassidy was rather pleasing. With the monikers in hand, we started trudging our way back to the car. It was an old graveyard, and the spongy, uneven earth was difficult to traverse.

My heels kept sinking into the ground, making me slow. We were almost to the gravel path when the sensation of icy tentacles running around my brain and covering my eyes gripped me.

I tried to call out but wasn't sure if any sound escaped my

lips. All I saw was a squat tombstone rushing towards my face when I was completely overtaken by the vision.

GEORGE

At the sound of Rosemond's gasp, I frantically spun around, already shouting her name. Ethan's shocked eyes met mine for a split-second, before he too turned towards her, but it was too late.

We heard the thud of her head striking a tombstone, and then she lay unmoving. Pushing Ethan aside, I dove to her, carefully rolling her onto my lap, not caring that the muddy ground was soaking through my trousers.

I released an uneven breath in relief when I saw her eyes darting beneath her closed lids. She was deep in a vision—and still alive. For a moment, my fear had been that I had lost her to a blow to the head. I cringed, she wasn't mine to lose.

"What happened?" Ethan inquired.

I gathered myself together. "She..." My mind raced as I tried to decide what to tell him.

Ethan sank to his haunches across from me. "It wasn't a seizure—look at her eye movement." He pulled an overly white handkerchief from his pocket and handed it to me.

A goose-egg was rising on the edge of her hairline. Blood had welled up and was running down the side of her face. I firmly pressed the cloth to the wound. A minuscule sort of whimper slid through her lips, but I kept the pressure up to minimize the swelling.

"George, do you know what's wrong?" He paused. "You do, don't you?" Ethan questioned with a determined tone in his voice.

I decided upon answering with the truth but still wanted to keep his knowledge of our world to a minimum. "She is *special*." I met his concerned eyes. "She is having a vision. When they happen, she loses consciousness."

"Like she...communes with spirits?" he asked, his face twisting in disbelief.

"No, she sees bits of the past or sometimes, the future. I know. I was skeptical too. My first reaction was to scoff at my father for sending me to escort a fortune-teller. But have my assurance, she is the genuine article. A seer or a prophetess or whatever you would like to call her. So was her mother."

He was silent for a long moment, and then he spoke again. "That is why people want to take her and kill you," he stated, as the bits of conversation he had overheard over the last week fell into place.

"If the wrong people get ahold of her, it would not only be bad for her, but bad for the world."

He grinned. "The entire world?" he questioned, assuming it was some form of hyperbole or exaggeration.

Gravely serious, I reiterated, "The *entire* world."

The grin melted from his face, and he swallowed. "You're serious."

I nodded in affirmation. "Wish I weren't." But I knew full well the hopelessness was clear on my face. Rosemond started to stir. Her hand went to her head before her eyes fluttered open, but I didn't release her. I raised the kerchief from her upper forehead, but blood immediately bubbled up. Returning the cloth, I put pressure on it once again. She started to struggle to sit up. "Lie still. My apologies, I couldn't get to you quick enough."

"Not your fault," she mumbled, still looking a little dazed.

"What did you see?"

Her eyes instantly went to Ethan, and she sighed. "You told him." It wasn't a question.

Ethan had already recovered. "Yes, I'm just shocked you haven't seen how madly in love you will fall with me. That is assuming you haven't fallen for me already."

She started to laugh but abruptly stopped and moaned. "Oh." After it appeared that the pain in her head had receded, she suggested, "Maybe we should only walk around in soft places from now on."

"Or invest in a helmet. You would be quite fetching in one." I quipped. She looked at me surprised that I had made the comment. In fact, I was. *Ethan's influence, no doubt.* Then it suddenly felt awkward that she was lying in my lap once again.

She put her hand over mine. "I can do that now." I carefully slid my hand out from under hers, keeping the cloth in place.

"You prepared to sit up?" I asked, not really wanting to relinquish my grip on her.

"I may need another minute. Blow to the head and all." The colour seemed to drain away from her face even further.

"What did you see?" I asked again.

She gave me the same answer that she gave me last time I had asked the same question. "Something that needs to be altered."

A frown tugged down at the corners of my mouth. I could sense Ethan looking at me and tipped my head up to return his gaze.

Ethan pointed at Rosemond and me. "The sun is setting. Should we get you two out of the mud? Or would you prefer to freeze? It looks like it will rain at any moment.

"Yes, best not to be out after dark," I confirmed.

Ethan gingerly pulled Rosemond to her feet, waiting until she was steady before releasing her. After a few steps, he placed his hand on her elbow and kept it there as we made our way to the motorcar. "How often do you have visions?" Ethan asked.

Her voice was hesitant. "I have only had a few. They seem to be a gift shortly after we turn eighteen. As terrible as they are, they can be useful." She glanced at me when she said it, making me wonder exactly what she saw.

We were at our out-of-the-way lodgings almost straight away and received only a few sideways glances as we walked through the small lobby in our muddied state. As we entered the living room, I turned to Ethan. "There may be an answer to the telegram I sent my father. Would—"

"Of course, you clean up," he replied, cutting me off in his typical good-natured way. "I'll get some supper too. I'm famished." And without another word, he was halfway down the hall.

"Thank you, friend," I murmured too late.

I shut the door and found Rosemond, standing in the middle of the room, lost in thought. She was staring at a spot on the rug and biting the thumbnail of her right hand. Not once had I seen her bite her nails before. I went into the bedroom I was sharing with Ethan and pulled out some clean clothing. When I returned to the living room, Rosemond hadn't moved.

"How is your head?"

She stared at me blankly as if I had spoken in some obscure language.

"What did you see that has you so rattled?"

She shook her head. "I'm not sure. This one was very fragmented, more so than usual." The line between her brows deepened.

"I saw a hand go through the glass of a windshield. I heard Ethan cry out in pain. You screamed my name. It felt as though my limbs were filled with mud. Then the car was stopped, maybe we crashed. A deep voice said, 'You should have called your Slayers.' Followed by a horrible sound of metal being twisted or torn. I actually heard more than saw. But there are chunks of time missing. There was no way to know where we were. I couldn't see what we were wearing. I don't even know what car we were in. I just know that you and Ethan will get hurt or worse, and it is my fault." Her voice rising at the end.

"Rosemond, none of this is your fault."

"Says the man who was shot and almost died saving me."

"You did not shoot me. If you had, then it would be your fault. You cannot control the actions of others." I sighed, knowing nothing I said could completely ease her mind. "Go, clean up. Ethan should be back shortly with the food."

Rosemond nodded and wandered to her room. It was evident from the sound that she was rifling through one of her bags. She emerged a minute later with some fresh clothes, holding them out from her body to keep them clean. "George, I do appreciate all you have done for me. I know that risking your life was not part of the plan."

I opened my mouth to speak, but she put up her hand to stop me.

"Please, my desire was simply to say thank you. I am not looking for reassurances."

Nodding, I kept my mouth shut.

Rosemond turned, and my eyes followed her until she disappeared into the bathroom, the door clicking tightly shut.

～

ETHAN'S DISEMBODIED VOICE CAME FROM THE OTHER BED. "Are you going to tell me what's bothering you? Or are you going to fret until sunrise?"

"How do you know you didn't just wake me?"

"I was practically your roommate for years. I know the sounds of your sleep. You, my friend, are troubled. Was it the telegram? Or the girl you are in love with?"

I grimaced, despite knowing he couldn't see me in the absolute dark of the room. "I am not in love with the girl," I said flatly.

"Me either, she's hideous, both inside and out," he replied, but the smile in his voice was quite evident. "And you didn't almost trample me to death when she fell this afternoon either."

"She hit her head. I was concerned." My voice was entirely too defensive.

"Restatement: So, George, was it the telegram or the girl you are *not* in love with?"

I thought for a few moments, though that was all I had been doing for hours. But now I was being forced to put those thoughts into actual words. "Since I was twelve years old, my singular goal was to teach at Cambridge. There was a tour of the campus I took with my parents, and that was it. I know you thought me crazy for being so determined when we were so young, but I could see it...*taste* it. It was a battle to be allowed to attend our school; without that type of prep school, there wouldn't have been a remote possibility of acceptance into Cambridge."

"Rosemond said she was surprised you'd been able to go to any sort of public or even private college. The knowledge seemed to shock her."

"Yes, I have been living life in public. Part of me wonders if this put Rosemond in danger." Suddenly, I felt as if something large, heavy, and ugly sat on my chest. But then again, my public life wouldn't explain the attack at her home. There hadn't been enough advanced notice to connect me to her. That was coordinated and planned. I became aware of the silence. "You are dying to ask me questions, aren't you?"

He chuckled. "I have been for eight and a half years, but I've learned not to push you." He paused. "Rosemond also told me you kept your air of mystery to protect me from your world."

"You and Rosemond seem to have done a lot of talking."

"You were unconscious for three days. Did you expect us to sit in silence and wait for you to wake? Or is it jealousy speaking?"

I ignored the jealousy comment and continued. "The telegram. My father sent word that despite my delay, the position at Cambridge was not lost. Originally, the plan was for me to be on an airship for mail transport two days ago. Someone had fallen ill, and I was to replace a teaching assistant until I could be given a class in the spring. This was my toehold. This was everything for which I have been working."

"Why the dilemma if you didn't lose the position? I would think you would be relieved," Ethan said in the tone he used when he was only saying a fraction of what he thought.

"I didn't say there was one. I'm simply worried that it won't be possible to teach Rosemond enough and get her settled before my departure."

"Ah," Ethan responded. A long while later, when I thought he may have drifted off to sleep, he spoke one last time. His voice was soft and pensive. "George, just because you set yourself on a path, it doesn't mean you need to stay on it."

My lips parted, wanting to reply, but I remained silent. His words to me were as heavy as the weight on my chest.

CHAPTER 12

HERO

ROSEMOND

The lobby smelled of old books and ink from newsprint. George and I stood, trying not to stare through the plate glass windows at Ethan speaking to the clerk. I stuck my hand in the pocket of my wool coat and felt the twenty dollar bill. I still couldn't believe Ethan had goaded George into betting that he could get a duplicate birth certificate for me. And twenty dollars was an extravagant amount.

I glanced over George's shoulder into the office again. Ethan was leaning rather flirtatiously across the counter, and the thirty-something clerk was covering her mouth and giggling. Ethan began writing something on a piece of paper, and while he was seemingly distracted, I noticed her check her deep-red lipstick that matched the pattern on her dress. Then, she surreptitiously fluffed her blonde bob. He placed his hand on the paper and slowly slid it over to her, his eyes never leaving hers. She seemed to melt a little when he spoke again.

I whispered, "George, I think you may have lost the bet."

He didn't answer. I placed my hand on his elbow, and he seemed to jolt from his current train of thought. He gave me a tight-lipped smile. "My apologies. You said something?" He seemed adrift or maybe sad.

I grinned at him. "Yes, I think you may have lost your wager."

He scowled, but I wasn't sure if it was about the bet. He casually turned and sat on a bench at the far side of the lobby while peering into the office. He shook his head, and I saw a grin flicker on his face, but he sobered again when he glanced at me.

I strolled over joining him, and was able to glimpse Ethan once again. He had the clerk's hand in his and was writing on her palm. Somehow I doubted there was a lack of paper in the office.

"You may be correct," he finally answered.

The bell on the door of the clerk's office jingled, announcing Ethan's exit. He walked past us, as if he didn't know us, and departed the building. We waited a minute, and then made our way out. Ethan was waiting for us in the motorcar.

"George, you may have to pay me double," Ethan stated in a puffed up manner.

"I don't believe that was part of the bargain," George replied disapprovingly.

"Yes, but I managed to finesse two birth certificates, one for myself and one for my dear cousin Vivian. Who, I might add, would string me up if I didn't fix things. After all, I was responsible for setting our home ablaze."

"One for you?" George questioned.

"Of course, what challenge is it only procuring one? I may have taken the liberty to jot a few extra names down during our visit to the cemetery yesterday."

I batted my eyes at Ethan. "And cousin, how do I not know my own kin's name?"

"Sorry, darling, it must be the bump on the head," Ethan laughed.

"Or smoke inhalation from the fictitious fire," I added.

"Yes, terrible fire." He took my hand and lightly kissed my knuckles. "Fredrick Lassiter, nice to meet you."

George interrupted our banter. "Freddy, when will you have the documents?"

"Meeting her for a late supper tonight. She will bring them with her."

"I see you are suffering for the cause," George remarked.

"Yes, terribly." Ethan put his hand on his chest and gave me a martyred look.

I couldn't help but giggle. It made me feel a little foolish, knowing the clerk had been reduced to the same state just moments ago, but I couldn't help myself. George, on the other hand, did not seem amused. In fact, he had been remarkably somber all morning. Almost cold.

WHEN EVENING ARRIVED, GEORGE AND I DINED ON OUR supper while well-disguised in the same restaurant as Ethan and his date. I almost felt sorry for the clerk, with Ethan shamelessly unleashing his charms on her. My gaze rested on George, who still seemed distracted, but his eyes would dart to the doorways and to every new person who entered. I knew he was constantly assessing threats.

"George? Are you going to speak with me at all this evening? Or will I be reduced to eavesdropping for my entertainment?"

"Rosemond," he whispered, but it almost sounded like a plea. I found his manner today confusing. He had been so much more open after we'd arrived at Ethan's home. And now, it seemed he was retreating back behind the controlled façade I had originally met, but even more so now.

His beautiful hazel eyes smoldered for a second, then his face smoothed. He said my name again, but this time it was as if I were a stranger. His tone was polite, and not at all unkind, but I had grown accustomed to a warmth in his voice whenever he had said my name. "I am to be called back to England in a few weeks. I have four, five weeks at most."

"Oh." I struggled to keep the disappointment from my expression. "I suppose I will be quite ready by then."

"Yes, you are a quick study, and you should have all the supplies you need by then." He gave me a ghostly smile, but it never managed to reach his eyes. I wished I knew what caused this change in him. After the exchange, we fell silent, with only the sounds of the other patrons in the eatery.

I had tried to will myself to put up some protective walls—knowing his presence was temporary from the start. His leaving was inevitable. Chastising myself was all I could do as I glared at the food on my plate. It no longer looked appetizing; I simply pushed it around until it was time to leave.

We shadowed Ethan as he walked the clerk to her car. She would have taken him home had he asked, her body language screamed of desire. He stood and watched her drive off. Once she was safely away, he strolled to our vehicle and slipped into the backseat. I watched as he pulled some paperwork from his inside coat pocket.

"She came through," George commented.

"Of course she did," he replied, as if there could have been no other outcome.

"Just because she thought you would bed her," I interjected matter-of-factly.

"Rosemond, I am appalled. Such frankness. In fact, I may have to start calling you Frank. You don't seem to pull any punches, do you?"

I swiveled around in my seat, a little farther to face him. "Would you prefer I swoon and coo like the other girls?"

He leaned towards me, splitting the space between us in the car. Even in the barely-there light, his eyes burned blue. "No, I much prefer my women strong and sassy. Much more of a challenge." And then he laughed and leaned back before I could swat him away. At that moment George started the engine to return to the hotel.

ONCE WE WERE BACK, I WASHED UP, PUT ON MY ROBE, AND joined the boys in the living room of the small suite. They were quietly playing cards, but it wasn't any game I recognized. Suddenly there was a flurry of motion and George slapped the back of Ethan's hand, Ethan then let out a whoop and slapped George's other hand. Then there was another flurry of cards being smacked down onto the table. "You, my friend, owe me a drink," Ethan exclaimed.

"And where in this dry town am I supposed to acquire said 'drink'?"

"You will have to owe me one. I like it when you owe me." There was a satisfied smirk on Ethan's face that told me there were many stories that could be told. I settled the rest of the way into the couch and curled my legs beneath me. "Oh, Frank."

I looked up at Ethan and pursed my lips in frustration with myself for responding to his stupid new nickname.

"Catch." He tossed a leather book to me. A smile cracked my sour expression when I realized it was the poetry book I'd been reading in his home. "George said your books were ruined in the rain."

Hugging the book to my chest, I felt genuinely touched. "Thank you." I glanced at George, but his head was turned so I couldn't see his face.

"Do you want us to deal you in?" Ethan asked.

I raised an eyebrow. "I prefer not to have my hand slapped in the deranged version of whatever game you are playing, thank you very much."

"Suit yourself," he replied with an accompanying shrug.

The boys acted like grade-schoolers while I happily read my Renaissance poetry for the remainder of the evening.

The faint click of George's pocket watch drew my attention. "It is eleven," he murmured.

Ethan stretched his long limbs and yawned rather theatrically. "I suppose it's time to go to bed."

George grew more serious before he focused on me. "We will leave at first light and head to the next town of appropriate size. I would like to have the paperwork for a minimum of four identities, preferably six. I have seen persons on the run burn through three rather quickly. And as the speed of communication increases, the more difficult it will be to hide."

My smile was thin but pleasant. "I will see both of you at first light then." Closing the door , I practically fell into bed. The night seemed endless though; maybe I was overly tired. Maybe I couldn't keep the change in George from running through my head over and over and over again. Maybe...

~

I WOKE WHEN ETHAN PLOPPED HIMSELF ON MY BED AND LAY on his side facing me. I squinted at him and scowled. "What are you doing in here?"

"The knocking didn't wake you. George was too polite to burst in. I, on the other hand..." He looked at me suggestively.

I rolled my eyes and grabbed the pillow from beneath my head and hit him.

He laughed and then stuffed the pillow under his head. He quieted and looked at me thoughtfully. "Are you well? I don't think I have seen you oversleep before."

I tried to smile, but little more happened than the edge of my lip quirking upwards. "Bad dreams."

He frowned and opened his mouth to say something but paused. "Well, don't take too long getting up. George seems to be all business today."

Forcing myself into a sitting position, I looked down at Ethan, who seemed entirely too comfortable on my bed. My voice was the softest of whispers. "Did I do something to offend George?"

Ethan didn't look surprised by my question and it made my heart sink. "George is a person with a clear vision of where he is going. And when something upsets the paradigm he has constructed, he struggles. Be assured that you have done nothing wrong. Just ignore it. He won't be so snarly in a few days."

My eyes narrowed once again. "Your words are suspiciously careful."

He stood abruptly and headed for the door. "And you, my darling, Frank, have ten minutes to get ready."

I flopped back onto the bed and pulled the covers over my head. "Just leave me."

He chuckled. "Nine minutes," he crooned as he closed the door.

TWENTY MINUTES LATER WE WERE ON THE ROAD TO THE next town of appropriate size. This time we hadn't the need of tromping through a graveyard; the town archives were separate from the clerk's office. I was fully prepared to spin my yarn to acquire the needed documents, but when Ethan saw the clerk, he quickly ushered me from view. "Please, let me do this one," he pleaded.

"I need to practice," I argued.

Ethan didn't release my arm. "Please, did you see her? She looks like a naughty librarian."

I think rolling my eyes was becoming my standard response to him. "Go. Have at it. Heaven forbid my education keep you from a woman."

He grinned devilishly, gave me a peck on the forehead, and was in the office before I could reconsider.

George touched my elbow lightly. "Why don't we wait over

there?" He pointed to a stone planter with a wide ledge to perch on.

We sat in silence for a while. George was so still, I wondered if he was breathing. It was nearly noon, and his eyes were in the shadow cast by his hat. His eyes were focused down the street, and I allowed myself to regard him.

He appeared to be fighting a larger gravitational pull than everyone else on the planet. Dark circles under his eyes matched the ones under my own. It seemed I wasn't the only one having trouble sleeping. The wind picked up, and the chill caused me to shudder. George's gaze swept my way again, so I quickly scrutinized a passing motorcar.

He moved behind me, but I refused to look over at him. Then I felt the warmth of his jacket as he placed it around my shoulders. "Thank you," I stammered.

He regarded me with an odd expression, catching the hitch in my voice, but he didn't say anything. An ethereal smile passed over his face, then was gone. His visage returned to the smooth, expressionless blank slate to which I was now growing accustomed.

I cleared my throat, and our eyes met. When they did, it felt as if they were locked together, and I was powerless to look away. The beat of my heart seemed to respond, and I felt a little short of breath.

George broke the contact by closing his eyes, and his breathing most definitely quickened. He rubbed his palms on his slacks as if they were sweating, then stood to his feet. He laced his fingers behind his neck and paced one direction, then back the other. The emotion simmering under the surface was palpable, but nothing happened. He still didn't speak to me; he simply paced until Ethan came out a few minutes later.

It was impossible to keep myself from smiling at Ethan and his triumphant demeanor. "Another dinner date?"

"Why would you think otherwise?"

"No, I expected this result. But I do wonder how all these women recover after you break their hearts."

"Don't worry, Frank. I always let them down easy." He offered me his arm. Looping my right arm through his, I held George's coat shut with my left.

As before, George and I dined in disguise while Ethan had his meal with "the naughty librarian." She also looked like she wanted to tuck Ethan into her pocket and take him home.

WHEN WE RETURNED TO OUR NEW LODGINGS, I WAS lagging behind Ethan, who had the room key and had already disappeared inside. After trotting up three steps, the heel on my t-strap shoes caught on something; I overcorrected and completely lost my balance. I twisted in an effort to get my hands out, but George already had me.

Suddenly, my hands were on his shoulders, and his hands on my waist. I had stumbled down to the step above him—we were face-to-face. Neither of us budged an inch. I once again felt powerless to move. We stood there, time stretching out before us. It took every ounce of my control not to lean in the three remaining inches and press my lips to his.

The sputter of a passing car a moment later seemed to snap us out of it. "Are you all right?" George asked.

Not trusting my voice, I nodded.

It felt almost painful to remove my hands from him, and this frustrated me. He had been so distant the last few days, though he'd never once treated me poorly. He was nothing less than a gentleman. It simply felt...professional. I stood up straight, but when I went to take a step realized I had, in fact, turned my ankle. Pausing, I let out a small whimper under my breath.

"Let's keep your weight off of it." And with that, George looped my arm around his neck and slipped his good arm around my waist, helping me up the rest of the stairs. When we shuffled in the door, Ethan was sitting with his feet resting on the table reading. He popped up, looking utterly shocked. I wondered what he thought had happened.

The boys helped me to a chair. George knelt in front of me and unbuckled my heel, sliding it from my foot. He slowly probed my ankle with his fingers, being both firm and gentle. "It seems to be only a twist, nothing permanent. It's best if you rest it tonight. Keep it elevated. We should see if they have ice available."

"I'll check on the ice," Ethan said before leaving our room.

George had his hand on my calf, and it was very distracting. My desire was to run my finger over the scar cutting through his eyebrow, and then touch where it picked up again on his pouty bottom lip. I held my breath and leaned back, resenting the feeling of yearning.

"Let me help you to a more comfortable chair," he said in the gentlest of tones. George helped me take a few steps, then eased me into the seat. He assisted me in swiveling to the side and propped my foot up.

Without asking, he retrieved a blanket and my book. There was a small kettle and hotplate in the room, and he put it on to make tea. He was no longer favoring his right shoulder as he had previously; he appeared to have full movement again.

Shortly after, Ethan returned with ice and wrapped it in a towel, draping it over my ankle. This attention was a nice feeling, though it made me feel a little guilty.

GEORGE

We played a more subdued game of cards while Rosemond read her poetry. Her face seemed to reflect whatever she read. Sometimes she smiled softly, other times she frowned. Once, it appeared as if tears might spill down her rosy cheeks. Ethan was winning due to my distraction. My heart was simply not in the game. My heart wanted to be with the girl across the room, but my head still urged me to keep my distance.

When we began our third game of cards, I glanced back at her again. She seemed slightly agitated, and a moment later she asked, "Ethan? Would you mind helping me to my room?"

"Of course, I am but your slave," he teased.

"Thank you." She marked her page with a piece of paper and slammed it shut while Ethan walked over.

When Ethan returned from Rosemond's room, I asked, "What was she reading?"

"She did seem to be blushing, didn't she?" he grinned, and walked over to the chair scooping up the book, opening it to the marked page. A wide smile spread across his face. "Hero and Leander."

"Whose version?"

"Marlowe," Ethan replied and tossed the book back on the chair. "I do like his ending, everything except the last few lines."

"Of course you would. Leander seduces the girl, and she

falls madly in love with him. But you know that is not how the original ends."

"I prefer to stop reading before the tragedy sets in," he replied smugly.

"How does that not surprise me?" I asked, more rhetorically than anything.

"You know, George, sometimes the hero does get the girl."

"Not without sacrifice, my friend. Not without great sacrifice."

CHAPTER 13

YELLOW

ROSEMOND

My ankle was minimally sore in the morning, so we set to work. In the next two days, we were able to acquire another birth certificate in a nearby town. Once again, Ethan convinced me to let him procure it, despite the fact that the clerk had to be in her eighties. It seemed Ethan's gift of persuasion worked on women of any age. But I was to try in the next town, no matter how good-looking the clerk might be. George wanted to get one more before heading to New York.

I woke the following morning, thinking of the color yellow. I kept seeing it everywhere: in the stripe on a man's tie, the bow in a little girl's hair, embellishments on the neckline of a woman's dress. Even the sun seemed to be more yellow today.

The clerk in this town was a gentlemanly, older man with a shock of white hair that stood up much like Ethan's. He wore a monocle with a delicate gold chain that hung to a clip on his collar. He managed to keep the eyepiece in place no matter what the expression on his face.

Unfortunately, that expression was rather disagreeable. I quickly found flirtation was not my forte. I took a deep breath and allowed all the sorrows of the last couple of weeks rush to the surface, and within moments, tears pooled at the rims of my eyes. I despised myself for the manipulation, but this was going to be a necessary evil if I was to survive on my own.

When the first tear plunged down my cheek, the clerk offered me his handkerchief with speed. I dabbed the corners of my eyes. In seconds, his tune changed, and he began the process of typing up the duplicate certificate for me. It seemed he had no idea what to do with an emotional woman. Once he'd completed the document, I thanked him profusely, returned his hanky, and found my way to the boys.

"And how, Frank, did you do?" Ethan asked, when we had strolled a safe distance from the Record's Office.

Before I could respond, George answered. "She has it in her handbag."

"What gave me away?"

George ran his fingers over my knuckles. "The grip on your bag changed. When you entered, you were squeezing the top shut because you were nervous. When you exited, you were cupping it from the bottom as if there were something precious inside."

I coolly responded, "I'll have to work on that." My heart quickened when I realized how many details he had noticed about me.

Ethan lit up a cigarette, and the smoke wafted behind us as we walked another block. I stopped and spied into the huge window of the general store. It was a fair-sized place with what looked like at least ten rows of shelves packed with goods. They had a small grocery section with some fresh fruit. "Do you think we could get some apples and cheese?"

George grinned and pushed the door open, waiting for me to enter. Ethan had just finished his cigarette as we arrived and crushed it under foot on the pavement while following us inside.

Since it was late in the season, George sorted through the apples to find some nice ones. I searched for a strong cheese. As I leaned over the small selection, I picked up on the scent of tobacco behind me. "Stalking me?" I said without turning.

"Not sure of your choice in cheeses," Ethan answered in a bored voice.

"Are you terribly disappointed you don't have a dinner date? I could see if Mr. Graham is available. The monocle is awfully attractive." I glanced at him over my shoulder.

"I'll make sure I pick one up," he responded, before he started to wander off. "Where is that eyeglass section..." He muttered happily under his breath. I couldn't help but be amused.

A deep, gravelly voice spoke from a couple of yards away, "I will be back in a moment to help you folks. There's a vendor at the back door."

George responded, "Take your time, sir."

I smiled at the heavyset shopkeeper as he waddled to the back, pushing his white shirt cuffs up his forearm. Moments later, the booming commotion of boxes being unloaded into the back of the store were the only melody available. I meandered up and down the aisles, feeling pleased that I had gotten the paperwork without any help. I'd even found the name on my own this time.

Slow footsteps of someone coming from the back of the store echoed behind me. "Can I help you find anything, miss?" A young man, not much older than myself, with straight dark hair and dark eyes, looked at me attentively.

"Thank you, no. I have what I need." I held up the cheese.

He eyed George and Ethan who were examining something I couldn't see. "And you, sirs? May I help you with anything?"

"We are fine, thank you," Ethan replied.

The worker started towards the back again and stopped at the end of the aisle. "We just got in a few boxes of ladies' things if you would like to take a look. You may find something to your liking." He seemed very earnest.

I looked to George for approval; he paused to inspect the worker and then nodded that it was okay. Following him, I entered the the storeroom. Just inside, was an open box with an assortment of gloves and handbags. Picking through them, I came upon a beautiful lavender bag with beading. I had always wanted a fancy gown in this color. My thoughts drifted to the grand balls I'd read about in so many books. It was a frivolous thought though, and I quickly quelled it.

The worker spoke again. "If you need stockings, there are some in that container there. He pointed to an open crate on the far side of the storeroom near the back exit, and then went about unboxing some other items.

My favorite pair of stockings had been ruined when I fell in the graveyard. I crossed the room, but before there was time to bend down to look inside the box, a hand clamped over my mouth and started dragging me backwards out into an alley behind the store. Desperately, I flailed, unable to knock something over to alert the boys.

I jabbed my elbow into my abductor's ribs as hard as possible, but it felt like his torso was protected by something hard, like thick leather. Then, I attempted to stomp on his foot with my heels, but it was of no use. He had heavy-duty boots shielding his feet.

Gritting my teeth, I tore at the hand over my mouth with one hand, while with the other I frantically tried to pull up my skirt to get at the knife in my garter. Seeing what I was doing, he forced me against the wall of the adjacent building, my forehead pressed to the bricks.

He tore my skirt clear to the waist as he stripped the knife from me. "You have anything else on you, baby?" he whispered into my ear.

His hot breath made my stomach lurch. He leaned into me hard, pressing his whole body against mine, searching for other weapons.

His breathing hitched as he ran his free hand all over me. My arms, shoulders, hips, at first. He seemed to grow bolder when I couldn't wriggle away. He paused his hand under my breast, then plunged down, his fingers lingering between my thighs for far too long.

He wanted power over me.

He wanted to hurt me.

His hand over my mouth shifted, and I bit down until I could taste blood. He grunted and ripped his hand away.

Before I had a breath to scream, he'd spun me around to face him and slammed me back into the wall.

He held the arm with his bleeding hand across my throat. His forearm was cutting off enough air that it was difficult to breathe. Then a jolt of recognition hit me. It was the man from the train with the yellow scarf.

All the yellow I'd been seeing all day—it had been a warning.

"You remember me then, Sheba?" He smiled, revealing a mouthful of stained teeth.

Calling me a Sheba while he pressed his body against mine again increased my alarm. I didn't need him to find me attractive—*he wanted to do far more than hurt me.*

I glanced at the back door of the general store and noticed the lifeless legs of the shopkeeper behind a box. Yellow Scarf put the knife into the hand I had chomped and reached into his pocket with the other.

He spoke to a conspirator I couldn't see. "Go through the front and pull the car around. Buy us some more time. Make some comment about her wanting to buy up the whole supply of women's things."

"Yes, sir." The other one replied.

Yellow Scarf tossed the keys, and I heard them snatched out of the air and footsteps grow softer as the accomplice followed orders.

"So, are you the daughter of that Seer bitch?" He sneered.

I bit my lip and didn't respond, despite my surge of anger. He was trying to get me to give something away.

He leaned into me harder. I was beginning to become lightheaded from the arm across my throat.

He continued, "She died horribly. So...sooo slowly. The blue dress she wore ran red."

I closed my eyes, wishing for enough air to scream. He knew the color of my mother's dress when she died. My knees began to tremble and feel weak.

Then I heard the cocking of a gun. George's voice was steady. "Release her now or I will cut you down."

Yellow Scarf looked at the mouth of the alley, and then back at me. He put the knife back in his free hand, and then pressed the tip over my heart. "Come any closer, and I kill her."

"You won't. Your masters want her alive."

Yellow Scarf cursed and spat on the ground as George continued to gradually close the distance. "You're right. I won't kill her, but they don't need her whole. They just want live blood." He raised the knife and hovered it an inch from my eye. I was petrified, barely able to stay on my feet. At the same time, it was evident that moving meant being blinded.

"You don't need to do this; we can come to some sort of an arrangement," George bargained.

Yellow Scarf laughed in a bitter burst. "You can offer me *nothing*. They can offer me eternal life. If I bring in an actual Seer, I can write my own ticket."

"We have money, more than you could ever spend." George tried one more time.

"Won't do me any good when I'm dead. Back away," Yellow Scarf warned. He placed the blade to the side of my eye and pressed it just hard enough to break the skin. A slow drop of blood began to trail down my face.

"Stop!" George's voice cracked, his icy control gone.

Yellow Scarf eased the knife back and held it out towards George. "Put the pistol down there." He used the tip of the knife to motion to the ground. "Now back away slowly."

George nodded. "Whatever you want."

At that moment, a cracking sound like that of a bat hitting a ball rang out. Yellow Scarf pitched forward into me, then fell away. With his weight against me suddenly gone I was tumbling forwards, unable to right myself. At that instant,

Ethan caught me and held me until my mind caught up to what was happening. I looked around Ethan at Yellow Scarf sprawled on the damp pavement, unconscious, or possibly dead.

Ethan propped me back against the wall. "Can you stand?"

"Yes," I breathed, through trembling lips.

Ethan bent and picked up the knife, then sank to his haunches to check Yellow Scarf's pulse.

Not two seconds later, George had my face his hands and was searching my expression. He rubbed the blood away from my cheek with his thumb. "Are you all right?" he asked, his voice fraught with emotion.

I nodded in affirmation, too choked to speak. My body began to tremble so hard I felt myself begin to slide down the wall. George pulled me to his chest and held tight. He squeezed me, and I clung to him equally as hard. I wanted to cry but forced myself to not fall apart.

"He wasn't alone," I was finally able to push out.

"Yes, the boy. We took care of him." He paused for a beat. "We need to get out of here."

I nodded again.

George kept his arm around me, as we started moving towards the street. Our motorcar was one block away. I kept one arm around George and the other holding my torn skirt together. When we arrived at the vehicle, Ethan climbed into the driver's seat and immediately started the engine. George opened the back door for me and helped me inside, hesitating when I didn't immediately release his hand. Then, followed me into the back, shutting the door. Ethan veered onto the road before George had even settled onto the seat.

The shaking hadn't subsided. I had killed two men and

jumped from a train, but I was more rattled by this attack. George still had my hand, but he released it to wrap his arm around me. He whispered my name in a reassuring fashion against my temple, but not even that could abate my quaking.

"I'm sorry," I whispered after a few minutes, feeling embarrassed.

"There is no need to apologize."

"This makes me feel weak."

He leaned away just enough to look me in the eyes. His face was more open than I had seen it in days. "Rosemond, you are one of the strongest people I have ever met. Having a nervous response after the fact is not going to change that."

I nodded in reply and tucked myself farther under his arm, resting my head against his chest. He didn't stiffen or pull away as expected; he simply drew me closer and held me as we rumbled down the road.

GEORGE

At the sound of Rosemond's scream, I launched myself into her room with Ethan on my heels. We found her soaked in sweat, her chest heaving.

"I am so sorry. It was a dream," she gasped. "I'm sorry...I'm sorry...my own scream woke me."

Circling the room, I checked the lock on the window and noticed Ethan poking his head into the closet. It seemed we both needed reassurance, too. I sank to my knees next to the bed, refraining from sitting beside her on the mattress. "Are you all right? Was it a nightmare? Or something more?"

She squeezed her eyes shut and pushed the damp tendrils of hair from her face. "Everything is fine. I'm sorry I woke you.

Please go back to bed." But never once did she open her eyes when she spoke, her voice rough.

Ethan dropped himself on the bed at her side, jostling her. Her eyes snapped open. He grinned at her. "If you need company, I am happy to stay." He patted the space next to her. "Your bed is so much cozier than mine." He leaned toward her in a tauntingly flirtatious manner. I felt myself bristle.

The haunted look leaked from her face. She giggled as she put her palm on his forehead and pushed him back. He laughed in return and stood.

"You can't blame a fellow for trying." He wagged his eyebrows and sauntered towards the door, looking satisfied that she had smiled.

Ethan glanced at me, and we had a silent exchange. He knew that I would stay for a while. He left the door wide open and turned out the light in the living room. I stood to my feet, dragged over the chintz-covered chair next to the bed, and took a seat. She had sat at my bedside for days; the least I could do was stay until she was asleep.

"George, I am really quite fine."

"Do you want me to leave? I don't mind staying for a while." With effort my tone was neutral.

She exhaled and seemed to struggle for a moment. "Truthfully..." There was a long pause. "I am terrified to be alone right now."

"Then it's settled."

She seemed to accept this and slid back under the covers. I turned off the light and sunk into the oversized chair, propping my feet up on the end of the bed.

It was silent for a long while. All I could hear was her soft breath and the occasional gust of wind flexing the glass in the window. Moonlight filtered in and illuminated Rosemond's dark hair as it spilled over the pillow. She opened her eyes and caught me staring at her.

"Are you close to your family?" she asked.

"Yes," I replied. "When I went away to boarding school, things were strained for a while. They didn't understand why I would reject our family legacy within the Watchers. I think my father hoped that I would come alongside him and help quell some of the problems in the Concilium. Sometimes, he has been the only reason the two factions haven't split entirely."

"I didn't realize there were problems. My parents never spoke of such things."

"Yes—one group wants to actively hunt vampires to extinction. I don't really understand it. They are still sentient beings; they have a right to life as long as they don't harm others. I believe your father had been in agreement with mine."

"They knew one another?"

"Yes."

"I suppose you may know more about my family history than I do."

I fell silent for a few moments. "I may."

"What do you know?"

Hesitating, I remembered my father's warning to tell her as little as possible. But at this juncture I couldn't see keeping it from her. She had a right to know her importance.

"Please," she whispered, prompting me.

I exhaled. "I know that your father is from a long line of Watchers who have helped to keep the Concilium in power. And that your mother is of the Lux...a line of Seers thought to have all been killed off during the French Revolution and that Queen Agrona of the French coven desires someone from your line more than anything else. It appears you may be the last one."

"Surely that can't be true."

"It very may well be. Your gifts are passed down only through the mother, and sometimes it skips generations. Only a handful of people even knew your mother was one of them."

"Do you," she hesitated, "still have all of your family? I'm sorry." She swallowed hard. "I shouldn't have asked that."

"It's fine. Yes, my parents are still happily married after twenty-five years. And I have a fifteen-year-old sister named Agatha. We are polar opposites, but I adore her. She has the personality to be a powerful force in the Concilium."

"Having family is good," she whispered.

"I wish…" I didn't finish my sentence. It seemed a superficial thing to say.

She humored me. "I know. Thank you." There was another long pause. "I hadn't thought of it until now, but I'm an orphan."

The weight on my chest returned, and I took a risk. Holding my breath, I took her hand and held it. My desire was to say things like, "You will never be alone," but it wasn't necessarily true. We had two weeks until my departure. She was exhausted and beautiful and vulnerable. We looked at one another, our hands linked in the moonlit room. After a while, her eyes drifted closed, and I wondered if she had gone to sleep.

"Would you tell me a story, George? Maybe something of your childhood…something happy. I know your character. I would like to know your past."

She wanted to know *me*. After an internal debate, I obliged her and talked deep into the night until she finally fell asleep.

Before standing to leave, I leaned down and kissed the hand I had been holding for hours.

Ethan had kissed her hand a half dozen times, and I could only bring myself to do it when she was unconscious. Sighing, I padded on bare feet to the living room and seated myself at the kitchen table. I wasn't sure how to behave tomorrow.

If I let my heart guide me, will I be able to keep my focus and protect her?

I had made a terrible miscalculation today and almost lost her. I pinched the bridge of my nose and prayed that I could make the proper decision.

CHAPTER 14

DISAPPOINTED

ROSEMOND

Sitting in the tiny two-bedroom apartment in New York was becoming more than I could bear. In his attempt to keep me safe, George was caging me. He was doing what he thought was best; maybe it *was* the best. But staying indoors and out of sight forever was *not* an option.

"George said you should stay away from the window unless you change your appearance," Ethan warned.

I glared at him. He didn't deserve it, but I couldn't help myself. "Yes, warden."

He sighed. "I'm afraid George is the warden. I am but a simple guard."

For a long moment, I studied Ethan. "A guard who hasn't been himself in days."

"I suppose not." He shrugged. Sitting next to him on the couch, I pulled the neatly folded blanket from the side table onto my lap. I spread it over my legs so that I could modestly sit cross-legged and face him.

"It's me, isn't it? You have seen the blackness of my soul and can't wait to get away," I joked, straight-faced.

"Yes, that is it, of course. I just don't want to be rude to George, you see. Biding my time." He smiled a little, but he kept his eyes on his hands that were busy folding and unfolding the slip of white paper George had left with instructions.

I pushed at his shoulder. "Ethan, now you are worrying me. I don't care much for the quiet Ethan."

He finally met my gaze. "I killed a man, Rosemond—I'd do it again to save you. He was an evil sort, but I still killed him with my own two hands."

"Oh, Ethan." I breathed. Then my memory went to him checking Yellow Scarf's pulse after striking him over the head. The shock had been so great that I hadn't thought as to whether or not he had lived. My assumption was that Yellow Scarf had survived. It was selfish of me. Picking up his hand, I kissed it and held the back of it to my cheek. "I wish I could say something...do something that could ease your mind."

"This life you and George live. I don't know how you do it."

I kept his hand between mine and lowered it to my lap. "We do what we have to. There are horrible things out there, much worse than you have seen."

"What could be worse than murder?"

I didn't answer. "It was not murder, Ethan. Do not take that on."

"Have you ever had to?" He didn't finish.

"Kill someone?"

He nodded.

"On the train. They would have killed George. I had seen it in a vision, and I struck before they could."

"You are strong, aren't you?" he commented more than asked.

"Or there is something terribly wrong with me. I shouldn't find all this acceptable, should I?" Looking at his pained expression I realized just how very good Ethan was.

He squeezed my left hand and pulled it to his lips. "You, my dear, are perfect. And I, on the other hand, need a smoke."

He stood wearily and went to the window. He flicked the lock open, pushed the window all the way up, and ducked through the opening to the fire escape. I watched as the breeze picked up the smoke and swirled it away.

As I studied his back, I felt the need to go to church and fall prostrate at the altar begging forgiveness for bringing such sorrow into both Ethan and George's lives.

My father had kept me hidden away all those years. I was like the siren depicted in Ethan's painting, and bound to pull both of them to their deaths. I curled up on the couch and closed my eyes, hoping sleep would rescue me from my thoughts.

GEORGE

After entering the apartment feeling a sense of accomplishment, I immediately hushed myself noting Rosemond asleep on the davenport. I placed on the table the blank documents that I had acquired during my time out. It took me a moment to work the embossing stamp out of my pocket. This would give legitimacy to anything Rosemond would need to create.

"How long has she been asleep?" I asked.

"An hour or so. She may die of boredom soon. I may die of boredom. Are you almost done?" Ethan's last sentence sounded conflicted.

"Almost. I still need to gather some sample documents so she knows how to fill in the forgeries convincingly."

"You should take the poor girl out, my friend."

"I suppose. Maybe tomorrow or the next day. I should have a new location secured by then."

Ethan exhaled with exasperated. "George, *no*." He put both his hands in his hair like he meant to tear it out. "I mean out, out. Like for a meal and talking and whatever comes natural."

Sighing, I whispered back. "Ethan, it is not a good idea."

He jabbed his finger in my direction. "George, sometimes I think you are a complete blockhead. You have one of the most amazing girls I have ever met right there in front of you, and you two are crazy about each other."

"She is?" Somehow this took me off-guard.

"George, you are an idiot. Of course she is—she is just too much of a lady to do anything about it." He stood and walked towards the front door. "I am not trying to be arrogant, but think about this, George. Have you ever seen a woman give you more attention than me? I am not in prison, so I am going out for a walk and to buy more cigarettes. Just wake up." He dramatically flailed his arms and went out the door, shutting it quietly, despite his mood.

I stood there, half-stunned. It was true, when with Ethan, I had always been invisible to women. Rosemond obviously enjoyed his company, but had never once played the moony-eyed girl other women were reduced to.

Sitting at the table, watching her sleep I wished I had

Ethan's artistic talent to capture how she looked. How her long waves framed her face, and how the blush on her cheek was the perfect shade. Her bottom lip was slightly fuller than the top, and when she frowned, it was the most adorable pout.

I stood and strode to the room Ethan and I shared, shutting the door before doing something stupid.

Like kissing her awake.

Or professing my undying love for her.

ROSEMOND

I woke, feeling stiff from sleeping too long. The glow of an approaching sunset warmed the room. Apparently, I had slept the entire afternoon away. The smell of cigarette smoke drifted in from the window. Sleepily, I shuffled over and hoisted the frame up the rest of the way and sat on the sill. "It looks like George came back. Did he go out again?"

"He was asleep last time I checked."

I scrutinized the tin can stuffed with cigarette butts. "How long have you been out here?"

Ethan held up an empty container of cigarettes. "This long."

"Did either of you eat?"

"No, but if you are hungry, I can get something. There is a market around the corner and two doors down. I don't think you saw it since we came from the other direction."

I chuckled. "And since I have been locked inside my tower like some mythical princess."

"Yes, there is that." He ground the butt out making a small sizzling sound on the side of the can, and tossed it in with the abundance of the others. It appeared as if he had been chain smoking for hours. He groaned, "I'm in need of a long hot bath. All this sitting around has worn me out."

I stood and gave him room to climb back through the window.

He glanced towards his room, then back at me, as if he wanted to say something. He was being quiet Ethan again, and then his familiar grin lit his face. "Of course, you could always join me. I'm delightfully good at scrubbing backs."

I let out a single laugh and pushed at him.

He shrugged. "One day, you may say yes." He laughed and disappeared into the bathroom.

I SAT IN THE EMPTY LIVING ROOM FOR WHAT SEEMED TO BE ages, having had checked the cabinets twice for food. Ethan must've fallen asleep in the tub, and I felt reluctant to knock, concerned he might come flying out stark naked.

After deliberating a moment, I decided that it was ridiculous to be barred from the market when it was so close. After putting on my coat and twisting my hair up into a knot, I grabbed my hat and pulled it low on my head. After a glance in the mirror next to the door, I was satisfied the camouflage was sufficient, so I swept up the keys and a couple of dollars from the table. But before freeing the latch, I decided to write a note:

> DON'T BE ANGRY. I WENT TO THE MARKET FOR
> FOOD.
> WILL BE BACK IN A FEW MINUTES. –FRANK

Feeling almost giddy at the prospect of getting out of the teensy apartment, I glided down the three flights of stairs. When I was about four steps out onto the street, there were a few misgivings—I hadn't considered the fact that it was dark outside, but I quickly dismissed it, made a left and went around the corner.

The market was only two doors down. It was brightly lit and very reassuring. A car was parked out front, and a well-dressed man was leaning inside the passenger-side window, talking to someone about picking him up in a few minutes after they dropped off his associate. I didn't really look at them, but he had a very nice voice—deep and resonant.

Before reaching the market, I noticed the window of the neighboring store and stopped. Beautiful evening gowns were being displayed on headless mannequins. I placed my hand on the glass and looked longingly inside. There was a lavender one with beading all over the bodice, just like the evening bag I'd coveted in the general store before my almost-abduction.

It was easy to imagine myself in the gown, dancing with George. Pushing the thought from my mind, I suddenly felt someone behind me and heard the voice from the man who'd been leaning into the car. "You would look beautiful in it."

I spun around and felt my face flush with heat but was afraid to actually look at him. "Oh, thank you," I whispered looking at the ground. "I'm sorry. I need to get inside." I indicated the market and started towards it.

"My apologies. I didn't mean to startle you, but I meant what I said."

This time I met his gaze and was shocked. He had the oddest eyes I'd ever seen, like citrine gemstones or yellow sapphires. They were set on a chiseled face with a square jaw and high cheekbones. His straight, dark blond hair was almost the same color as Ethan's.

As I took a half step back I noticed his physique, even under the coat and suit, seemed to rival that of a Slayer. He looked like his photo should be splashed across the tabloids to render women speechless.

Snapping out of my gawk, I sputtered, "Thank you. Maybe someday I will have need of such things."

He looked at me very piercingly. "Come to my club tonight."

I felt a tremendous pull, and part of me wanted to do exactly as he had said. I resisted the urge to follow him like an eager puppy. "Thank you, but I have other plans."

He cocked his head to the side and seemed genuinely surprised by my response. "Interesting," he murmured under his breath.

His response struck me as odd, and possibly, a little insulting. *Did he expect me to fall at his feet? I just met him.* "It was nice meeting you. Good evening." I nodded and stepped around him, entering the market. I could feel the weight of his stare on my back as I entered. Once inside, the magnetic pull I had felt towards him receded.

I picked up a small basket near the door and threaded my way down the aisles, picking up fruit, bread, cheese, and preserves. When I stepped into the last aisle, I saw the yellow-eyed man from outside talking to another man in a grey hat near the checkout counter. Yellow Eyes whispered something and patted his associate's back. The grey hatted man said, "Yes, sir," and exited the market.

I continued towards the god-like gentleman at the end of the aisle slowly, while looking for soap.

Suddenly, he was a few feet away from me. I hadn't heard him move. "We meet again," he said.

"Yes, shocking, since you watched me walk in."

He raised his eyebrows a little.

"I'm sorry. That didn't sound so harsh in my head. I was going for facetiousness, not biting sarcasm." I bit down on my lip to stop myself before I began speed-talking and really embarrassing myself.

"If you are really sorry, you will tell me your name." He had the same intense expression as before.

"Awfully demanding, aren't we," I replied, my voice lighter.

"Then I'll start. Pleased to meet you. My name is Cadeyn Bradshaw." He offered me his gloved hand.

I stood and looked at it for a moment and then finally shook it. "Mine is Eloise," looking him straight in the eye as I lied.

He cocked his head to the side again. "What is your real name?" he asked, with more intrigue than irritation.

I shook my head. *Why did I have to be a terrible liar?* "Vivian." This time the lie was more convincing. After all, it *was* one of my identities.

A slow smile spread across his face that made my heart quicken. "Nice to meet you, Vivian. Do you live around here?"

"Just visiting friends for a time."

"Then you *definitely* need to come to my club. You can bring any of your lady friends."

"Terribly sorry, but we are quite busy, though the invitation is appreciated." Needing an excuse to look away, I spotted the soap on the shelf next to us and put it into my basket. Giving him a small smile, I headed towards the cashier. Half way there I heard something tiny hit the floor, noticed the button had fallen off of my overcoat and bent to retrieve it. When I stood, Cadeyn was in front of me.

He smiled the warmest of smiles. "Are you going to make me beg?" he asked in a tone so warm that it could have melted the polar ice caps.

I felt drawn to him again as he stood partially blocking my way. "I...I'm sorry. We really are too busy."

He stepped aside gracefully and let me pass. After paying for the goods, I made my way into the night. Two steps outside the door, the bottom of my shopping bag gave way. Exasperated, I dropped the spent bag and ran after an orange before it could roll into the gutter, scooping up an apple on the way. I spun around and started back towards the rest of the groceries, but Cadeyn was already there with two new bags dropping in the last of my groceries.

I noticed the man with the grey hat had returned and was standing next to Cadeyn near the doorway. I cautiously approached, not trusting his companion, and was acutely aware of a car pulling up on the street behind me. My heart started to hammer.

Cadeyn held out the bags towards me. I put the apple and orange in one hand and took the bags. "Thank you," I said hesitantly.

He smiled. "There is no need to be nervous. We aren't planning on snatching you up," he chuckled and tilted his head to the side again. "I would like to see you once more this evening, though." He motioned to his companion.

The man with the grey hat gave me a curt nod. "Miss." Then, he walked around and stood by the back door of the motorcar, with his hand on the door handle.

My heart calmed a little. Cadeyn reached into his inside

coat pocket and pulled out a business card. It was white, with an address printed on it in elegant script. "This is the address to my club. Use my name to get in at the door. It's a gin joint, and there will be a fabulous band." He took my free hand and bent to kiss my knuckles. "And there will be dancing." His kiss was slow and soft and made me feel a little unsteady on my feet. He straightened up, but his hand lingered on mine for a moment. "I hope to see you later tonight or tomorrow."

I didn't reply. I simply stood there mute, watching him as Grey Hat opened the door for him. Grey Hat climbed in the front passenger seat as Cadeyn rolled down the back window. He didn't say anything, just looked at me with enough desire to make my stomach do a flip-flop. Even after the car had gone, I stood for a few moments wondering if this was what all the girls felt in the penny dreadfuls I had read.

Cadeyn Bradshaw was mesmerizing.

Finally, collecting myself, I proceeded back. I entered the apartment building next door and watched for several minutes to see if anyone had followed. Then, when satisfied, I slipped into my building and started up the three flights of stairs, moving one bag into each hand for balance.

Somehow the groceries seemed heavier than before, but of course, I was climbing steep steps. When I reached the landing at the top of the second flight, hurried footsteps scuffled from above.

Alarmed, I backed through the exit into the second floor hall and peeked through the cracked door to see who was racing down the stairs. When George and Ethan's figures tore by, I swung the door open and bellowed their names. They came to an abrupt halt, and when I surveyed George's expression, I knew this wasn't going to be pleasant.

Ethan reached me first and took the bags, starting back up the stairs without a word. He was pale, and the look of panic in his blue eyes lingered as they bore into me.

I was afraid to look at George again, so I started up the stairs behind Ethan. We entered the apartment, and Ethan placed the bags on the kitchen counter, then went to the back window. He frowned over at me, his disappointment evident, and slipped out to the fire escape to have a smoke.

George was behind me.

His voice was low and too calm. "What in the bloody hell were you thinking?"

I kept my back to him. "I am sorry. My intent was not to frighten you. We needed food."

He walked around to face me and emotion leaked into his tone. "Why, after all we have done, would you risk yourself like that?"

"I didn't think. I—"

"No, you didn't think, did you?!" he replied, his voice rising. His face was red, and his eyes burned.

"It was just for food. I said I was sorry." My voice rose to match his.

Now there was no way around it; he was yelling. "Never leave here unaccompanied! *Ever!* You have to think. If something had happened to you!" He slammed his hand on the table.

"I said I was sorry. There is nothing else I can do!"

"Say you will never do it again!" he thundered.

I should have said I wouldn't, but he was yelling at me and it made me irrationally angry. So I refused. "You aren't my keeper!" I half-growled and half-shouted. Spinning around, I grabbed onto both bags of groceries and stomped to my room, slamming the door behind me. Shame immediately overcame me as I tossed the bags onto the bed and flopped onto it.

After several deep breaths, I ferreted through the bags and noticed why one had seemed so heavy. A parcel wrapped in rose-colored paper, with a white ribbon around it, had been placed inside. I tugged it onto my lap and loosed the ribbon and then the paper, gasping when I realized what was inside— the gorgeous lavender gown from the window.

I ran my fingers over the silky fabric, tilting some of the beads back and forth to watch them shimmer.

This must be the most expensive garment I have ever touched.

A SHORT WHILE LATER IT WAS EVIDENT THAT ETHAN HAD come back inside. Heated words were soon exchanged between the boys. Obviously, I was the source of the argument.

It made me feel trapped. I sat folding and unfolding my hands in my lap as emotion bubbled inside me chaotically. Everything in my life had been outside of my control, and I was tired of it. I was weary of schedules and training and hiding. I just wanted to be a normal girl on a normal Friday night. I wanted to go to a club and dance with a pretty boy and not worry about tomorrow and the reality of my being hunted. Besides, I would be on my own in a matter of weeks.

I made my decision. *George is already furious with me, how much worse can it get?* I slipped into the gown and primped in front of the small oval mirror hanging over the nightstand. I searched for a fountain pen and, upon finding one, I wrote a note on the bag of groceries.

NEEDED TO FEEL NORMAL, IF ONLY FOR A SINGLE NIGHT.

I'M SORRY. WENT TO A SPEAKEASY ON 10TH AND LEXINGTON. —VIVIAN

I screwed the cap back on the fountain pen and tossed it next to the note on the bed. I hadn't heard voices in a while, so I cracked the door open. George wasn't there, and Ethan seemed to be asleep on the couch. I was afraid I would wake him if I went out the door, so I tip-toed to the open window to go down the fire escape. If George heard me, he would probably assume it was Ethan going out for another smoke.

As I eased the window closed, I regarded Ethan's motionless form and had the dreadful thought that he would be better off if I never came back.

CHAPTER 15

GREEN

ROSEMOND

The intimidating metal door before me with heavy rivets around the edges was reminiscent of the hull of a ship—*unwelcome* might as well have been stamped on it. Part of me wondered if I were in the wrong place, but it *was* an illegal club. It would have to be inconspicuous, otherwise the police would be banging down the door. I glanced up and down the street—this was the correct address.

Clutching the business card in my palm, I raised my hand to knock, but before I could, a small viewing hole opened up and a set of man's eyes appeared. They were almost black and were topped with a set of disapproving brows.

"He-llo..." I hesitated in the middle of the word. "Cadeyn invited me? Cadeyn Bradshaw." It sounded more like a question, so I quickly held up the card he'd given me.

The man stared at me for a long, uncomfortable moment, making me feel like I had committed some appalling crime and he was deciding upon my fate. Then, when I thought he was going to say something, the viewing port slammed shut.

I stood, stunned for a moment, blinking at the door, and started to leave. At that moment, the clank of heavy bolts sliding free echoed down the alley, and I stopped just as the door creaked open.

A colossal man with black hair and pale skin towered over me. He swung his arm towards the interior, prompting me to enter. The sound of music swept into the entryway, along with the smell of cigarette smoke and some sort of savory food. I stepped over the threshold, and he shut the door behind me, locking it.

"Miss Vivian," the large man uttered, his voice on the low side of bass.

I smiled and nodded. "Yes."

The right corner of his mouth twitched upwards and I realized he was the man with the grey hat. "He said you would come tonight. Please, follow me. I'll take you to the bar and find him."

He led me through another doorway, and the sound seemed to wrap around me, making me feel alive. A band played in the far corner, and the place was brimming with energy and people. Elegantly dressed patrons were sporting the latest fashions—bright colors and beads and feathers. Lips painted in deep reds, sipping on cocktails. Rosy-cheeked men and women having riotous fun on the dance floor. While secret conversations happened in darkened corners on scarlet-colored couches that were placed throughout. I couldn't believe the size of the club. Cadeyn and his associates must've taken over the basements of multiple buildings.

"Miss Vivian," Grey Hat said. He was trying to usher me to the coat-check girl.

He helped me out of my coat and handed it to the attendant. She smiled at me, with mischief playing in her eyes, and handed me a ticket for my coat. "Have fun, doll." Then she snapped the gum in her mouth and nudged Grey Hat. They shared some type of look that I didn't understand.

"This way," he motioned, and suddenly he was halfway down a small set of stairs, holding his hand out to help me. I placed my hand in his and let him assist me down the steps. His hand was firm and a bit cold.

Weaving our way through the crowd, we arrived at the bar. Grey Hat motioned to the athletic-looking bartender with a light olive complexion who walked over with some swagger. "Billy, whatever she wants. It's on the house." Grey Hat turned to me. "I'm Breton, by the way." He smirked, and then melted into the crowd.

The bartender was grinning at me. His dark brown eyes were playful as he leaned in on both elbows to speak over the noise. "You heard the man: anything you want." It seemed more like an advance than the request for a drink order.

"I really wouldn't know what to order," I felt silly admitting it, but my only experience with alcohol had been champagne at a wedding in Canada.

"How much fun do you want to have tonight?" he asked, sounding a little overly-friendly. He ran his fingers through his short dark hair and waited for my answer.

"A fair amount," I answered.

"As you wish." His grin turned crooked as he pulled out a fancy-looking stemmed glass and slowly poured a liquid into the bottom.

"It's green," I stated in surprise.

"This spirit has fennel and green star anise. It tints the liquid." He pulled a fancy slotted spoon out and placed it over the top of the glass, followed by a sugar cube. Then he slowly trickled iced water over the sugar cube.

"What is it?"

"Absinthe," he replied, his expression part dare.

I'd heard of absinthe, but had never seen it or tasted it, for that matter. It was the rage in many of the bohemian writer and artist communities in both Europe and America. I felt a nervous, but wanted to try it.

A normal girl at a party for one night, I reminded myself, as I slid onto a stool.

Bartender Billy finished pouring the last of the ice water over the cube and removed the slotted spoon. He gave it one small stir and slid the drink towards me across the bar top. He leaned towards me murmuring, just loud enough for me to hear over the din of background noise. "Bottoms up."

Holding my breath, I picked up the glass and took a sip. The mixture of tastes was indescribable, and I was certainly not adverse to the idea of drinking more. Taking a larger swallow, I felt the burn of the alcohol go down my throat and warm my stomach.

My eyes closed as the warmth went back up to my head and my muscles began to relax. After a moment, and another swallow, the stress in my shoulders dissipated. After yet another swallow, I was over halfway through the glass and feeling rather delightful.

I liked the feel of my skin.

When I opened my eyes, Bartender Billy was eyeing me like he was a cat and I was a parakeet. His expression made me more aware of how I was dressed. My perfect lavender gown was more revealing than anything I'd ever worn. I felt a little naked without sleeves; a shiver ran up my almost bare back. After another swallow I didn't care. Billy leaned towards me and then froze.

Someone was behind me. Hands appeared on the bar on both sides of me.

Billy Bartender reverently addressed the owner of the hands, "Good evening, Mr. Bradshaw. I'm sorry. I didn't realize she was with you." He winked at me and slipped off to the other end of the bar with speed. I felt Cadeyn backup a step as I swiveled on my stool to admire him.

He picked up my hand and kissed my knuckles slowly as he looked me in the eyes. It took an effort to remember to breathe.

"I trust you have been treated well?" he asked.

"Yes, very well."

"I'm glad you came," he said with a confident gleam.

"According to your friend Mr. Breton, you were expecting me."

He grinned. "I had hoped you would come. Would you like to finish that? Then dance?"

I nodded and took another sip, feeling the alcohol burn down my throat again. "How long have you run this club?"

"A few years. My brother and I are on sabbatical from our other job. We thought we would indulge in the New York nightlife for a while."

"What is your normal line of work?"

He tilted his head to the side and thought for a second. "We specialize in security," he replied ambiguously.

Taking the last swallow, I opened my mouth to ask him

another question, but he held up his hand to stop me. "Dance with me?"

Nodding, I placed my glass on the bar and slid off my stool. My head was woozier when standing. He placed his cool hand on my elbow and I wondered if Breton had retrieved him from outside—both their hands were cool.

The tune the band was playing ebbed into something slow and sensual. When we reached the dance floor, Cadeyn turned me, placing my hands on his shoulders as he slipped his to my waist. Another shiver ran through me as his fingertips brushed the bare skin of my back.

We danced amongst the press of bodies for song after song. The longer we danced, the more he touched me, and the less opposed I was to having his hands on me. It was almost as if I were under a spell.

A large man, who must have been Cadeyn's brother, interrupted us. He had the same yellow eyes, but appeared to be older. Cadeyn led me back to the bar.

"I have to take care of something. Wait here a few minutes?" he asked, whispering into my ear.

I nodded, not sure where my voice had fled to.

He smiled and kissed my hand, then the inside of my wrist in parting.

Bartender Billy poured me another glass of absinthe, and I drank it despite still feeling the impact of the first glass. I felt free.

Cadeyn returned a few minutes later. "Would you like to go somewhere else or dance some more?"

"Dance more, if you don't mind?"

He leaned down to my ear again. "*Anything.*"

I swallowed, looking into his magnetic eyes and shadowed

him back to the dance floor, which seemed even more crowded now. His body was against mine as we swayed to the music. Again, I thought of how magnificent my skin felt as Cadeyn ran his hands over my back—his cool fingers leaving a trail of warmth that urged me on. I was completely enraptured.

At the short silence between songs, we stopped moving. He gazed down at me, and there was a change in him—a seriousness to his expression. I was keenly aware that he would kiss me soon.

He drew me closer to him as he leaned down. My eyes went to his lips, but all I could think was that Cadeyn wasn't the one I wanted to kiss. I quickly turned my face, and he kissed my cheek instead. Then he kissed the hollow under my cheekbone and whispered into my ear, "You are different, aren't you?"

My breath was uneven. My head was swimming from the drink, yet I was aware enough to realize I didn't want him touching me anymore.

I wanted George. Regret coursed through me and filled my body, but I didn't know how to disentangle myself from him.

He kissed under my jawline, and when he reached my neck, I involuntarily leaned my head back to give him more access. Some sort of epiphany was floating just out of reach. I twisted in his arms so my back was to him. It didn't slow him down. I glanced around the room, which had become so dim that it seemed more shadow than light. We were so close to the other couples that anything could be going on, and it would still be obscured.

Cadeyn ran his hands over my hips and pulled me closer. When he did, the metal of his belt buckle felt cool against the feverish skin of my lower back.

I wanted to move away, and he must have sensed it. He ran his hands down my arms and gently took my wrists in his hands. He crisscrossed my arms across my torso as we moved to the seductive tune the band was playing. Slowly he raised my right arm upwards over my left shoulder, while holding my other arm against my ribs.

He bent and kissed my palm, and then the inside of my wrist. And just as the elusive element I had been struggling to reach was within my grasp, he bit down.

It hurt for a fleeting moment, then there was a delicious feeling, as if every cell in my body sang out in exquisite relief.

He was a vampire, and he was feeding on me, and I was powerless to stop him. Truthfully, as the effects of his bite surged through my body, I didn't want to fight.

I wanted to feel this way—forever.

My knees gave way, but he held me up as if I weighed nothing. He ran his tongue over the bite mark and turned me around in his arms so we were face-to-face again.

I rasped, "Are you going to kill me?"

He held me up with one arm and cupped my face with the other, looking at me as if I was a puzzle he wanted to unravel. "You know what I am and can see through all the glamours." He blinked slowly. "You are *magnificent*; why would I harm you?"

"I'm food," I replied, remembering George's words.

"Humans can be so much more than food." He ran small circles on my cheek with his thumb. "They can be companions and lovers." He paused. "I have never, in all my years, tasted anything like you."

"I'm sure you say that to all the girls," I replied, feeling silly.

Cadeyn smiled, and I hated the fact that I noticed how attractive he was, how his face lit up. "No, I don't speak with anyone like this." The smile faded from his face. "What are you?" he asked. We weren't dancing anymore.

We were standing still in the middle of a shifting sea of people. He drew me close and ran his nose down the side of my face; it seemed as if he was breathing me in.

I felt someone behind me, and Cadeyn straightened up as a hand clamped his shoulder. "Someone is near. Come with me," the owner of the hand stated.

"Gareth, we looked once already. Leave me be." He shrugged the hand off, and I felt as if the world was spinning.

Gareth.

He was the vamp from the train station and in the car when Yellow Scarf tried to abduct me. *Does he know I am standing right next to him?* He didn't appear to recognize me. Maybe he hadn't gotten a clear view of my appearance.

"This is an order, brother," Gareth barked.

Cadeyn squeezed me tighter. "I will be there in a moment. Let me see to my guest."

Then Gareth was gone.

Cadeyn backed me up into the far corner of club next to the dance floor. It was all shadows here. He leaned me against the wall. "I would like you to wait for me here. I can't compel you to stay. Will you wait for me?"

My head bobbed in agreement but knew the first chance I got I would try to get to the exit.

He glowered, and the next thing I knew, my head was leaned back and his mouth was on my neck. His fangs punctured my throat. There was a brief moment of pain, and then the ecstasy of the bite. It occurred to me he was flooding me with whatever substance they emit. He moved me a couple of feet to my left and put my hands on a column. I clutched it, unable to stand on my own. "I'll see you in a few minutes." Then he vanished like his brother.

Clinging to the column, I tried to make my legs to work. I was desperately trying to tune into my need for flight, but I felt so incredibly *good*. My true desire was to find one of those velvet couches and lie down and enjoy the euphoria. Then I couldn't remember what I needed to do. I wasn't sure how long I'd been standing here when someone grabbed me by the arms.

"Rosemond, we need to leave right now." It was George, his voice a hoarse whisper.

A flood of emotions rushed through my veins; I tried to pull away, but he was grabbing onto me too tight.

George's face a mask of calm. "This isn't a game, and this is not the place to punish me." His eyes were pleading with me to listen.

"George," I said harshly, fighting against his grip. He pulled me closer, his face strained.

"Please don't attract any more attention," he commanded through clenched teeth. His breath washed over my face.

"George," I repeated, but this time it sounded more like a caress. "George. George..." I placed my hands flat on his chest and felt his body go rigid. The liquor and vampire hormone were surging through my veins, urging me forward.

I was staring at the tiny scar that created a dent in his bottom lip. Before my mind could say no, my index finger was tracing the scar, while my other hand went to the back of his neck. His skin was softer than I expected. I thought for a moment that he shuddered. I looked up at him through my lashes and whispered almost breathlessly. "I do like your name, George."

He leaned his head forward, his lips parted slightly as he searched my face. Releasing a shaky breath, I ran both of my hands up his neck and into his hair. It felt like strands of silk it was so fine. I glanced back at his face and noticed that his eyes were closed, his brows pinned together, and hands moved to my waist.

"Do you not want to kiss me, George?" I asked.

He pressed his forehead to mine; it felt as if he was trembling. I could feel every point our bodies were touching, and still wanted to be closer.

He swallowed and sucked in a breath through his teeth. "We need to go," he whispered, so softly it took me a moment to process what he had said. Then it took another moment for the denial to register, and my cheeks to burn with embarrassment and rejection.

I felt a fool—throwing myself at him.

I tried to wrench myself from his grip, but he still had his hands around my waist. He'd gathered the fabric of my dress in his hands and was squeezing it, holding me there. I dropped my hands to my sides. He finally met my eyes and gave me a withering look, then shook his head as if he was arguing with someone over my shoulder.

Grasping my hand, he towed me through the crowd zigzagging towards the door. I didn't fight him. The coat-check girl chirped as we approached her station. George spun around and blinked at her, dropping my hand.

Coat-Check Girl handed him my coat, leaning forward suggestively, and batting her jewel-encrusted lashes. He blinked at her, but there was no reaction. She might as well have been trying to tempt an inanimate object. When that didn't work, I saw something feral rise up in her, but she stayed behind her counter.

George helped me into my coat. I was unsteady on my feet and swayed towards him. He steadied me, and in so doing, buttoned me up. My cheeks burned again when I looked at his lips, still wanting to kiss them.

He took my hand again, but this time he laced his fingers through mine. As if I needed something else confusing me.

We were almost out the door when a cool hand encircled my other wrist. Cadeyn's winning smile greeted me.

"I thought you were going to wait for me?" he purred, but he was obviously upset.

George yanked on my arm, not realizing Cadeyn had stopped me. I knew George had turned when he squeezed my hand. I watched Cadeyn's eyes as they flicked to George, George's hand on mine, and then back to me. There was recognition in his expression. He smiled as his eyes slid back to George again.

I stammered for a second. "I-I'm sorry, but I have to go."

Cadeyn pressed closer, and I could feel his breath spill over my left shoulder. He placed his finger under my chin and tilted it upwards, completely ignoring George. That warm sensation from his touch made me want to step towards him—to follow him anywhere.

Cadeyn bent to my ear. "Stay with me," he murmured, with so much warmth, I felt as if I could take flight. "You are of value, and I don't want to let you slip through my fingers. I could give you more than he or anyone else could." He had kissed the hollow under my cheek before I even realized he was going to kiss me. My mind felt sluggish and churned with the liquor and Cadeyn's promise.

I was jostled as George moved to stand between us, pushing Cadeyn's hand from my face with a swift movement. At some point, I realized George must have put on gloves. When Cadeyn dropped his hand, I was able to think more clearly.

"Leave her be," George growled in a tone so cold it stunned me.

Cadeyn straightened up, the edge of his lip curling into a grin that was more a challenge than smile. His yellow eyes narrowed. "I could rip out your throat before you have a chance to unsheathe the Durateus blades in your belt, Watcher."

"You wouldn't want to startle all your prey." George thrust his chin towards the crowd. "It takes time and money to set up a place like this."

Cadeyn nodded at the coat-check girl and pointed to the bar. "Go." She immediately moved where he'd ordered her to travel.

I suddenly felt sicker than before as I glanced around the room. There were so many vampires: Breton, Billy the bartender, the coat-check girl, and others.

It was obvious to see that they stood apart. They were unearthly, attractive, and mesmerizing—beings of sheer power. It occurred to me that Cadeyn had been trying to compel me to come here at the market. Of course, it had been my resistance that fascinated him. Increasing his desire to seduce or maybe hunt would be a better word. I was a rare challenge.

George faced Cadeyn fearlessly. "Let us go peaceably, and I won't report this to the Concilium."

Cadeyn angled his head to the side. "Dead Watchers don't report *anything*." The humor had drained from his face and had been replaced with something lethal.

George released a humorless chuckle and asked Cadeyn, "How are you feeling?"

I clutched some of George's coat in my hands.

Cadeyn stared at his hand where George had touched him and staggered back a couple of steps; his forehead was slick with sweat. He opened his mouth to speak, but nothing came out except a rasp of air. His look became murderous.

George held up a small vial made of amber glass between two of his fingers. "We will be leaving now. I suggest you find this." George flung the vial into the pulsing crowd heaving with music and booze and hunger.

Cadeyn was off after it before I could register his movement, and I was being dragged out the door into the stinging rain.

George hauled me into the backseat of a running motorcar as we exited. Ethan was driving, and we charged into the night.

CHAPTER 16

HARMED

ROSEMOND

We had only gone a block before I shrieked and started to frantically climb over the seat to the front. George grabbed at my waist. "Rosemond, have you gone mad?"

I kicked at him. "Ethan! You can't be driving!" Images of my dream came rushing to the surface with bits I hadn't remembered. I was wearing *this* dress. That awful moment was *now*.

Ethan glanced at me as I half-rolled and half-plopped onto the seat next to him with no sort of dignity. My head was still spinning from absinthe and Cadeyn. "It's fine Rosemond—we anticipated everything."

Glancing back at George, I noticed he was digging in a canvas bag. He pulled out two Durateus throwing blades and handed them to me. I took them, despite the fact it wasn't possible for me to throw with any accuracy right now. Ethan made a hard right, causing me to slide into him.

"Sorry." I used his shoulder to push myself back. Then he took a hard left, and I slid the other way.

"Almost there," George said urgently, but in my haze I had no idea what he meant.

At that moment, something large landed on the hood of the motorcar making the metal groan. My eyes shot to the source of the noise, and I watched as Gareth cocked his arm back to punch through the windshield. Ethan slammed on the brakes, and I flew into the dash as Gareth disappeared over the front of the hood, but it didn't feel like his weight had left the motorcar.

Ethan floored the gas pedal, and the motorcar lurched forward, making a turn into a wide alley, where we came to an abrupt halt. We were trapped.

Suddenly, the driver's side door was ripped from the hinges and tossed away. I grabbed at Ethan as he was stolen from the car. The drink removing my inhibitions, I followed, flinging myself at Gareth. I landed on his back and looped my left arm around his neck and my legs around his waist. He acted as if I weren't even there. Fear shot through me because Ethan was no longer visible.

Reaching around Gareth, I drove one of my blades into his chest, attempting to hit his heart. I failed. Gareth shuddered violently and dropped Ethan to the ground.

Gareth then reached around and ripped me from his back as he stumbled forward. His expression was vicious until he realized it was me. He cursed and abruptly shoved me to the ground next to Ethan. George appeared behind Gareth and hit the backs of his knees with a metal pipe. Gareth stumbled forward as he dislodged the knife from his chest.

George moved evasively as Gareth spun and moved

towards him. I scrambled for my other knife, but before I could take action, a loud whistle at the entrance to the alley drew his attention, and all motion stopped.

A woman's voice called out, "Gareth, I think we have some unfinished business."

Gareth ceased his advances towards George and stood up. He smoothed his elegant coat and scowled at the woman. She was still a silhouette, and I couldn't make anything out besides the fact that she was tall, thin, and sounded vaguely familiar.

With sneering coolness he replied, "Sariel, I hadn't thought we would meet again."

A savage laugh escaped her. "Your men are sloppy, Gareth. Maybe you should learn to do the job yourself instead of sending your neophytes."

George interrupted, "Sariel, above you!"

A shadowy figure dropped from the roof a yard from her, just as a motorcar sped by the alley. Its headlights flashed and illuminated Sara and the vampire attempting to ambush her. I recognized the coat-check girl, but within three deft moves Sara had sent the girl's head rolling towards us.

Gareth's posture changed, and it was obvious, even from behind, that he was furious. I sidled next to Ethan. He was clutching his ribcage with his right arm, left arm hanging limp, cheek covered in blood, and scarlet was soaking through his shirt. He was pale and looked as if he might lose consciousness.

I reached to check Ethan's wound when another figure dropped from the roof between us and Sara, not four feet from our location. It was Breton, quickly followed by Cadeyn and Billy. A moment later, three more I hadn't met landed. We were cut off from Sara and escape.

Cadeyn peered back at me and his eyes tightened, his expression unreadable. He seemed to have to force himself to look away. Sara was still standing in the mouth of the alley. She seemed unfazed by the show of power. "Is that all?" she asked.

Gareth laughed. "You. One Slayer. Against all of us. You know you are no match for us. You will not escape. We will take our prize and destroy the rest of you." The group of vampires crept forward as Gareth spoke, leaving us behind.

"Never claimed to be alone, my darling Gareth." Her voice was sweetly venomous. I'd never expected to hear a Slayer speak in such a casual manner to a vampire.

Ethan grimaced, his eyes flitting to the innermost part of the alley. I'd been so rapt with the events unfolding in front of me that I hadn't noticed the group of people creep in from behind. An entire unit of Watchers, the combat variety who worked with Slayers, had inched in behind us. I peeped back to the mouth of the alley and noticed that Sara was now flanked by four people. By the size of them, they were all Slayers.

My focus returned to Ethan as I knelt next to him. It was hard to see clearly in the darkness, but it was evident that his arm was badly broken. I tried to peel his fingers away from his ribs to see the source of the blood.

In a forced whisper I spoke to him. "You fight, you hear me. I will never forgive myself for this."

Then the battle began. The clash of metal rang out over the smashing of bodies. George slid next to me as I bent over Ethan. A second later, a warm hand went over my mouth and another around my waist, hoisting me up. At that moment George was in front of me with his index finger pressed to his lips. I calmed, and whoever had me released my mouth.

Two men pushed at me to back up, then unfolded a

stretcher and began moving Ethan. He groaned through clenched teeth but remained remarkably silent. At least ten Watchers had entered the alley and were surrounding us. The ones closest to the mêlée had their weapons drawn.

Next we were being ushered to an open door in the inner-most corner of the dead end. George held my upper arm firmly, keeping me steady. My head hadn't entirely cleared, even with the frantic beat of my heart. One man led point, two with Ethan, then George and I and one man in the rear. The others stayed behind, possibly to guard our exit or to join in the fight.

Our group hurried down multiple hallways, and George kept me on track. We hadn't gone far when there was a horrific cacophony behind us. We picked up speed, but with carrying Ethan there was no way to evade the vampires for long.

I whispered to George, "Cadeyn and Gareth want *me*. Can we lead them away so they can evacuate Ethan?"

The Watcher behind me replied, "That may be our best bet, sir."

"Do it," George exhaled under his breath.

We were at a three-way intersection in the building. The man on-point and the two carrying Ethan went straight for the exit out the front.

After waiting a moment, I gaped at George nervously. It was terrifying to let our pursuers get closer. The Watcher who stayed with us stepped over to me, bent on one knee, and grabbed the hem of my dress, tearing a swatch from it. Then, he snagged it on the doorframe opposite the staircase and motioned for us to go upwards.

George took my hand and started up ahead of me. We had

made it to the second floor before sounds of our pursuers filtered up the stairwell.

We stopped and held our breath. Through the slats in the bannister, I could make out the top of Cadeyn's head and, a second later, the top of Billy's. I surveyed the hall—all of the doors were closed and some of them boarded up. The building hadn't looked abandoned from downstairs, but it was quite obvious from up here. The cavernous mouth of an open elevator was right behind me, with no lift in sight.

When no one mounted the stairs, it appeared they'd taken the bait and went down the hall we'd marked with the fabric from my dress. We slinked up the stairs, trying not to make a sound. When we reached the next landing, the hair on the back of my neck stood on end.

Billy was standing half-way up the next bank of stairs, as still as a stone monument. And Cadeyn casually leaned against the wall behind us, the open elevator shaft next to him. George squeezed my hand, and I his.

Cadeyn peered at George. "There is nowhere for you to go. Leave the girl, and I will forgive you the ruse. Your cleverness will be rewarded with your life and that of your Watcher friend."

George choked, "I won't leave her."

Cadeyn smiled cruelly and looked at our entwined hands. "Your fondness for her will get you killed."

Dropping George's hand, I said "I will go with you if you release them." In that instant, I remembered the Durateus blade shoved in my garter.

George glared at me and scanned the room. I had already surveyed it and could see no other course of action. If we had a

Slayer with us, we could fight. But we were no match against them.

George asked Cadeyn, "Will you give her to your queen?"

"Now that I know she is the one we have been searching for, I am duty-bound." Cadeyn's voice was cool and professional.

"But you want to keep her for yourself?" George questioned. I wondered why he had asked. Was he stalling?

Cadeyn's nostrils flared, and he motioned for me to come to him. Taking a gulp of air, I squeezed George's elbow and moved towards Cadeyn.

When I was midway between both groups, George cried out, "No! You'll hit her!"

Shots shattered the hush and Cadeyn wrapped his arms around me, placing his body between myself and the source of the gunfire. He made a guttural sound as the bullets found his back, and when they did, he lost his footing. Then everything went dark as I felt the weightlessness of falling.

It took a only split-second to realize we'd tumbled through the doorway of the elevator shaft. Somehow Cadeyn had managed to swing himself below me, and I curled myself on top of him before we hit.

Fireworks exploded behind my lids as I tried to suck air back into my lungs. When I managed to actually breathe and open my eyes, I examined the shaft. Dim light spilled in from the second and third floors. More gunshots rang out, followed by a scream, and then all went silent.

My desire was to call out for George, but I still struggled to draw air. I rolled the rest of the way off of Cadeyn, and assessed myself. Nothing broken and nothing punctured.

Possible internal damage. Groaning, I attempted to sit up, but my head swam. I must have hit my head on Cadeyn's jaw.

My second attempt to sit upright was more successful. When I did, he stirred for the first time. I felt a horrible range of mixed emotions swirl inside my gut. Foremost was fear, but he had saved my life twice in a matter of seconds, making me wonder if that should count for something.

Cadeyn's voice, barely audible, rose to my ears. "You are unharmed?"

"Yes."

He exhaled in relief.

I pulled out my knife. "You would save me to give me to your queen? Why does she want me?"

He moaned, and in the little light there was, I could tell his eyes had rolled back into his head. He was in tremendous pain and I had to ward off the desire to offer him my wrist. The connection was stronger than I thought possible. I clenched my teeth and fought the urge.

"I would give you to her," he finally said through the agony he was experiencing as his body knit itself back together. After a moment, he added, "If you are going to kill me for it, do it now."

"H-how did you..." my voice trailed when I started to feel myself lose my nerve. My grip on the knife tightened.

He expression became thoughtful. "I drank from you. We are connected. I can feel what you feel. Any heightened emotion."

"The blood bond," I murmured. The knowledge seemed to be revealed in my memory. Learning these things in books was so different than experiencing them. I peered down at Cadeyn, who still wasn't moving much.

"You saved my life, twice, in the last few minutes. For that I owe you. But, I cannot have you pursuing me."

There was no judgment in his voice. "Do what you must." Then he closed his eyes.

Hesitating for a moment, I held the blade over his heart. A small whimper escaped my lips, and I whispered, "I'm sorry." The blade easily slipped between his ribs, followed by a whoosh of air escaping his lungs—then nothing.

My body protested as I mounted the ladder, but I was able to force myself to climb anyway. The doors on the first floor wouldn't budge, so I continued to climb. When I reached the second, I was able to pry them open enough to slide through.

My wish was to call out George's name again. Sobs threatened to erupt from me, and my mind went wild as I traversed the final set of stairs to our last location. The thought of George being dead was unbearable.

I reached the top step and noticed dark liquid pooling on the landing. Relief shook me when my eyes fell on George as he hunched over the Watcher who'd stayed with us, his hands gripping George's shirt. The Watcher said something to George, and then his hands went limp. George crossed his arms over his chest and whispered what I knew to be the last rites of a Watcher. Without thought my eyes closed as he recited the words.

The moment George was finished, he noticed me and dashed over. He embraced me so fiercely that I couldn't breathe. His face was buried in my hair. "Thought I had lost you forever." He spoke in a broken voice.

"I was sure you were gone." My voice a sob. There were so many things that were begging to be said, but this wasn't the time.

"We need to go. Can you run?"

I nodded mutely. He grabbed my hand and the nearly empty bag of weapons, then led me downstairs. Within a minute, we were on the street, running away from the bloody scene and into the night.

GEORGE

We covered a few blocks quickly and ducked into an alley to rest for a moment. Rosemond looked a little green. "Where are we going?" she gasped between breaths.

"To Ethan," I replied.

She made a sound of surprise and half-laughed.

"Did I say something amusing?"

She shook her head. "No. I just thought I would have to fight you to take me to him."

"Would you have let me take you anywhere else?"

"No."

"I know you, Rosemond Le Clair," I answered simply. After another moment I asked, "You ready? We need to get out of the open."

"Yes," she replied, but the pained look on her face said she wasn't.

I removed a small coded map from my pocket and examined it for a moment. Then we took a serpentine route to the building adjacent to Ethan's location. Sariel's team had prepared a room for emergency medical treatment. We entered a side door, wound through the lobby, and went down to the basement. Once there, I slid back a panel hiding the secret entrance to the basement of the neighboring building.

A few minutes later, we stood outside the apartment door.

I reached out to take the doorknob, but couldn't bring myself to cross the threshold. Terror at what I might find was incapacitating.

"Rosemond," I whispered, "we need to be prepared. Ethan didn't look good when they left with him."

"I will never forgive myself."

She was paler than I had ever seen her. Her bottom lip trembled, and part of me wanted to comfort her, yet the other part was still quite angry with her. I opened my mouth to speak, but she held up her hand to stop me.

"Don't. Please, don't. I deserved to die in that elevator shaft for running off like that."

"Rosemond—"

She shook her head and refused to meet my gaze.

Sighing, I turned the knob, swinging the door open to reveal the chaotic scene in the apartment before us. Sariel was standing vigil, looking like a tired angel. Two of the Slayers were wounded and had medical staff attending them. A body of a fallen warrior was on the floor covered in a sheet. Two of the Watchers appeared to have been already been patched up. I searched the area for Ethan, fear rising in me that he was the one under the sheet.

Sariel cleared her throat, then jut her chin in the direction of one of the bedroom doors. I nodded and tried to read her face.

Gently, I pushed the door open and observed Ethan's unmoving body, his forearm draped carelessly over the edge of the bed. He was an alarming shade of white. Rosemond pushed past me and dropped to her knees next to him. Ethan's eyes opened leisurely. Rosemond made a weepy sort of sound of relief and took the hand of his uninjured arm and pressed it to her cheek.

"I am *so* sorry, Ethan. You should hate me forever."

He smiled lazily at her. "If I wasn't blissfully drugged, I might be angry. Your people know what they are doing." He slurred something unintelligible. Then he seemed to sober up for a brief moment. "Tomorrow, you will tell me what in the hell that was that attacked us. 'No' is not an option." Then he mumbled something else and drifted off to sleep.

Rosemond sniffled, and I caught her hand before she reached to wipe at her face. "Whose blood is this?"

She looked at the blood that was painting her fingertips and smudged all the way up her arm. "I-I don't know. I don't think it's mine."

My eyes widened, and I urgently helped her to her feet, almost dragging her to the loo. Flipping the water on, I pulled her hands to the sink, washing away the drying blood while checking her for cuts. "Did you ingest any?" I asked, trying to keep panic from my voice. If she was exposed to any of Cadeyn's blood after being bitten, she would turn. The thought was unendurable.

"No. None in my eyes. None in my mouth." Her voice was hoarse. "How long were you at the club?" she asked in barely a whisper.

I finished checking her for cuts. None could be found. Releasing a shaky breath in relief, I answered, "Long enough."

She squeezed her eyes shut, and pulled away from me. But then something changed, and her body seemed to undulate.

"I'm going to be sick," she gasped, as she dove for the toilet. She barely made it before she started heaving. I dropped down next to her and swept her hair out of her face, holding it back with one hand. Then I stretched and reached the sink and managed to dampen a towel for her. She sobbed between each heave. "Don't be nice to me, George. Just leave me be. I don't deserve it."

My internal debate as to what to say only lasted a moment. "I don't believe anything I do or say will be worse than any punishment you will inflict on yourself." I sighed, "It was stupid sneaking out. I'll get over it."

"People *died*, George."

"Not Ethan. Not you. Not me. That place had been under observation for months. Sariel's team was itching to go in. How do you think I got there so quickly? And with so much support? They were waiting for them to violate any of the rules. It was a feeding ground, but Gareth's coven hadn't actually harmed anyone. But their intent to kidnap you? That was what Sariel had been waiting for. It would have happened eventually. And when it did...people would have died."

She made eye contact for the first time since we had entered the water closet. Her lips looked mildly purplish, and she started to shiver almost violently. I grabbed a towel from the rack, then wrapped it around her and pulled her into my arms to try to warm her.

I had the feeling that there was more in that drink they gave her than just the absinthe.

It was going to be a long night.

CHAPTER 17

BARRIERS

ROSEMOND

A confusing mixture of sensations bombarded me when I woke. My stomach felt raw and empty, and my throat felt as if I had swallowed crushed glass. I was lying on my side on a cold hard surface; then I realized why I wasn't freezing. Gentle breath tickled the back of my shoulder and the warmth from George's arm was around me. Bits of memory trickled to the surface. *He stayed up with me all night.*

A flood of shame, regret, fear, humiliation, and any other emotion that could be attached to the idiocy of my actions yesterday crashed around inside me. I gently picked up George's arm that was resting on my side and placed it on his hip. Rolling away, I sat on my knees, watching him for a moment.

He was sleeping soundly, but the worry line between his brows was creased. His mouth kept parting a tiny bit, like when he wanted to say something, but held it in instead. When I found myself staring at his lips—his full lips with the endearing scar on the bottom one, I forced myself to stand. He suddenly looked cold, and I pulled some towels from the shelf to cover him.

Tip-toeing to the sink, I twisted the faucet on to little more than a drip and washed my face. A stack of new toothbrushes and toothpowder had been supplied. I took the liberty of using one and felt infinitely better after scrubbing away the wretched film from my mouth. I dabbed my face and mouth dry, then went for the door. Before opening it, I watched him for another moment, feeling like a coward leaving before he had woken. Biting my lip, I exited, unable to face him.

The living room was larger than I'd remembered. Sara was sitting at an oversized kitchen table placed in the corner near a window. Golden light streamed through making her blonde hair a halo around her face. *A tired angel.* Had I thought that? Or maybe George had said it last night. I crept over and sat next to her at the table.

My voice was low so as to not wake some of the Watchers recovering not far away. "I am glad to see you are all right. When we fled my home, I feared the worst."

She smiled, "I feared they'd caught up with you. It seems we both have blessings for which we should be thankful."

My throat felt choked. "Agreed."

I frowned. "I am sorry for the trouble I caused. Going into that place was not one of my finer moments."

She seemed surprised by my candor. "You should have followed the advice of the people protecting you, but everyone makes mistakes. Learn from them. If you repent and mean it and turn from that behavior, then there is nothing for which to be sorry."

"But the men that—"

"You and George drew the vamps out. We had been waiting for an opportunity. Gareth and his men are far too aware of what we will and will not do."

"That's what George said to me." I sat quietly for a moment. "Did you get them all?"

She shook her head. "No. The ones who counted the most escaped. Gareth and Breton. I wanted to ask you about the ones who followed you."

After thinking for a second, I became aware that some parts of the night were hazy. "The only one who survived was Cadeyn." I paused. "He could still be at the bottom of an elevator shaft. I staked him and left him behind."

"You didn't kill him?"

"I-I couldn't. He saved my life—twice. The Watcher with us fired his weapon, and the bullets would have hit me. Cadeyn shielded me and took the rounds in his back. It was almost as if the Watcher fired *at* me. Then we fell into the elevator shaft and down three stories. Cadeyn held me and took the impact of the fall. I just couldn't finish him after that. He had done me no wrong."

"I understand." She looked as if she did. She may have been disappointed, but she hid it well.

"When I climbed out of the shaft, George was the only one left alive. He will have to fill you in on the rest."

"Of course."

"I should probably check on Ethan."

She nodded at me with a thin smile. I dismissed myself and entered Ethan's bedroom. He was resting peacefully. His color looked better, and my fears eased. Now that it was obvious he was recovering, my exhaustion closed in on me.

There was nowhere to sleep in the tiny room except on the bed with Ethan, and I wasn't about to return to the bathroom floor with George. Slipping out, I checked the other bedroom and cracked the door open to find four people asleep. A few moments later, I returned to Ethan's room. Creeping around the bed, I curled up as far away from him as possible; within moments, sleep stole me away.

GEORGE

Her fragrance was still on me. She hadn't been gone for long; the tile was still warm where she had been. It was difficult to fight my disappointment. I had not realized how much I wanted the excuse to wake up next to her until now. I folded the towels she must have covered me with and washed up. All while trying to clear my mind.

When I emerged from the washroom, Sariel pointed her chin towards Ethan's room just like she had done last night. I nodded in return and headed for the bedroom. Ethan was in the same position, but looked much improved. Rosemond had herself curled into a tiny ball, her arms hugging her legs, and chin touching her knees. Wondering how she could be comfortable, I watched them both for a minute, then returned to the living area.

Spinning the kitchen chair around backwards, I sat close to Sariel. "Do we know who leaked the information?" I whispered.

She shook her head, and then stopped. Sariel sat eerily still for a moment, and then I watched understanding spread across her features. She tilted her head to the side. "Maybe."

I nodded and regarded those in the room. She was the only person in this task-force I trusted completely. Sariel touched my elbow, and my shoulders sagged knowing what she was thinking. "We aren't safe here. How soon should we leave?" I mouthed.

She leaned in and practically pressed her lips to my ear. "I need a day. I have a plan. No one has left this place yet. One of us should be the only person to leave. It ought to give me enough time."

The day was achingly slow. Sariel was gone for hours, but even once she returned I was unable to get her alone without drawing suspicion. She wasn't the only one I couldn't seem to converse with. There was an odd dynamic between Rosemond and me. No matter where I moved, Rosemond seemed to be on the opposite end of the room. When I looked at her, she looked away.

Before the evening meal, I had reached my limit. When Rosemond was walking towards Ethan's room, I caught up to her, placed my hand on her lower back, and ushered her towards the other bedroom.

When she moved like she was going to slip around me, I clasped her arm. Though I held her with the lightest of touches, I despised the fact that it was necessary to manhandle her in any way. When I swung open the door it revealed three men resting inside. "Gentlemen, may I have the room please?"

The most senior of the Watchers jumped up. "Of course, sir." He hit the shoulder of one of the other men, and they left the room briskly.

I nudged Rosemond inside and shut the door. Walking in, I

sat on the edge of the bed, giving her space, and stared up at her. She stood like stone next to the door and fixed her gaze on the floor.

My voice was hoarse, though I tried to keep it smooth. "Rosemond, would you please speak to me?"

"George, I haven't spoken, because I have nothing to say."

"Please, be angry, be sad, be—something. This silence is killing me."

She shook her head, her eyes still glued to the floor. "Both you and Sariel have told me that last night's conflict was inevitable, but it still doesn't change the fact that my foolish actions started it. And Ethan hurt..."

"This is more than guilt over sneaking out. Are you angry because I yelled at you?"

"I am not that childish, George. I was in the wrong."

"Then why won't you even look at me?"

"Because—" her voice faltered, and she didn't continue.

I stood and moved towards her a few steps. "Because?"

She held out her hands, wanting me to stop my approach, still refusing look at me. "Please, don't. I—"

"What, Rosemond?"

She sighed. "I am mortified beyond belief, George. Isn't that enough?" She turned to open the door, but I quickly placed my hand on it to keep it shut. She leaned her forehead against the door.

"The club? Is that what this is about? Cadeyn?"

"Not him, but...the club." Her posture straightened, but she kept her back to me. I could see my breath ruffling the hair cascading down her back. "George, I would like a new handler. Or if you think I am ready, help out of the city. I can make a go of it alone."

My stomach dropped. "You don't want to be around me anymore?"

She placed her hands flat on the door as tears choked her voice. "George, I can't be around you. I threw myself at you last night, and it is unbearable. I feel humiliated on top of everything else. I understand; I do. It is your duty to protect me. I am a job. So please, just let me go. Please..."

A crazed sort of laugh escaped my lips. "This is why you won't look at me?"

She finally turned and met my gaze. I watched her ball up her fist and thought for a moment that she was going to punch me. "You laugh at me."

"No," I whispered, and felt every barrier I had so carefully constructed crack with a single blink of her eyes.

When she looked at me with her rosy, tear-stained cheeks, I framed her face in my hands and pressed my lips to hers. She made a startled sound, and then wrapped her hands around my waist and pulled me closer.

I feared that I would never be able to let go of her. The barriers weren't just cracked; they were tumbling to the ground and turning to dust.

I love her.

More than I had thought possible, and the confirmation of her lips made it seem more than my body could contain. I pressed her to the wall, wanting to be closer still.

Our breath was uneven as I ran my hands up her neck and into her luxurious hair and then over her shoulders and down her arms and back again.

She tasted sweet and minty and like the promise of infinite possibilities. Like futures as bright as the sun.

I whispered into her neck, "I have wanted to kiss you since

the first moment I saw you. And didn't kiss you last night, because if...when I did, I wanted you to remember it."

I didn't let her respond and kissed her again. A faint moan escaped her, and it was the most beautiful sound. She had fist-fuls of my shirt and kept pulling me closer still.

I was hers and hers entirely.

I didn't know if my heart would allow me to leave...*ever*.

CHAPTER 18

WANTS

ROSEMOND

"Are you surprised we haven't heard from Sara?" I asked, trying to draw more information from George without pushing. "It's been a week since the ambush."

His full lips were pressed into a thin line as he stared at the road. The window was cracked open, and the smell of newly wet earth wafted inside. "No. She said it may take some time."

"And you still don't have a clue as to what her plan is?"

"No." He glanced at me for half a second, and then his eyes were focused on the road again. He exhaled and patted the pocket with the telegram he had picked up in town. He still hadn't opened it. He drew in a breath and changed the subject. "Ethan will like what you got him." He wore a faint smile, but it never reached his eyes.

"I hope so. He hasn't seemed himself."

"He will bounce back."

"I hope so."

"He was seriously wounded and found out about our world all in one night; even someone as unflappable as Ethan had to take pause."

"I suppose so," I replied, still worried.

George reached over and took my hand. I immediately felt more at ease. His touch seemed to be a healing balm. I hadn't known how much I had needed to be touched.

We pulled onto the long dirt road that led to the country house in which we were staying. As soon as we were through the front door, I pulled off the blonde wig and spectacles I was wearing and ran my fingers through my hair, loosening the large pin curls. Before I could head to the back of the house to check on Ethan, George put the bags on the floor and caught me around the waist, twirling me to face him. He had a hopeless look on his face that frightened me. We had faced so many dangers in the last few weeks, but this look truly unnerved me.

"What is it, George?" I whispered.

His lips were downturned as he regarded me through his lashes. "I simply," he paused, and then instead of finishing his thought, he kissed me.

Dropping the wig and glasses on the floor, I kissed him heartily in return. I ran my hands over his chest, up his neck, and into his hair. His arms wrapped around me tightly as he pulled me closer, to the point that my toes were barely touching the floor.

I loved the feel of his hands on me and the feel of his lips on mine, always the perfect balance of tenderness and want. It seemed as if he was shaking ever so slightly as he released me and pressed his forehead to mine.

"We should check on Ethan and start preparing some food," he murmured.

I nodded in agreement, still not wanting to let him go.

~

WE SPENT THE NEXT HALF HOUR PREPARING THE MEAL IN silence while Ethan looked out the back window. Once everything was in the oven, George excused himself and went out onto the porch by himself. I retrieved the gift I had bought for Ethan and found him still staring out the window. Sitting next to him on the wicker love seat, the cushion groaned as I settled in.

Ethan grinned, but there was something somber beneath the twinkle in his eye. "Did you have a nice trip to town with the Warden?"

I giggled. "It was rather nice to be out of the cottage. I wish you would have come with us."

"If something had happened, I would have been an impediment."

"That is why you refused?"

"One of many reasons, love," he replied.

"I bought you something." I handed him the flat parcel in plain brown wrapping. He placed it on his lap. I reached over and untied the string, holding the package closed. He glanced at me with an expression that could only be described as grateful and frustrated at the same time, as his left arm was still snug in a sling from the bad break.

"Buying me gifts? Won't George be terribly jealous?"

"Terribly—he may throw himself off a cliff or something."

"Understandable, the way you look longingly at me all the time. I am hard to resist."

There was no restraining my smile. He hadn't really flirted

with me since the attack, at least not while he wasn't highly drugged. "Are you going to open it?" I asked, referring to the gift.

He watched me for a long moment before breaking his eyes away to look at the package on his lap. He finally peeled back the paper with one hand to reveal a leather-bound artist's journal. Inside the book, every fifth page was lined, while the rest were blank. The heavy stock of the paper was perfect for sketching. I reached into my purse and pulled out a drawstring bag filled with a few pencils. He stared at them and didn't say anything.

"Your drawing hand isn't injured, so I thought this might help pass the time."

"I never said thank you."

In confusion, I tilted my head to the side. "I just gave it to you."

He shook his head. "No, the night we were attacked. You tried to save me. I still have this vision of you appearing over that creature's shoulder, hanging on for dear life, and plunging that knife into his chest."

"Oh," I uttered, surprised, while feeling the darkness of that night wash over me. "I'm afraid it was rather futile. I was a dog nipping at the heels of a war horse."

There was a spark in his eyes for a second. "Just proves once again that you are desperately in love with me."

"Shhhh. Don't tell, George." I whispered.

He pursed his lips, his eyes on the journal again. "You deserve a normal life, Rosemond. One in which you aren't running from monsters."

My voice was more melancholy than I wished. "Ethan, I can't help what I am. It is rather hard to disappear completely."

I paused, "I suspect my life will be one of putting down roots only to tear them up again. But I have known that my whole life. I accept it."

"You and George have told me about vampires and your Concilium of the Watchers. Even about other immortals walking on the earth. But there is one thing you haven't told me. What are you? George told me a little, but not enough to understand. Why do they want you so badly that they would send people and vampires to their death to retrieve you?"

I wilted. "George probably knows more than I do." I played with the ribbon on the drawstring bag lying between us. "I am a Seer. I have dreams and visions about the past and the future. There is a vampire queen, an Ancient, one of the original people cursed by God to walk in darkness. She wants people from my bloodline for something. But it has been kept from me."

"So only people from your bloodline are Seers? Or are you special amongst them?"

"That would be a question for George." I paused as a revelation hit me. "He should have returned to England already, shouldn't he?"

Ethan batted his eyelashes at me. "Yes, but I think he has found a reason to stay."

My hand covered the small, coy smile dancing on my lips as my cheeks flushed. "I didn't expect him to stay for me."

"Any man would be a fool not to stay for you," he grinned. The twinkle in his astonishingly blue eyes had returned.

I laughed. "You flatter me, Ethan. You shouldn't. No man could ever have a simple life with me."

"Is that what you want? Something simple?"

"What I want..." I shook my head. "My desires are of no

consequence. Suitors should beware. I'm afraid you were spot on—I am like the siren you depicted in the painting. I'm just waiting to pull them under and ruin their lives."

"Were your parents not happy?"

"No, they were desperately in love, for eighteen years. But because of who my mother is...was...my father was killed."

He took my hand and kissed my knuckles. "Still worth it."

Laughing again, I pulled my hand back while rolling my eyes. Then I peeped out the window. George was slowly pacing back and forth. I watched as the heat from his breath puffed out around him.

Keeping my eyes on George, I commented, "We picked up a telegram at Western Union. He still hasn't opened it." I paused for a moment. "I heard the two of you talking late last night. Do you know what it's about?"

"He didn't tell you?"

"No."

Ethan sighed. "He cabled his father a few days ago and told him he was staying. I assume this is the response."

In shock, the blood drained from my face. My voice was a whisper, more to myself. "He did that? I thought he had the position at Cambridge waiting for him. All his dreams. How could he give all that up?"

"I thought we covered this already."

We both watched George through the window. He kept reaching into the pocket for the telegram, and then he would pull his hand away empty. I didn't want to get my hopes up.

"You want him to stay, don't you? You love him." It was a statement more than a question.

"Yes." My voice was breathy and hesitant. I hadn't said those words to George. It was no use to say otherwise; Ethan would see right through me. I struggled with the fact that I had felt so much in such a short time. My logical brain fought against it.

Our attention was drawn outside. George had finally stilled and leaned against the bannister attached to the back steps. He drew in a deep breath, then held it as he pulled the envelope from his breast pocket and tore off a thin strip at the end. He slid the contents out and read them as he exhaled. His face was expressionless. I think both Ethan and I were holding our collective breaths while we waited for his reaction. George placed the telegram on top of the envelope, then crushed it in his hand and closed his eyes.

"That isn't good," Ethan remarked.

George's cool demeanor crumbled as he suddenly punched the railing. Instantly, I was on my feet and out the door before what I was doing registered. I stood above him at the top of the steps. His shoulders slumped and he clutched his hand.

"George, are you all right?"

"Nothing is broken," he muttered. He glanced over at me, then sat on the step. I cautiously approached and perched myself on the step to his left. When he didn't speak, I took his injured hand in mine and pressed it to my lips, then held the back of his hand to my cheek. He sighed.

"Are you going to tell me what was in the telegram?"

"My father's disappointment," he replied, his voice rough.

I felt as if my heart was pushing frigid water through my veins and had to will myself to keep steady. "You are leaving. He ordered you back."

George had that same hopeless expression he'd had in the entryway when we returned from shopping. "I won't go."

I hoped he couldn't see how painful my next words were.

"Don't sacrifice everything for me. Don't alienate your family and give up your dreams. It may not feel like it now, but you will resent me later." I didn't know if the last statement was true, but I'd heard about it happening to others. Once it was out though, it felt false. I bit my lip before I could retract the last statement.

"Rosemond." He gave a bitter sort of laugh. "I am young, but I know my mind. All the dreams. All the plans. They mean nothing without you." He turned the hand I had pressed to my cheek so he could cup my chin. "I love you. I want to be with you." He swallowed. "Forever."

He did it.

He said the words.

"We don't always get what we want, George."

He dropped his hand while shifting his body to view the yard. "I have never been lost before, Rosemond. Not like this."

My eyes stung, and I pressed my lids shut trying to stifle the tears as moisture dampened my lashes. It was nearly impossible to force myself to be logical.

All I wanted was to tell him that I loved him—and to memorize his face, his neck, his hands, his everything with my lips.

I wanted to be crushed in his embrace and allow myself to forget every sorrow I had ever felt. He could do that for me. I sucked in a breath and offered him my hand. "Walk with me."

GEORGE

She stood there, her arm outstretched and her bottom lip about to tremble. The sun shone behind her, framing her silhouette with golden light. I cringed and shoved the telegram in my pocket. Taking her hand, we started walking a large circle around the wooded yard. I was thankful for the proliferation of trees allowing us the freedom of outside; it was easier to breathe out here.

After ambling a hundred meters or so, she looped her arm through mine but remained silent. Halfway through our second round, she finally spoke, but before she did, she dropped her arms to her sides and walked a few feet away.

"George, you aren't going to like what I have to say."

A knot instantly rose in my throat. "Don't," I gasped.

"We need to be smart about this." She turned her back to me. "You need to do what your father said and return home. You have a life waiting for you." Her voice faltered. "And you have been living in the open. You said because of that, short-term training would be the only wise course."

I gently grabbed her arm. After a moment, she turned and backed up two steps into a tree, still refusing to look at me, so I took her chin in my hand, forcing eye contact.

"Is that what *you* want?" I asked.

She tried to look away. "George."

"Is that what *you* want?" I asked again more firmly.

There was a change in her, and her expression became that of stone. She pushed my hand away from her face, keeping my wrist tight in her grip. "Wants are not part of my life. Tomorrow we will go into town and take the pictures for the identification packages. You will arrange a meeting with Sariel where she can take over my safe-keeping. We will send Ethan home. And you will do what your father says."

"Rosemond." I said pleadingly, but I had nothing to refute. My suggestions were emotional. There was no flaw in her plan to exploit.

"I will eat in my room this evening. See you in the morning." She pushed past me and returned to the house. I watched as Ethan tried to speak with her when she hurried by him, but she never broke her stride. In fact, she didn't turn left to go to the kitchen. I saw her disappear in the direction of the rooms. I stood stunned.

Reaching into my pocket, I pulled out the crumpled telegram, running my eyes over the message one last time. Three short sentences had stolen everything from me. *Everything.*

CHAPTER 19

COLDEST

ROSEMOND

It had been a silent morning. I'd expected George to act coldly or angrily towards me, but there had only been kindness. His eyes seemed to be damming back a storm, but he never uttered a word. There had been no sound other than footsteps on wood floors, the scrape of forks on porcelain, and the splash of water in a sink. Now I sat in the backseat of the motorcar behind Ethan as we waited for George to lock up the house.

Ethan shattered the quiet with the gentlest of voices. "George doesn't love easily. You know that, don't you?"

A muffled sound had to suffice as a response.

Ethan continued. "When he does love, it is completely. Are you—"

"Please, stop."

He turned in his seat and appraised me. "So you *do* still feel something."

"How could you think I wouldn't?" I retorted incredulously

and instantly felt horrible. There was no reason to be sharp with Ethan.

"George said it was as if you flipped a switch yesterday afternoon. Like you were a different person."

"Would he have listened to me if I had told him my true feelings?"

He dropped his arm over the back of his seat and took my hand. "He isn't gone, yet."

I jumped when the driver's side door opened. George slid into the car, his eyes stopping for a split-second on our clasped hands before he cranked over the engine.

Ethan gave my hand a little squeeze and sent me a concerned look before turning to face front. After that, there was no conversation for the entirety of our journey.

WHEN WE PARKED BEHIND A BUILDING, I DREW OUT MY father's pocket watch from my purse and noted the time. It had taken forty-five minutes to travel to the town with the little photo studio. When we entered the shop, a small, scholarly looking man greeted us. He had a fabulous waxed mustache that had been out of fashion for a decade, but somehow it fit him. His small, round spectacles enlarged his dark eyes making him appear owl-like.

George shook the photographer's hand. "Hello, I'm Basil Adkins. We have the 11:00 AM appointment." I turned away quickly hearing the name he had used. When we'd first met, I had told him I'd expected his name to be something like Basil or Nigel. It seemed like that conversation had been years ago.

"Ah, yes. The actors and the actress." He bowed a little.

"Step through there. Everything is set up. Please." He motioned us through a doorway next to the counter marked "Studio."

We trailed behind him into a sizable room equipped with hand-painted backdrops, one dark and one light, on the back wall. There were screens where we could change in opposite corners. George put down the bags, and we went to work getting dressed. The next two hours were spent having our photos taken. Most of them were of me with different wigs in various colors. Both George and Ethan had several pictures taken with an assortment of facial hair and hats. *Too bad there isn't a pretty assistant for Ethan to flirt with.*

He must have been sick to death of the cloud that had been hanging over us since I'd commanded George to follow his father's orders.

I sank onto the chair behind the changing screen as the boys were taking the last set of pictures. There was a small mirror at eye level, and I stared into it, the pain evident in my eyes. Ethan must have done something funny, because George laughed for the first time in two days. I made a decision and quickly twisted my hair into a swirl at the base of my neck and came out looking as myself.

The photographer was busy with Ethan, who had on a ridiculous mustache, and George was smiling at the pose Ethan was holding. His charm had to have been emblazoned onto the film. George turned towards me and instantly noticed there was a change. He approached, but didn't speak, the smile dissipating from his face.

He stood in front of me, partially costumed, so close that his shallow breath displaced a small feather that had found its way to my lapel. I reached up and pulled the glasses from his face and folded them closed in my hands. His body leaned ever so slightly forward, and it was all I could do not to rise up on my tip-toes and kiss him. His welcoming lips were so close.

"I want a picture. Of the three of us. The real us."

"Rosemond, you know we—"

I placed two of my fingers over his lips and felt him melt. "*Please*," knowing he wouldn't deny me.

George nodded in consent just as the photographer turned towards him. "Is that going to be it, Mr. Adkins?"

George's face looked a little flushed. "Just one more. The three of us—without costumes." I saw Ethan give George a look; even with his limited knowledge he knew this was not protocol.

"Wonderful!" the photographer proclaimed. He pulled his camera back to get a wider angle. Ethan removed the mustache and primped in the mirror for a moment. "Miss, if you wouldn't mind standing in the middle." I was directed to the X inked in red on the carpet.

I dutifully stood on the designated spot as he arranged the boys around me; George on my right and Ethan on the left. He draped a coat over Ethan's arm to hide the cast, and then added a fern on a pedestal in the background. The photographer tilted his head to the side and examined us. Then he stepped forward, brought George's hand to my elbow, and turned Ethan slightly more towards me.

As the photographer dipped under the drape on the back of his camera, George gently squeezed my arm. The yearning I felt from such a simple gesture was agonizing. I could feel the warmth of his hand through the thin fabric of my sleeve. We froze in our positions until we were told otherwise. "Splendid," the photographer announced.

I turned towards George and whispered, "Thank you."

He swallowed and nodded his head, but didn't speak. He cleared his throat, dropping his hand from my elbow, and turned to the photographer. They were discussing something about "closing the shop" and a "rush job" and "well-compensated."

Ethan sidled up next to me, drawing my attention. He bent to my ear. "Not gone yet," was all he said.

I glared at him.

He shrugged his shoulders and mouthed: "What?" his expression innocent. He turned to George. "Basil, I'm famished. You buying?"

George turned. "I thought you were the one with the giant pocketbook."

"Doesn't mean I don't want to be wined and dined," he lifted his eyebrow suggestively.

"Do you have everything you need?" George asked the photographer.

"Yes, Mr. Adkins. See you in four hours' time." The photographer trailed behind us to the door, and once we were on the street, he waved to us and flipped the sign to closed.

"He is able to develop them and get them to us today?" I asked George, surprised.

"Yes. He is closing the store. He has his own dark room and equipment." He thought for a moment, "I would like to get you two settled, then send out some communications."

I sulked. Communications equaled George leaving in my mind, even though I had told him to do so. I looped my arm through Ethan's. "Guess it will just be the two of us."

"I suppose it is acceptable for *you* to wine and dine me."

"Who says I am paying?" I retorted.

He flashed a smile. "I do. With George's money of course."

"How silly of me. *Of course*, I'll pay," I giggled. There was a small restaurant ahead, and George's eyes were trained on it. When we were two store fronts away, he dropped back and gently tugged at my elbow and urged me towards an alley. I pulled Ethan in after us.

George spoke in hushed tones. "Are you armed?"

"Always." After the train and the club, I was determined to be armed at all times—to the extent that I had weapons neatly folded in my towel while showering.

Ethan asked, "You are?"

In silence, I opened my purse just enough he could see the revolver tucked inside. Then I reached up to my hat, where there was a beautiful broach sticking out of the flowers adorning the side. I tugged at the broach to reveal it was really a small blade. He wasn't really that surprised until I pulled my skirts close to my leg to reveal the Durateus blade strapped to each thigh.

"Anything else?" Ethan asked.

I batted my eyelashes: "Wouldn't you like to know."

George pulled a few bills from his wallet and a handkerchief, handing them to me. When I felt through the cloth, I realized he was giving me more ammunition. I nodded. Then he turned to Ethan, lifted his pant leg, and drew a small pistol from the hidden holster. "Keep this in your pocket."

"You really think we will need all this? I thought it would be safe. It's noon." Ethan asked.

"Just a precaution—they have human familiars. Well-trained humans are not to be underestimated."

Ethan seemed a little pale. "No, that wouldn't be prudent."

"We should get to that restaurant," I urged.

Ethan started towards the street. I glanced at George and let out my breath in surprise, not realizing he was so close. We seemed to hold each other with our eyes for a long moment. Once again it was a battle to control the urge to kiss him.

He leaned towards me as if I had my own gravitational pull. It took every ounce of strength to squeeze his elbow, give him a tight-lipped smile, and quickly follow after Ethan. As soon as George couldn't see my face, I squeezed my eyes shut and grimaced in pain, praying not to plow into something. If I had let him kiss me, it wouldn't be possible to let him go.

GEORGE

I inquired with the hostess as to where the Western Union was located, then ordered food, having the restaurant hold it for an extra twenty minutes. As quickly as possible, I covered the two blocks' distance to send my communications.

Once inside the cable office, I composed coded messages to my father informing him that I would be returning home and then a message to Sariel that I needed her to take on my duties. As per Watcher protocol, the same message was sent to five separate relay stations with five response locations. I would pick up the replies two towns away in the late afternoon after setting up in a new safe house.

When returning, I took an alternate route back to the eatery. Stress was gnawing away at my nerves and I was holding it in my chest. It felt as if there was a wedge threatening to separate my ribs and crush my heart. But worse than the pain was the fear that my attention was too fragmented to see threats.

A hectic eddy of imperatives swirled in my brain, pelting

me with everything from protocols to items I still needed to teach Rosemond. I cringed. In an effort to be extra cautious, I circled around the back and entered through the rear of the restaurant.

Ethan was holding Rosemond's hand across the table and speaking with an odd intensity. I started to bristle, but realized it wasn't a demonstration of intimacy. She glanced over, noticing my approach, then her attention went back to Ethan pleadingly and whispered, "Ethan...*please.*"

Ethan released her hand, and she drew it back, clutching her napkin. He smiled in greeting, but I saw the worry before he whisked it away.

Rosemond stood. Her face was exceptionally pale. "If you can excuse me for a moment, I need to visit the ladies room."

Instead of sitting, I headed to the water closets in the back. As I did a security sweep, I could feel her disapproval. It seemed as if she could barely contain it.

"It's clear. Meet you at the table," I whispered.

She nodded in affirmation, but didn't speak. I wanted to hear her voice. She had done nothing more than that necessary for basic communication, besides her request for the photo. I was beginning to wonder if she had really felt anything for me at all. She hadn't reciprocated in words when I had expressed my love for her.

After returning to the table, I positioned myself to see the back exit and water closets and pinned Ethan with a foul expression. "What were you saying to her?"

"Nothing to be concerned about. Just trying to make a point."

I looked at him utterly confused. "About what?"

Ethan rubbed at his forehead and blew out a lungful of air. "That it is acceptable to choose happiness sometimes."

A few minutes later, Rosemond returned to the table, still pale as the linens. For a moment, it seemed as if the edges of her eyes were red. She spent the remainder of the meal avoiding eye contact with both Ethan and I. I wished it possible to see inside that stubborn head of hers.

Maybe Socrates was right when he said that,

"The hottest love has the coldest end."

This is a coldness I don't know if I can bear.

CHAPTER 20

ASK

ROSEMOND

"Ethan, bend the knee. Feet at a 45 degree angle." I patted his leg, and he relaxed into the stance. "Hold both arms out towards the target, like so." Demonstrating, I held my left arm in front of me, with the right hand gripping the blade.

"There are three main types of holds." I held up the knife and spun it in my hand, demonstrating as I showed him each. "Hammer hold, modified hammer hold, and blade hold. I prefer the blade hold, but if the knife is extremely sharp, one of the other holds may be better. You should start with one of the hammer holds."

"And how long have you been throwing knives?"

I shrugged. "Since childhood—weapons training was part of life. I can always masquerade as a circus performer."

"I believe the knives are usually thrown *at* the beautiful women, not *by* them," he joked, prodding me.

"And that is where you are mistaken," I replied, not letting him ruffle me. I let the blade fly, hitting the center mark on the makeshift target.

"That was lucky," he said smugly, eyeing the trunk of the sprawling Sugar Maple tree.

Rolling my eyes, I picked up three more blades. My grin grew wide as the breeze blew strands of hair over my eyes. I blinked and tucked them behind my ear. "Should we make a wager?"

"Sure. I lose, you talk to George. You win, you talk to George?"

"You are a certifiable riot," I retorted, deadpan. "And, I have talked to George."

Ethan let out that same bitter sort of laugh that I wasn't used to hearing from him. "If by talking, you mean answering with one word whenever in his presence, then, yes." He held me with his eyes. "You haven't talked to him since your walk in the yard of the cottage."

Gritting my teeth, I turned towards the target and threw each blade in rapid succession. I didn't look at where they landed. My shoulders drooped. "Ethan, I am trying to do what is the most logical. Please, speak of this no more." My voice uncontrollably husky. My worry was that he could see my resolve breaking.

"Ros—" he stopped. "Your hand," his tone softened.

"What? Oh." There was a crimson trail down my palm. Droplets were splattering on the brown brick patio.

He took my hand and started escorting me towards the house. "Let's get that cleaned up."

Tugging my hand out of his, I snapped. "I can do it. You practice."

His mouth pressed into a hard line. "You can let people help you. You can let people in."

I turned my back and paused, never having thought of myself as closed off before. "What good does that do? No one gets to stay. Not my parents. Not my sister." I faltered, choking back bile. "Not George. It will be better this way."

He spoke at my back. "George isn't dead. He wants to be with you. *You* want to be with him."

"Don't you remember? I don't get to have wants, just musts."

"Someday someone will stay, if you are brave enough to let him."

His challenge stung. Spinning around, I rushed into the house, trying to escape his words. Quickly washing my hand in the bathroom, I wound a bandage around it while continuing to my room. The moment the door was shut, I kicked off my shoes and crawled under the covers that smelled too much of dust. I prayed that sleep would take me from my present misery before George returned from picking up the telegrams.

GEORGE

The small two-bedroom house where we were hiding was quiet when I parked in front of it. After exiting the motorcar, I stood and listened. There was the sound of a wolf in the distance, a hint of music from a radio, the smell of burning firewood, and the whisper of leaves in the breeze. I felt unsettled but wasn't sure if it was my emotional unrest or a danger that I was sensing. Slowly creeping to the door, I swept my eyes over the newly darkened landscape, dismayed I hadn't made it back before nightfall.

Lugging a few groceries, I unlocked the door and proceeded down the narrow entry, towards the music that could be heard from outside. I rounded the corner into the cramped living area. Ethan sat on the leather davenport with his elbows on his knees and head in his hands. He didn't look up at me. "Hello, George. Get everything you need?"

"Yes. Uneventful." I paused. "Is everything all right?"

He finally looked up and eased back against the couch. "Yes. Tired, I guess. Rosemond had me out throwing knives all afternoon."

"She's quite good."

"I noticed. Pray I'm never the recipient. Her groupings on the target were impeccable, even after I upset her."

Feeling myself bristle, I asked, "You upset her?"

"Teased her a little too much," he replied, but his voice wasn't quite right.

I nodded, but didn't feel any resolution. "Has she turned in already?"

"Appears so. She cleaned up a cut...haven't seen her since. I tried to get her to eat something, but she wouldn't come to her door. She said she wasn't hungry."

Drawing a train ticket out of my breast coat pocket, I handed it to him. He stared at the thick slip of paper, turning it over in his hands a couple of times. "So, this is really it?"

"Yes," I replied tersely. Frowning, I shook my head. "My apologies. It is dated a week from now. I depart in the morning, and Sariel will arrive tomorrow afternoon. My hope was that you would stay with her for a few days...help with the transition."

"Anything you need."

"Are you terribly disappointed?"

He regarded me for a long moment. It was unnerving to see him so serious. "It just wasn't the ending for which I'd hoped."

"Nor I, my friend."

I walked away, almost lethargically, heading to Rosemond's bedroom. After arriving, I stood outside, working up my nerve to knock, steeling myself against her indifference. Holding my breath, I drummed softly with my fingertips.

Her muffled voice barely made it through the door. "Ethan, my decision is made. *Please*."

"It's George. May I come in?"

Silence. I couldn't discern a noise in the room, not even the shifting of covers.

Finally, she replied. "Yes."

The door creaked as I swung it halfway open. She sat on the bed, feet on the floor with a blanket wrapped around her shoulders. For some reason, it appeared as if she had been sitting in this position for a long while. Her eyes were red. I approached her with caution.

My voice was soft. "I have some currency and some paperwork for you." I handed her the envelope.

She thumbed through the contents. When she flipped to a sheet with a series of numbers, she held it up questioningly and cocked her head to the side.

"Locations to send cables...if you need me in the future."

She nodded and focused on the floor once again. Her hair slid off her shoulders and hid her face from me. I stood there, locked in place, wanting to say so many things to her and debating on whether it was important to retain my pride. I sank to my knees in front of her; Rosemond's expression remained unreadable. She raised her chin, the muscle in her jaw flexing. I wanted to hold her hands, but she had tucked them under her legs.

I finally arrived at the conclusion that my pride meant nothing. Slumping my shoulders and leaning forward, I rested my head on her lap.

My voice came out impossibly thick. "Ask me to stay, and I will."

She didn't answer, but suddenly her warm hands were in my hair, smoothing it. While keeping my head on her lap, my arms circled her waist drawing her closer.

I wondered if she was feeling anything but pity for me. Then came the answer. A single teardrop fell to my cheek and I squeezed her a little closer. This was tearing her up too. She was simply stronger than me.

CHAPTER 21

DISTRACTION

ROSEMOND

Once I was finally able to wipe sleep from my eyes, I was grateful it was morning. After George had left, the night had been long and black and fitful. We had stayed locked in an embrace for what must have been an hour before he'd slipped from the room, breaking my heart with the look on his face.

No longer able to keep myself from him, I sprang from the bed running to the kitchen following the clank of flatware. My bare feet slapped the wooden floor as I sprinted the short distance.

Ethan looked at me alarmed as I flew into the room.

I spun in a circle, looking for George, tugging at my robe when it slipped off my shoulder.

"He's gone, Rosemond."

"*What?*" I cried.

"Didn't he tell you last night?"

"No...he..." My voice choked. I sucked in a stuttering

breath and sank onto a chair opposite Ethan with the realiza-tion. George had been saying goodbye last night. "You must think me despicable."

Ethan looked at me sympathetically. "No," he answered resolutely.

"You are still here. I thought you would've left too and that Sara would be here."

"She will be here in a few hours. You have *me* for another six days. Plenty of time to fall madly in love with me."

When a strangled sort of laugh escaped me, my eyes met Ethan's beautiful, blue ones. It was obvious that it was taking considerable effort for him to be cheerful. I was breaking everyone around me.

My bottom lip quivered as he held my gaze. "I'm glad you stayed, Ethan. So very glad."

GEORGE

It took me two full days to make my way back to New York, and I was grateful for the distraction of travel. In twenty-four hours I would board an airship and slip back into my old life. I glanced down the still-bustling city street. It had been raining all day, and the lights were doubled as they reflected in the pooled water.

Out of the corner of my eye, my attention was drawn to a black roadster. The passenger side bumper had a small dent where deep blue paint had transferred from another vehicle. There was a hitch in my step as I recalled seeing that same motorcar yesterday and the day before. *I am an imbecile.* I had been trailed and been too swathed in my own misery to notice.

Ambling down the street, I watched passersby in the

windows, tracking people in the shadows. I caught furtive looks from one, then two, then three casual observers. Rounding a corner, I stepped into a small general store that reminded me more of something one would find in a rural area rather than in New York.

Outside, one of the men I had identified lit up a cigarette and nonchalantly looked through the window. I amassed a few supplies: a pair of socks, a box of nails, and a coil of wire. I quickly filled the bottom of each sock with a liberal amount of nails and knotted the tops. Shoving them into my pocket, I casually strolled down the next aisle while wrapping my right hand with the wire, careful not to make it too tight and prevent me from using my pistol.

Nearing the end of the aisle, I bent down feigning interest in something. When out of sight for only a moment, the door squeaked open and closed. I stood and surveyed as three men lingered around the front counter. Two of them were new, which meant that there were at least two more outside.

Without backup it was necessary to avoid confrontation. Pinching the bridge of my nose, I walked to the front of the store and placed my items on the counter. Hiding my hand with the coiled wire, I asked the elderly clerk. "Sir, is there, by chance, a privy I could use? It is a long walk back to my lodgings."

He considered me with one bulging eye from beneath two prolifically wild grey eyebrows. "Where you from?"

"Oxford, or there about."

"Ah. Wife's from Wales." He chewed on his bottom lip for a moment. "Go ahead and go back. Through the door, the toilet is on the left in the back corner of the storage room."

"Much obliged." I patted the canned food and bar of soap I had picked up. "Do you mind holding these here for me?"

He nodded and made a sort of grunting sound of assent.

I turned and walked past the men who were now meandering near the first aisle. As I pushed through the 'Employee Only' door, I glanced out the storefront and took in the unmistakable profile of the man with the yellow scarf—he wasn't dead.

Once out of sight, my feet couldn't carry me quickly enough through the room thick with boxes. The back door was chained shut, so I swerved towards the water closet and locked myself inside. I listened through the door. There were no sounds of pursuit—yet. Turning, I noticed a small window above the loo and stepped up to open it up. The frame was sealed shut with ancient paint. I pulled out the small knife hidden in my belt buckle and sliced through the sealed frame. Once finished, I carefully freed the lock, my palms slick with perspiration.

Someone rapped the door. "Are you all right in there?" It wasn't the clerk's voice.

"Yes. Sorry. Stomach troubles. Be out momentarily."

I flushed the toilet with my toes while simultaneously wrenching the window open. To my relief, the opening was large enough to squeeze through. I strained to look outside. It appeared to be clear. Dashing to the sink, I flipped on the faucet, and then immediately hoisted myself through the opening and disappeared into the night.

ROSEMOND

Hands were shaking me, and my only desire was for whomever it was to cease. George had been gone for two days, and I wasn't ready to stop wallowing. After pushing the hand away, it went to my face.

"Rosemond!"

My eyes fluttered open, and the disorientation started to clear. It had to be the middle of the night and the pillow beneath my head was damp from tears. I sat up, almost knocking heads with Ethan and looked at him wildly. The events in my dream started to come more sharply into focus.

"What is it? You have been screaming in your sleep for over a minute."

Tears plummeted down my cheeks, as I shoved the covers away and stood up trying to put the pieces together. While pacing back and forth, I realized that I was only in my night-gown and alone with Ethan. It was completely inappropriate to be alone with him like this, but it was hard to care. When I glanced over at him, his eyes were fixed on my face.

"George is in trouble, and we have no way of reaching him until he returns to England." I swallowed. "It may be too late."

"Sara...she—"

I cut him off. "He has no reason to check in at this point." The speed of my pacing across the floor increased until Ethan finally caught my arm and pulled me down to sit next to him. "If I hadn't insisted he go back to his life...his family..."

After I had calmed, he stood up and held out his hand. "Let's go talk to Sara." I took his hand and let him help me up, but stopped to grab my robe before leaving the room.

The discussion didn't go as I thought it would. Sara insisted that we leave the house at once. If George was captured and compromised in any way, we could not be in this location. We were packed within ten minutes and rumbling down the dirt road with Sara at the wheel. Ethan, seeing my agitation, sat in the back with his arm around my shoulders and didn't complain when I squeezed his hand painfully hard.

I couldn't stop blaming myself...

blaming myself...

blaming myself...

GEORGE

The sun couldn't rise soon enough. I felt safer, though most of the men who had attempted to abduct me last night were human. I shoved my few possessions back into my rucksack and placed in the front flap the paperwork I needed to return to the bank. When I opened the front pocket, I noticed an extra slip of paper and pulled it out between my index and middle fingers. The name "Frank" was written in neat letters; I flipped it over and found it was the picture of Rosemond, Ethan, and I. *She must have placed it in my bag.*

I sat staring at the picture for a long while, running my finger around the curve of her cheek. "Damn her," I hissed, sticking the picture back in the pocket, suddenly feeling an avalanche of anger that she'd driven me away and frustration that I had allowed it.

Pulling out my pocket watch, I noted that the bank would already be open by the time I had walked there. Making one last spot check of the room, I strode out the door. Three sets of stairs, five blocks, and a hundred looks over the shoulder later, I arrived at First Trust and entered.

A small man with a weak chin and bulbous nose intercepted me. He was the boss who had delayed the transfer yesterday and had sent me off with more paperwork to fill out. I tried to shove down my annoyance and smiled back in greeting.

He made a kissing sound with his lips before he spoke. "Mr. Klein, I trust everything with the documents went smoothly?"

"Yes. I should have everything you need." I loosed the file of papers and the extra identification he had requested, handing them to him.

"Wonderful. Please, follow me."

He led me to a tidy desk in the corner with a nameplate reading: Wilbur Pines. He kept glancing at the gold clock on the wall. It made me feel unsettled. He prattled on about his plans once the weather warmed and other items in which I had no interest. I smiled thinly and nodded.

At exactly 9:15 AM, he stood up. "Well, Mr. Klein. I think that does it. The money will be in your accounts in two days' time."

"Thank you, Mr. Pines." We shook hands, and I started towards the side exit.

"Oh, Mr. Klein. There is work on the street just outside. It would be prudent to use the main exit." He motioned over to some posted signs.

Nodding curtly, I uttered, "Good day," and headed towards the main exit. Pushing open the brass and glass doors, I stepped outside.

The street was bustling with people. I stood at the top of the marble steps and drew in a deep breath and enjoyed the sunlight on my face. It was the first time the sun had cut through the clouds in weeks it seemed. I slowly traversed the steps and scanned the crowd to my left, accidentally colliding into a woman and knocking her bag to the ground.

"Terribly sorry," I stammered, fumbling to pick up the bag for her.

She stood there with an odd expression. I started to return her bag, but she remained still with her arms crossed, for a long moment, not taking it. After another moment, she seemed to snap out of it and looked embarrassed. "Oh, it's all right. I wasn't looking. I think I ran into you." She took the satchel and smiled a little flirtatiously, then disappeared into the crowd.

I watched her leave, perplexed, then headed in the opposite direction. A photographer was taking pictures of a building and some renovation work was being done. It was necessary to cross the street to avoid the construction, but for the life of me, I couldn't understand what they were doing. Dismissing it as not-my-problem, I traveled towards some taxis.

A few paces from the taxi queue, a large man opened a car door and stepped in my path. Something hard jammed into my back, and knocked me towards the motorcar with the open door. Catching my hand on the roof, I looked at the interior, all the while keeping myself from being shoved inside. The man with the yellow scarf was settled in the back seat and I knew if I allowed myself to be taken, no one would ever see me again.

I spun around, surprising the man behind me as I grabbed his shoulder and belt and thrust him inside the motorcar. Slamming the door with all my might, I crushed his legs that hung out of the car. The larger man who'd opened the door lunged at me, so I ducked down and planted a blade in his belly.

A flurry of movement broke out around the other side of the car, but I didn't wait to see what was coming. Picking up my bag, I bolted down the street, as fast as my legs could carry me, knocking people from my path should they have the misfortune of getting in my way.

Someone was pressing closer. The person grabbed my coat, so I shrugged it off without breaking stride or losing my bag. Reaching the next crossing, I ran into the street, narrowly being missed by a speeding motorcar. My pursuer was not so lucky. The screech of tires followed by a dull thud of impact resounded behind me.

Rounding the corner, I looped the bag over my head and shoulder. Men headed towards me with determined looks. I skidded into an alley without losing much speed by latching onto a pole and swinging around it. Then sprinted to a ladder leaned against the wall next to a fire escape. I climbed to the base and pulled the ladder up just before the men reached the bottom.

I gasped for air and continued to climb higher and higher. Glancing down, I saw that they had dumped over a waste bin and made it to the bottom rung of the ladder. I increased my speed, the muscles in my legs burning.

Mounting the roof, I ran to the first opening just as the roof access door burst open. Somehow the man with the yellow scarf was among those who emerged. I screeched to a halt and barreled towards the closest adjacent building and headed for it.

The wind whipped my face as I reached top speed. When I came to the edge, I jumped. My stomach lurched from weightlessness as my body propelled through the air towards the other building.

Then the dread hit—I wasn't going to make it. My body slammed into the face of the other building.

My fingers clung to the edge as my feet tried find purchase. My cheekbone throbbed from the impact, and I could smell blood trickling down the side of my face.

Desperation tore at me with the realization that I had no strength left to hoist myself up. I hung there panting as I felt my fingers slowly slip from the side.

CHAPTER 22

UNHINGED

ROSEMOND

Sara's tone was harsh as she leaned over the kitchen table. "Eat this, or I will feed it to you."

Hopeless, I rested my head on my arm. My voice was muffled by my sleeve. "I'm not hungry. I'm a grown woman and can make my own decisions."

"For me?" Ethan murmured softly.

Sighing, I looked at him. *He's never asked me for anything and this is his choice?*

Sitting up and growling internally, I picked up the fork and ate half a bowl of the thick stew, resenting every bite. It tasted good enough, but made me half sick as I hadn't eaten in so long.

I pushed myself back from the table, "Permission to leave the table?" My voice was sour. I waited for Sara to object, but she didn't, so I stood up. Then the disappointed expression on Ethan's face shamed me.

Biting my lip, I hurried up the stairs. My room was at the end of the long hall. I threw myself on the bed knowing these were the actions of a child, but my spiral downward seemed beyond my ability to control.

Voices drifted upwards through a vent. "Sara, do you think there is a reply yet? He left here five days ago. Surely he should be back in England."

"Yes, but we will have to wait. It is one thing to be gone for a few hours of daylight, but I won't leave her unguarded at night. Tomorrow morning. I'll go at first light."

"What about sending me? George has sent me to pick up messages. I don't mind. I want to know too. He's my best friend."

Sara's response couldn't be heard, but soon there was the rustling of papers. "If something happens and we aren't here, go to this location. I will send word to you." There was a pause. "Memorize it. Never carry anything with an address if it can be helped."

Not a minute later, the motorcar out front fired up. I listened until the sound could be heard no more. Suddenly, I felt the queasy signs of a vision coming. With my hands clamped to the sides of my head, I held my breath as the scene unfolded.

IN LESS THAN A SECOND, I REALIZED IT WAS THE SAME AS MY dream last night, but from a different perspective. Watching George running up and up...entering an elevator to the roof... the lift operator saying, "fifth floor"...a set of stairs... bursting through the door...seeing George running towards me and swerve the other direction...screaming for him to halt... reaching the edge of the building just as his arms gave out...his body arching backwards against the fall...seeing the five-story drop. A sob bubbled up from deep within me tearing me from the vision. No one could survive that fall.

"Rosemond." I was startled by Sara's presence.

I sat up and wiped the tears from my face with the backs of my hands. Before she could say anything I cried, "He fell five stories, Sara! He couldn't have—"

"Did you *see* him hit the ground? Did you *see* him die?"

"No." I sniffled.

"Then there is hope. We will soon know if he made his flight."

"I didn't think Slayers were capable of optimism," cringing immediately as I realized how rude that sounded.

She chuckled, low and throaty.

Relief washed over me. "I apologize for not being myself."

"I understand, Rosemond." She paused as she turned to leave. "Losing Zach at your mother's home was not easy for me. We all suffer losses. I am going to walk the perimeter."

"Thank you," I whispered and wondered if she'd heard me.

I DREW A BATH AND SOAKED IN THE TUB WHILE WAITING FOR something to do. The house was still silent after I crept to my room in search of a pair of socks. Cool air seemed to be slinking through the floorboards, giving me a chill with my wet hair.

The house had no radio. Needing distraction, I went to my bag—the only book I still had in my possession was the

Renaissance poetry Ethan had given me. With tome in hand, I returned to the living room and curled my legs under me.

Sliding my fingers next to the bookmark separating the leaves, warmth rushed to my cheeks. "Hero and Leander" stared up at me. My memory of being embarrassed and leaving the room after reading it for the first time returned. There was a notation that Marlowe never finished the poem. I wondered how it ended. Maybe Ethan knew.

Lost in thought, I sat in a holding pattern, waiting for Ethan. My lids began to feel heavy. Leaning my head back, I listened for a car as five nearly sleepless nights tugged at me.

The front door closing returned me to consciousness. My eyes felt like paste as I forced them to open. Ethan was standing in the doorway watching me. He didn't say anything, but he didn't need to. The slump of his shoulders and down-turned lips were all I needed to see.

"It's all my fault." I whimpered.

He was already sitting at my side, hugging me to his chest. "All this means is that he didn't make his flight."

"Five stories, Ethan. My vision. That's how far he had to fall."

I listened to the steady beat of his heart and the rhythm of his breath. Then I was struck with my horrible selfishness.

"How are you?"

His heart seemed to speed for a moment. "A beautiful woman in my arms. How could I have a single complaint?"

When I finally sat up, he pulled his arm back and rubbed it. We had sat there so long that it had probably fallen asleep. He hadn't asked me to move. "I'm serious, Ethan."

"I refuse to worry until we have confirmation." He tapped the book. "Reading again?"

I shrugged, knowing he was trying to distract me. "Finished the last bit of *Hero and Leander*." The heat returned to my cheeks. "It says Marlowe never finished. Do you know how it ends?"

He smiled again, but this time there was a large dose of flirt in his expression. "After the seduction? Why Rosemond, I'm shocked."

"It is quite clear as to what happened in the bedroom. That is not what I'm asking, and you know it."

He hesitated for a long moment and seriousness edged his tone. "They were so in love that he swam the channel night after night to spend it in her bed. One night, there was a horrible storm coming. She asked him to come anyway, but the sea was too rough and he lost track of the shore and drowned. The next morning, his naked body washed up on the shore right in front of the tower in which she resided. When she saw his lifeless figure, she was so overwhelmed with guilt and heartbreak that she threw herself from the tower. She died by his side."

Shaking my head, I knew the look on my face was pained.

"What?"

"The irony, we both caused our beloveds' deaths. She asked hers to come and I forced mine to go."

"Rosemond, you didn't—"

Feigning cheerfulness, I squeezed his hand to stop him. "You are going home tomorrow. You will have none of this to worry about."

"I'm not going anywhere."

Kissing the back of his hand, I stood. "We will see." I immediately stalked out of the room in search of Sara. It was imperative to get Ethan out of harm's way.

MY FISTS WERE BALLED IN FRUSTRATION. STUPID, CHARMING Ethan had already spoken to Sara about staying longer, and my arguments were not swaying her in the slightest. I pointed and jabbed my finger at her. "If he gets hurt, it's on you."

She looked at me blankly and blinked. "If you are to remain in the shadows, it is best to keep those already involved... involved. I prefer to have an extra set of eyes." Then her demeanor changed, and she shrugged. "And, he's not hard on the eyes."

My mouth dropped open in utter shock. I had no other arguments. "On *you*," I snarled and stormed from the room. I clomped down the hall passing Ethan. He was looking a little smug. My glare pinned him. "I hate you."

Ethan sighed. "Rosemond—" he said, followed by something else, but I was already halfway up the stairs.

Feeling petulant once again, I collapsed onto my bed and squeezed an armful of blankets to my chest. The moon was visible through the lace curtains. The evening ticked by slowly as the sad orb traveled sluggishly across the midnight sky.

I HAD SLEPT TOO LONG. THE SUN WAS GLARING THROUGH the overly thin window coverings. My stiff body felt as if I hadn't stirred all night. Sitting up, it was apparent I hadn't. I was still on top of the covers. My braided hair was still damp, just like my mood.

With effort, I made the decision to go downstairs, despite my desire to avoid socializing. I knew that food would be shoved at me again if I didn't eat of my own free will. Tromping, unladylike, down the stairs, I arrived in the kitchen to find Ethan reading the newspaper. It had yesterday's date printed at the top. He peeked over the top of it.

"Still hate me?" he asked with raised brows and a twinkle in his eyes.

Rolling my eyes at him, I headed for the pot on the stove. It was still hot, so I poured myself a cup of black tea and splashed a bit of fresh milk into my cup. Someone had obviously gone to the grocers. I slid onto a seat across from him. For some reason, his pretty-boy looks started to make me angry again. Maybe it was Sara's comment that he wasn't hard on the eyes.

Taking a sip of tea, I placed my cup on a saucer and it clattered as the cup missed a little, and tea sloshed over the edge as the cup settled into the grooves on the bottom. My hands flew to cover my face, and I stood to leave. "I am not fit to be in public."

"Please stay."

I furrowed my brow, "I will be grumpy at you, and despite the fact I do not like you right now, my preference is to avoid that." I picked up my tea once more and gulped it down. It was much too hot to drink that quickly, so it made my eyes water, and a small squeal escaped my lips. Turning abruptly, I left the room with my robe billowing behind me.

Knives. I needed to throw copious amounts of knives. Taking two stairs at a time, my feet carried me into the bedroom. There had to be a non-dress around here somewhere. I rummaged through the dresser and found some men's clothing: a pair of denim overalls and a button-down shirt. They would be a little large, but would work well. On my way downstairs I grabbed my blades and headed to the rear yard. A large maple tree towered over the lawn about thirty paces from the house. It was the perfect spot from which I could begin my knife therapy, complete with a natural side table.

Quickly covering the distance, I laid out my blades save one on a stump. I threw the knife hard and drove it into the tree, almost to the hilt. A moment later, the smell of maple filtered through the air on the slight breeze. Picking up three more blades, I flung them in rapid succession. The knot in my gut started to ease a little.

Hours must have gone by throwing, retrieving, and then throwing again. But every time my lids closed, all I could see were George's fingers slipping from the ledge. My powerlessness was killing me—as well as my need to know.

After gathering up my instruments of death, I headed back towards the house. My fingers were sticky and nicked and scraped from the activity. Ethan was sitting on the back steps. "You make an adorable tomboy."

I scowled and sat next to him.

He tugged on my braid.

"You disappointed with me?" My tone was miserable.

He leaned back, bracing himself with one arm behind him, and smirked. "You are very attractive when you are angry."

I couldn't help but roll my eyes, "Ethan—"

"I am worried about him too. We simply express it in different ways." He chewed on the inside of his cheek.

We talked then, like I hadn't talked to anyone before. He looked at me kindly, allowing me to blather on about all of my frustrations and fears. But I wasn't the only one to speak. I could see how very deep his soul was. He was a flirt, it wasn't an act, but he was so much more. After I could think of no more words needing to be conveyed, I felt like I had the ability to breathe once again. When we finished, the sun was already slipping towards the horizon. We had skipped lunch and spoken all day.

I looked at him steadily with the first smile to warm my face since my sending George away. "Ethan, I haven't had too many friends. Always kept apart. I am proud to call you one. Even if you insist on putting yourself in danger by staying around."

He smiled and cleared his throat, as if choked a little by emotion. "Let's get inside and make some food."

I glanced out at the yard as Sara passed by on her perimeter sweep. I was thankful she'd given me space today.

"Ethan." Stopping in my tracks. "I'm a dreadful person. I should have thought to tell you. The man you hit in the alley, the one we have been calling 'Yellow Scarf.' He's alive. You haven't killed anyone."

He looked tremendously relieved and conflicted all at once. "He is chasing George."

Immediately, I understood the conflicted part of his expression. "Yes, he was on the roof."

He ushered me through the door. My hope had been to ease some of his woes, even if only a little. But maybe the fact that he was one of George's pursuers had nullified that. In my heart, I knew Ethan would have killed him to save George.

NIGHT HAD FALLEN. MY EYES FLEW OPEN WHEN THE SOUNDS of quick steps down the hall startled me awake. My last memory was of reading in bed. The oil lamp was burning low. I raced to the door and opened it. Sara stopped in the hall at the top of the stairs and spun around to address me. "Get back in your room."

"Is something wrong?"

She pursed her lips. "Not sure. Something is off. I'll run the perimeter. Ethan is armed downstairs, so stay in here so you aren't mistaken for something you're not."

Nodding quickly, I shut the door, allowing her to get to her security sweep. I dove to my bag and drew out my newly sharpened and cleaned knives, then retrieved the pistol from beneath my pillow. After that there was nothing to do but wait.

Every creak in the house seemed to be magnified. I turned down the lamp until it was almost out and positioned myself in the corner near the window, wishing the lock on the door worked. The dog on the farm an acre from here started barking. When concentrating, I could hear that there were slow, even footsteps circling in the downstairs that must have been Ethan. Not knowing where Sara was increased my anxiety. Minutes ticked by. I dried my palms on my nightgown and gripped the pistol again.

Something was happening on the back porch. Sara exclaimed, but then her voice fell low. The boards on the deck creaked, and it sounded as if water was being pumped. I strained to hear more. More than anything, I wanted to peer out the window, but my instincts warned me not to give away my location.

The draft through the window carried in the smell of smoke. I risked a look through the lace and could see some flames at the base of the steps to the right. I prayed that the fire was in the burn barrel.

There were more voices. My anxiety climbed. It had been at least fifteen minutes since I'd heard the dog next door go unhinged. I was combating both fear and anger.

The anticipation was almost worse than an attack. Someone was inside. Quick steps up the stairs echoed down the hall and one door after another opened. *They're searching for me.*

I straightened up and raised the revolver, pointing it at the door. Drawing air into my lungs, I relaxed my shoulders, and put my finger on the trigger.

The second my door handle turned, I held my breath to steady my shot. The door swung open and something between a cry and a sob escaped me as my thumb decocked the pistol, almost dropping it as I cast it aside to run forward.

"*George,*" I gasped, already clinging to him and covering his face with kisses. "I thought you were dead. I saw you fall." His hair was wet, his skin icy, and he was shivering. He had on ill-fitting clothes that felt slightly damp.

He leaned back far enough to look in my eyes. There was a hint of a smile. "Still alive."

"I love you. I should have said it a dozen times. I love you. Please never leave again."

He tucked a strand of hair behind my ear. "I'm not going anywhere." His voice was relieved and breathy and serious.

I pulled him towards the bed and made him sit; gathering a blanket around him and pressing myself close, trying to warm him. "What happened to you?"

He shook his head. "It doesn't matter." He cupped my face and kissed me, and I felt as if I could melt into his arms and disappear. He sucked in a deep breath and spun around onto his knees in front of me and searched my face.

"When clinging to the ledge, thinking that was it. That I would be dead in moments in some trash ridden alley...alone. I had only one thought in my head." He swallowed. "You."

"George, you're freezing." I pulled the blanket around him again and he shook his head.

"Rosemond," he whispered. "I don't care about being cold. I'm trying to say something." He seemed tongue-tied.

"What is it?" I asked, suddenly feeling nervous.

"Marry me. Be with me always."

Letting out a small sob and nodding, my lips urgently on his, as he pulled me against his chest, I knew this night would change everything.

And I wanted nothing else.

CHAPTER 23

UNSAID

GEORGE

I kissed her bare shoulder blade, and she murmured in her sleep. Cool, blue early morning light was already lighting the room through the inadequate window dressings. Not being able to help myself, I ran my fingers leisurely down her arm and kissed the back of her neck, breathing in her scent.

She stirred and slowly rolled over, holding the covers in place. She gazed at me through heavy lids, yet somehow still looked radiant.

"I need to get to another room before the others wake. What rooms are they in?"

"Ethan is straight across the hall. Sara has been staying downstairs." She paused. "But it's doubtful you will fool anyone."

I furrowed my brow, feeling ashamed. "I won't spend another night in your bed until I have made you my wife."

She smiled and pressed her fingertip between my brows.

"Agreed, but I am as much to blame." She batted her lashes. "It was my duty to beat away the boy with ill intentions."

I pulled her hand to my mouth and kissed her palm. She sighed softly and took her hand back as she tucked the covers firmly around her. I propped myself up on one elbow, and her expression changed when the sheets slid off my shoulder. She reached out and ran her hand next to the bruising that had formed a band that looped beneath my left arm and around the right side of my neck. I placed my hand over hers and held it to my heart. "You indirectly saved my life, yet again."

Her face clouded with confusion.

I smiled wistfully, remembering those last moments before falling. "The photo. I had cursed you for putting it into my bag, not wanting the reminder of you. Some of Gareth and Cadeyn's men found me, and I fled. Normally, I would have shed my bag...to be faster...but the picture was in there. Not wanting to lose it or have it fall into their hands, I looped the bag over my head and ran with everything I had. You said you saw me hanging from the building?"

She nodded.

"When I slipped from the edge, I remember arching backwards and twisting as I plummeted at least two stories. Then the strap of my bag caught on a metal post that was bent upwards with a clothesline connected to the adjacent building. If it had been a few inches to the side, the pole would have impaled me. But it didn't, it stopped my fall, until it gave way. I managed to hold onto the clothesline until smashing into the other building. Then I was only a few meters up and was able to safely drop to the ground." I ran my fingers over the bruise from the strap and looking at her, "You putting that picture in my bag saved my life."

Her lips parted, about to respond, but the sound of movement came from downstairs.

"Blast," I hissed and rolled out of bed, pulling on my trousers. Piling up the rest of my clothing under my arm, I smiled at my beautiful-bride-to-be, then closed the door as silently as possible.

I turned to head to one of the bedrooms just as Ethan opened his door. He took in my shirtless form and my unbuttoned slacks and looked at me blankly. After a few beats, he walked slowly to the stairs without a word. My shoulders sagged slightly as I debated what to do. I could normally read Ethan's face, but not this time. I swept into one of the empty rooms and finished dressing, then hurried downstairs while fastening the last few buttons on my shirt.

Ethan was leaning forward on the sink, with straight arms, looking out the window. I walked up behind him. "Eth—" He whirled around, leading with his fist. I hit the floor hard and clutched my face in shock.

Ethan's voice was barely under control. "*George Yates*, I have thought many things about you in the past, but *womanizing bastard* was not one of them."

My head snapped up. "Womanizer? I..." I felt as if the breath was knocked from me.

He stood over me, his face still flushed with anger. "You said you weren't sure if you were going to stay, and yet you bed her?"

I shook my head in disbelief, "I have never been with anyone else...never wanted to..." I swallowed hard. "I'm not going *anywhere*. I asked her to be my wife."

Ethan's expression softened, but his mouth remained in a grim line. After a moment, his colour returned to normal and he exhaled in a gust offering me his good arm and pulled me up. "Maybe you should have married her *first*."

I sighed and nodded. "Yes. You are correct, of course." Walking to the table, I sat down hard and rubbed my still aching jaw.

Ethan still looked a little angry as he sat across from me. "I'm sorry. I shouldn't have hit you."

"I deserved it." I looked over at him feeling the weight of my actions.

He grinned a little. "I'm not really that sorry." Then his face became more serious for a moment. "She isn't one of those reckless flapper girls. She is the one you stay with forever. Respect that in the future." He knocked his knuckle on the table twice.

I nodded. *I might as well have my father here.*

"I have said all I will say." Ethan stood again. "I'm going to make some breakfast. Why don't you do something with that." He waved a hand in my general direction. He clearly wanted me out so he could compose himself for a minute.

Chuckling, I ran my hand through my hair, realizing it was sticking up in all directions, and my clothes were an exemplary display of disheveled.

"Yes, of course." I headed out towards the wardrobe in search of new clothing, with my stomach growling in hunger.

ROSEMOND

I walked into the kitchen, and the moment Ethan turned and looked at me, it was obvious he knew. Last night, I hadn't thought of what it would feel like to have Ethan know. My heart started beating a erratically, and nerves hit the pit of my stomach. Glancing around, looking for George. I could've sworn I'd heard his voice down here.

"He is getting cleaned up. Breakfast is almost ready," Ethan said. His tone was not one of cheerfulness as it usually was. He wasn't humming or whistling either.

I nodded and stood there awkwardly.

He motioned to the stove. "The grits need to simmer for a few more minutes. I'm going out for a smoke." He smiled thinly and went out the back door. I watched as he lit up and he exhaled a slow and steady stream of smoke. He rubbed at the knuckles on his right hand as the cigarette hung from his lips.

I swallowed and walked out the back door and leaned on the railing next to him, hating unsaid words. "Are you horribly disappointed?"

He e met my gaze for a long moment. His blue eyes were illuminated by the morning sun and seemed as if they were glowing orbs. "I didn't say anything, Frank."

"Am I being too blunt once again? Was I supposed to make small talk first?"

He coughed a laugh and leaned towards me. "No, that would make you like other women and not nearly as attractive."

A sigh of relief eased from me.

He took a long drag and flicked his spent cigarette into the rocks at the base of the steps, then put his arm around my shoulders. He exhaled smoke through his nose and looked at me with an odd expression. He nodded as if he had made some sort of decision and smiled once again.

"Come on, Frank. Breakfast should be ready. Now that

George is back, safe and sound, maybe you will actually eat. I don't like my women all skin and bones."

Rolling my eyes at him, I allowed him to escort me back inside.

George was stirring the grits when we walked back into the kitchen. There was some anxiety in his face when he looked over, but it quickly dissolved. I wasn't sure what had happened between George and Ethan, but there was a painful-looking, red mark on George's cheekbone. We sat with our bowls and ate our bounty, the awkwardness quickly dissipating as normal conversation flowed. While eating, George reached over and laced his fingers through mine under the table. My heart beat unevenly for a moment.

Then I recalled the events leading to George's arrival last night. "I saw flames outside last night. May I ask what was happening down here?"

Ethan almost choked on his food as a huge grin spread across his face. "Yes, George, what happened?"

There wasn't any humor on George's face. "It seems I was rather fragrant. Sariel made me strip down outside and wash up. Ethan burned my clothes."

"There was no way of getting rid of that smell."

I raised my brows and looked at George; despite the humor, my heart sped a little.

His shoulders slumped. "I escaped through the sewers and lived in them for a couple of days. I would rather not dwell on the events of late."

"Trust me—no one wants to smell *that* again," Ethan chortled. "Though, your expression when you realized Sara was serious about bathing outside was priceless."

I tilted my head, "How did you find us?"

"I went to your last location. Sariel left a crumpled piece of paper in the trash bin with a symbol that only I would know. It led me here. My guess is that she expected me to return. After dumping the motorcar a few kilometers away, I came in on foot."

Ethan scrubbed his chin with his napkin, still chuckling.

George leaned back so he could see down the hall. "Where is Sariel?"

I shrugged my shoulders. "She has been disappearing everyday into the barn. Something to do with her plan."

George wore a serious look and retreated into his head for a few long moments. He chewed on the inside of his cheek, and then looked at both Ethan and me. Standing abruptly, he walked to the stove and dished up a bowl of the grits. He leaned against the counter as the steam rose from the food. "I'll take her breakfast and see if I can help." George pointed at Ethan's cast. "How much longer?"

Ethan ran his slender fingers over the plaster. "Another week."

"Has Sariel said anything about it?"

"The cast?" Ethan clarified. "Yes. She wants me unimpaired, I think she said, before we can initiate her plan."

George scowled.

"What is it?" I asked.

He gave me a tight smile. "Nothing. I'm going to go and lend a hand." George took a spoon off of the counter and plopped it into the bowl as he headed outside.

"Her plan is dangerous," Ethan said.

"Did she tell you about it?"

He shook his head. "No, but George knows something. He

chews on the inside of his cheek when he is working through something he finds distressing."

I thought back. I had seen him do it before when he was troubled. "Are *you* worried?"

He exhaled slowly and raised an eyebrow. "I never worry."

CHAPTER 24

SUSPICIONS

ROSEMOND

Feverish heat and flames encircled me. Just over the crackle I could make out George screeching my name. I squinted in the direction of his voice. Through smoky glass, I could see he was a short distance away. Then, someone took my hand. It was Ethan, looking impossibly calm, despite the heat of the flames. We were in a motorcar and in mortal danger. My hands latched onto the front of his shirt as he pinned my face between his hands. "You ready?" he asked, just as sparks landed on my sleeve.

I WOKE, YELPING AND SITTING UP, WHILE TEARING THE blankets away, seizing my left forearm. Then the understanding hit that it was only a dream—a prophetic one. Its intense heat still lingered on my skin.

My door swung open. George entered, looking breathless. "Rosemond?"

It could only mean that I'd screamed. I shook my head and rubbed at my arm, still feeling the phantom burns. "I'm fine— a nightmare." But there was hesitation in my voice.

The tension left his body as he approached, but his eyes still swept the room. He sat on the edge of the bed. "Would you like to tell me about it?"

I paused and bit my bottom lip and changed the subject. "You worked with Sara all day. Did you both decide on anything?"

He raised an eyebrow and gave me a shrewd look, letting me know that the change of subject had not gone unnoticed. "She has already set things in motion in New York. We will work our way back that direction. It will most likely be two weeks before we," he paused, "have our performance."

"Performance? Are you going to share said plan?"

A small grin lifted the corner of his mouth. He spoke so quietly that I needed to lean in closer to hear him. "How do you feel about short engagements?"

Now he was changing the subject, but I certainly didn't mind the topic. I wiggled close enough that I'm sure he could feel my breath through the shoulder of his nightshirt. "I am not opposed to the idea." My tone was cautious, though my smile grew.

He took a stuttering breath and turned into me, placing his fingers under my chin and guiding my mouth to his. I loved his magnificent lips; the soft touch of them sent shivers down my spine as I looped my arms around his neck and pulled him closer. He gasped as the kisses became more intense. He leaned away not two inches, the tips of our noses still touching. "Next week."

I wasn't tracking with him. My only desire was to kiss him. "Hmm?" I murmured against his mouth.

George whispered, "Marry me next week."

Half-startled, I asked, "Are you serious?"

"Entirely. I don't see any reason to wait."

"You just want back between the sheets," I teased.

His hands dropped into his lap, and he became deathly serious. He wouldn't look at me as he shook his head back and forth, as if denying something, then he stilled. "The other night should not have happened. I have been berating myself for not respecting you more. I thought myself better than that. Can you ever forgive me?" The depth of his sorrow was dripping from his very being.

I reached and took his chin this time and made him look at me. "I should have said no. I had thought you dead and lost myself." I sighed. "Just marry me and make me an honest woman."

He covered my hand that was on his cheek and held it there with his eyes closed. "My only desire is to be with you." He leaned over and slowly kissed my cheek. "Have you recovered from your nightmare?"

I nodded.

"You still don't want to speak about it, do you?"

I shook my head.

He smiled sympathetically. "Get some rest." He stood, keeping my hand in his. Then he bent and kissed my knuckles. "Pleasant dreams, Miss Le Clair."

"And to you, Mr. Yates."

He shut the door behind him, and the look on his face before he did so said he was mine forever.

GEORGE

The sunlit hours of the next five days were consumed in the barn with Sariel working on her plan. Each evening was spent with Rosemond and Ethan trying not to dwell on the impending danger. By the time I crawled into bed at night, I was beyond exhausted and spent the midnight hours wishing I had already wed her so I could hold her even in my sleep.

Sariel and I spent the final day making a small scale model of the Studebaker to test our work one last time. It was time to show Rosemond and Ethan. I strode into the house and collected them. As the three of us walked outside, Ethan was poking a slim stick inside his cast to itch his arm. He seemed more than ready to have the plaster prison removed.

We entered to a stern Sariel. She nodded at Ethan and Rosemond and motioned them to take a seat on some wooden crates. Ethan appeared relaxed as usual. Rosemond seemed anxious after she sat down; before I could do anything to comfort her, Ethan seemed to notice and bumped her with his shoulder.

The strained look melted from her face, and she smiled over at him. He leaned over and whispered something in her ear; her face remained blank for a moment, and then she rolled her eyes in an exaggerated fashion and turned to look at me. She gave me a knowing look as if I had understood the joke. Since it was Ethan, I probably did.

I wanted to whisk her away at this moment, to keep that

unguarded look of adoration on her face and not show her that our possible salvation could end horribly with our deaths.

Sariel fixed her gaze on Rosemond and no one else. Her tone was gravely serious. "Rosemond, the only way to truly keep you safe is to fake your death. Unfortunately, as you know, vampires are not easily fooled. They fake their own deaths and take new identities as a matter of form. They need to see you die and believe it."

Rosemond nodded for Sariel to continue. She was still, and I could detect not a hint of nervousness now. She was brave and beautiful, taking in every detail. She pointed to the model. "They will see me burn," she stated matter-of-factly.

There was a slight hitch in Sariel's voice; it seemed she wasn't entirely used to Rosemond's intuitive nature. "Yes. The last week was spent in New York scouting locations. I found one with a blind corner, and the roof visibility is perfect. There are no overt places from which to escape. The vamps we want as witnesses prefer roofs to streets." She paused. "I have also established a clear line of communication with the coven through an informer. It is a certainty that we can have them where we want them if you are present." Sariel lifted her chin slightly pining Rosemond with her expression.

Rosemond shuddered almost imperceptibly. "Cadeyn," she whispered, understanding immediately.

"There is no better proof than the word of a member of the royal guard who actually knows you. If he and Gareth witness—"

Rosemond dropped her head into her hands. "What about the blood bond?"

The set of Sariel's mouth became hard. "He drank from you?" She seemed barely able to reign in the incredulous tone.

"Yes." Rosemond didn't make excuses as she could have. She hadn't known what he was, and she had been drugged. She accepted the weight of Sariel's disapproval.

Sariel scowled out the door. "The only way to break that bond is to stop your heart." Her words stung as they hung in the air, punctuated by silence.

I finally spoke. "He may not say anything, even if he suspects you are alive."

Sariel objected, "He is a member of the guard. It is his duty."

"Rosemond, didn't you say he *didn't* want to turn you over to the queen?"

"No, he didn't."

Painful flashes of memory returned of Rosemond in the club and on the dance floor with Cadeyn. I had stood by powerlessly and watched him feed on her. But it was more than feeding, it was a seduction. My collar suddenly felt like a noose around my throat, I tugged at it and released the top button. "The way he protected her...looked at her. I think he would remain silent."

"That is a rather large gamble."

"And the alternative? Stopping her heart?" I paused, needing to regain my control. I took a steadying breath before speaking again, "In the confusion he *may* believe she has died if we put enough distance between them. We know that some bonds are limited by distance."

"We don't know if *their* bond is." Sariel paced back and forth for the better part of a minute, her mouth downturned in the corners as she rubbed her forehead concentrating on some aspect of the plan. Suddenly, Sariel stopped all movement and looked at Rosemond as if seeing her for the first time. The fact that she had had some sort of revelation was clear on her face. If I wasn't mistaken, there may have been awe. "You aren't like other people are you?" she asked. It was obviously a leading question.

Rosemond looked at her confused.

"You are Lux Casta. The vamps determination has been nagging me. That is why they have sent their people to the slaughter without any concern."

Rosemond froze for a brief moment, then in a small voice answered, sounding almost grieved, "Yes, I'm the last of the line, though I didn't know until recently." She glanced at me.

Sariel laughed, but it was an ironic one.

Ethan looked at myself and then at Rosemond. "So, Frank, you didn't tell me everything."

"Almost," Rosemond muttered.

Sariel's gaze fell on me. "The risk is far too great. You should have told me."

"I wasn't at liberty and nothing has changed."

She exhaled harshly with nostrils flared. "As previously stated, I scouted locations in New York. I found a three-way intersection where we can crash the motorcar. There is a street grate that leads to the sewers beneath it."

Sariel picked up a stick and pointed to different parts of the model while she talked through each step. "1: You will have to hit a streetlamp hard enough to damage the car without damaging yourselves too badly. 2: Light a fire inside, and wait until the material we have coated the inside of the motorcar with blazes up. 3: Pull open the hatch we have installed in the floor. 4: Escape into the sewers and follow the map to my extraction team."

"How will they not see us beneath the motorcar?" Rosemond inquired astutely.

Walking to the car, I opened the driver's side door. "When we impact, one of us will pull this." I yanked on the lever. Three wooden plates flopped to the ground on both sides and in the rear, effectively blocking the view of our planned escape into the sewers. "They are made of wood, so they will burn away. We have coated them in flammable material, so even if they have police on their payroll, the evidence will burn away."

"And there will be bodies, of course," Ethan mused.

Sariel answered. "Yes. We have bodies lined up from the medical school. The interior of the vehicle has been coated with a chemical that will obscure all vision through the windows. But..." she paused. "You have to actually crash the motorcar. And it will be on fire.

"There is terrible risk in this plan. There are countless variables, in addition to the fact that we will have vampires closing in on us. If the impact jams the escape hatch, you could be trapped. Or if the smoke becomes too great in the interior, you could die of smoke inhalation before it is safe to slide into the sewers. If I had known what I was risking...a living member of the Lux Casta. Your value...I wou—"

"Nothing has changed," Rosemond interrupted. "This risk is what will make it believable. They have to be convinced." Her voice was even.

Sariel nodded and looked at Ethan. "How is your acting ability?"

"Phenomenal," he replied coolly.

"Then you will stay with me a half block from the accident."

Ethan nodded, but I objected. "The only time they have

seen Ethan was in that alley the night we were ambushed. Shouldn't he stay out of this? Just disappear?"

"They know he exists; we will figure something out for him in the future. Having a genuine reaction on the outside will be most beneficial. And it would be much too dangerous with three of you on the interior of the car. Not with the corpses taking up space." She held up her hand to stop any protests and walked to the model. "I wanted you to see how everything will burn with the chemical on it. With George's help, the mixture is perfect." She walked to the small wood burning stove and stuck a long twig into the coals until it was ablaze.

Without any fanfare, she strode to the model and lit it up. I watched Rosemond; her face never betrayed a single fear, but when sparks popped in the rear of the model, Ethan glanced worriedly at her. She had grabbed his hand and was squeezing it tightly. Had I not seen her gripping his fingers, she would have appeared to be completely indifferent.

After the demonstration, Sariel gave more instructions. I continued to try to read Rosemond's face, but despite my best efforts, I failed. There were only those few seconds she squeezed Ethan's hand that gave away any apprehension. But I feared it was more than mere apprehension and wondered if she had seen something in a vision.

My musings were interrupted by Sariel's voice. "George, can you stay for a moment?" I looked and realized Ethan and Rosemond were headed back to the house.

I returned my gaze to Sariel. "Of course."

ROSEMOND

Once inside the house, Ethan spun around to face me. After looking over my head and out the back window, he spoke. "Are you sure you want to do this?"

"There isn't really a choice. The only way to be safe is for them to see me die. I see no flaw in Sara's plan."

"Except for the part where you could be killed."

"I won't be."

He placed his hands on my upper arms and peered at me. His voice was gentle, but his words struck me. "You are afraid of fire."

I tried to pull away, but he didn't let go. "I'm not afraid of anything, except losing the people I care about." My mind went wild trying to figure out how he would have gleaned the information about my fear of fire.

"I would have thought that true if..."

An epiphany struck me. "My nightmares."

"Do you *have* simple nightmares? Or do you know something?"

Looking up at him, whatever expression I wore made him release me. I did know something—that he would end up in the motorcar with me and not George, but I had no comprehension of how that would be possible. Maybe it was incorrect —a remnant of a future that would have happened if George had not come back. "How did you know about my fear of dying by fire?"

"While George was gone, you screamed out in your sleep a few of the nights. I checked on you, but you were never fully awake. You asked me not to let you burn. You begged me. Then you would slip back into the oblivion of your dreams."

I tried to keep my voice as steady as possible. "I do have simple nightmares. I was heartbroken while George was gone. There is no reason to read anything into it."

His eyes tightened, only a hint of blue, peeping at me. "If you know something is going to go wrong—don't do this."

"I know nothing of the sort. I just know that I was frightened." That was true.

Suspicion held him and he opened his mouth to speak just as George entered. Ethan glanced at George and then back at me. He didn't say anything, but he pointed at me accusingly before he swept from the room.

George reached me and placed his hand on my elbow. "Did I interrupt something?"

"Nothing. He's just worried about the plan."

George lifted his hand and gently ran his fingertips across my cheek. "If anything happens to you, I won't survive it."

"It would feel like that, but you would go on living. You would move on. And you would find a way to be happy—truly happy. I wouldn't want it any other way." I wasn't exactly sure why I said it.

He gave me the same suspicious look Ethan had given me moments before. "There are some things from which you can never recover."

CHAPTER 25

THE FOX

GEORGE

I scowled, frustrated that I couldn't do this myself. We were in a rural area, no more than an hour from New York, and Sariel didn't want me making any unnecessary public appearances after the last time that I was in the city. Ethan, now sans cast, was doing all the runs for food and sending all of the communications. Though I had equal authority, Sariel was correct to keep me indoors. Tomorrow there would be a visit to a church and then our staged accident the following night.

The jingle of keys drew my attention. Ethan was standing near the front door with a list in hand and keys swinging on his long fingers as he hummed our old school's theme song.

"Ethan, would you mind making an extra stop for me?"

Ethan's easy smile widened. "Anything."

I closed the space between us and spoke softly. "I don't have a ring...for tomorrow."

He narrowed his eyes at me. "You mean I have less than a day to pilfer her from you? Probably need to up my game."

"Ha," I couldn't help but chuckle. "I thought you preferred them doe-eyed and swoony."

Ethan's grin became much more devilish. "I thought we'd established this. *Sassy.* I like my women sassy. And the answer to your question is: yes. I will find something for her."

"Thank you, my friend." I patted him on the shoulder

"What are best men for?"

"Oh, did I ask you to be my best man?"

"No, and frankly I cried myself to sleep over it last night. It was very thoughtless of you." He swung the front door open.

"Hmmm...I'll have to ask you at some point. Will you want a ring, too?"

He smiled again as he tossed the keys into the air and snatched them back into his palm. "I'll see you in a couple of hours. Try not to miss me too much." Then he loped down the front steps and slid into the driver's seat of the Model A.

I closed the door as he fired up the engine. The sound of it grew faint as I walked to the atrium in the rear of the house. Rosemond was sitting with her legs curled beneath her and a book propped in her lap. At second glance, I realized it was the same book of poetry Ethan had given her, but she wasn't reading. Her worried gaze was fixed on some point out the window. She hadn't noticed my entrance.

"Are you getting cold feet?"

Her head snapped in my direction, but the troubled look lingered for a moment before it melted away. My heart hammered in my chest, wondering if she really was having second thoughts.

She smiled. "Marrying you is one of the few things of which

I am certain. The plan failing and burning to death in the motorcar isn't." I released the breath I was holding.

I sat next to her, placing my arm around her shoulders and pulling her towards me. She nestled her forehead against my neck.

"Ethan said you had nightmares about burning while I was gone."

"Ethan has a big mouth," she replied flatly.

"You aren't denying it."

"There are many moving parts in this plan. Wouldn't any rational human being fear that something could go wrong? Burning to death is not my first choice."

"I suppose I can't argue with that logic, but you didn't know about the car at that point, unless you've already seen it."

"Just nightmares," she breathed, almost inaudibly.

She slid her hands around my torso, hugging me. In doing so I could feel her heart sprinting.

"Is that all you are worried about?" I started running my fingers through her hair near her temple.

She murmured against my neck, but didn't answer.

"Rosemond?"

"I'm sorry." She paused. "Nothing that can't wait."

I wanted to push, but the slight hitch in her voice indicated she wasn't ready to share. I couldn't help myself. "It isn't about marrying me, is it?"

She drew back, keeping her hand on my chest and locking her gaze on me. Her voice was brimming with emotion, "I have *no* doubts, George Yates. I plan to be your wife." Her brow furrowed. "Are *you* having doubts?"

Leaning in, I brushed her lips lightly with mine, and

watched her lids flutter closed. "No doubts," I whispered. "No doubts at all."

ROSEMOND

I woke, still nestled against George on the high-backed wicker love seat. He'd fallen asleep too; his breathing was still slow and even. His white dress shirt was wrinkled where I'd been leaning against him and had gathered it in my hand. A hint of a smile played on his lips, they were—happy and unguarded. I wondered, once this was over, how often I would see this peaceful expression.

After a moment, I realized why I'd woken: the house phone had rung. I rubbed at my eyes and glanced out the back window, trying to discern the time. The sun was still high in the sky; it was early afternoon.

Sara was speaking in a hushed tone. At first she spoke to an operator, then she said, "Are you sure? Both the post office *and* Western Union?" There was a long pause. "Yes. Yes. That would be wise. No, go South." A longer pause. "See you in a few hours. Be careful."

The identity of the person who called was nagging me, as well as, the fact that Ethan hadn't seemed to have returned from his run into town. Disentangling myself from George was the last thing I desired, but something was wrong, I knew it in my gut. After getting up, I drew a blanket from the adjacent chair and lightly placed it over George. He stirred, his hand moving absently to where I'd been nestled, then he slipped deeper into sleep. He'd hardly allowed himself to rest at all over the last five days.

I tiptoed out of the room in search of Sara and found her

standing at the table packing some items into a knapsack. When her eyes met mine my heart skipped a beat.

"What's happened? Is Ethan all right?"

She kept her eyes on the bag. "Ethan is fine. I need to go to town and send some cables."

"Didn't Ethan just do that for you?"

She pursed her lips. "Different messages." She finally answered after a very pregnant pause. "I want you and George armed."

"You want me to wake him?"

"No." She replied grimly. "He will probably need the sleep." She slung the bag over her shoulder and headed towards the front door.

"Please, tell me something."

"There may be...a complication. Let's not worry. Yet."

"You realize that makes me worry even more."

Sara gave me a pained look and headed out the front door. I stood there with my imagination racing wildly ahead, clenching the back of one of the kitchen chairs.

I DIDN'T MENTION TO GEORGE THAT SOMETHING WAS wrong when he woke. I had no hint as to whether it was about New York, our wedding, false identities, or Cadeyn's coven. It could've been any of those or none of them or all of them. Not knowing was driving me mad. I grit my teeth and stared out the front window through the sheers as I listened to George happily humming in the back of the house. The tune sounded as if it was the same one Ethan had been humming earlier.

Ethan rumbled up in the Model A, and Sara pulled in

behind him in the other motorcar. Ethan climbed out of the driver's seat and hauled a couple of bags out from the back, placing them on the running boards.

When Sara walked up to him with a stack of papers draped over her arm, he stopped and leaned against the door of the vehicle. He wrapped his arm around his torso like he was in pain, and his coloring said the same thing. I felt as if I'd been punched, the worry hit me so hard. Sara was speaking fervently to him, but I was already out the door and bounding my way down the steps towards them.

"Ethan, are you all right?"

He looked up at me half-alarmed then turned away. I could have sworn he cursed under his breath, but he didn't answer me.

"Ethan, are you hurt?" I asked again just feet away. When he still didn't answer, I touched his arm, and he shrugged away from me. It stung my feelings and I snatched my hand back. He glanced back, realizing what he'd done. His face fell.

"Rosemond, I'm sorry. *I* am fine." He compressed his lips and grimaced, looking to Sara.

She placed her hand on my shoulder and started ushering me towards the house. "We need to have a meeting."

I followed along woodenly and glanced over my shoulder at Ethan. He'd collected the bags and was following us inside. Ethan looked as though he had opened Pandora's Box and was about to watch its contents devour the world.

We filed in, walking to the back of the house. When George saw the expressions on Sara and Ethan's faces he dropped the knife on the counter and fell silent. The clank of the steel blade on the tile seemed to reverberate in the room.

"What's happened?" he asked searching Ethan's face.

"I think you should sit down, George." Sara said with more compassion than I'd ever heard in her voice.

"Tell me," he replied without moving.

Ethan plopped a stack of newspapers and miscellaneous documents onto the kitchen table, drawing our attention. "When I went to Western Union, I found this." He pulled a folded sheet of paper from the top of the stack and handed it to George. I quickly sidled up next to him.

George slowly unfolded the paper. The letters in bold print across the top read: "WANTED." My eyes slid to a candid photograph of George. It wasn't a mug shot like those on most Wanted Posters. My heart sank as the byline above the picture glared at me: "The Fox, wanted for Crimes Internationally."

I continued to read every detail: "The reward offered in this case will be paid to the person or persons who cause the arrest or detention and turn the Prisoner over to an authorized Officer." My eyes skipped to beneath the likeness of George. "No. 18276 fled the scene in the Financial District in Upper Manhattan on Dec. 11, 1928. Wanted in conjunction with international crimes including: breaking and entering, burglary, kidnapping, and murder.

"Description: Nationality British, Age 22-24, Height 5'10", Weight 165-175, Build Athletic-Boxer, Complexion Fair, Hair Dark Brown and Thick Wavy, Eyes Large Hazel/Mixed, Mouth Med, Lips Full, Chin Dimple, Cheek Defined. Marks and Scars. Scar through Left Brow and on Lower Lip, Body scarring from Bullet Wound, Various marks from Knife Wounds.

"Relatives: Possible relations in British Isles. Traveling with a dark-haired female companion. Probable the female is under duress, as she was taken from the scene of an earlier robbery.

Safety of the woman is of utmost importance, additional reward for her safe return. Call special task force if spotted."

George swayed on his feet, so I quickly grabbed his arm and led him to a seat at the table. I stood behind him, placing my hands on his shoulders, not wanting to stop touching him, needing the comfort. Ethan sat across from us, and no one spoke for a long while.

After several minutes, George stated, "I assume there was more than one poster."

Ethan nodded and patted the large stack of papers. "I pulled the flyer from Western Union when they weren't looking. Then, I checked the Post Office and Police Station...even in the local diner. I wondered if there was a write up in the paper, so I picked one up at the local newsstand. It referenced a previous article, so my next move was to procure the older issues they still had in stock. I telephoned Sara wondering if I should go farther into New York and see if the Wanted posters were in town. They were. When confirmed, I raced back here."

George dropped his head in his hands and took a few deep breaths. Nothing I could do would ease his pain—or mine. He stood and stepped away from the table. My hands dropped to my sides seeing the defeated slope of his shoulders.

He finally faced all of us before exiting. "They will have covered all their bases. There will not be a place in this world where I can hide. And you will never be safe in my vicinity." His voice faltered, and he rasped. "At the very least, I'm ruined." He turned toward the hallway. I made two quick steps after him, but he held up his hand to stop me. "Please," was all he said, and his expression broke my heart.

Swallowing hard, I let him go. I stood there for a moment,

not sure what to do. When I glanced at both Ethan and Sara, the looks of pity on their faces were unbearable, so I fled from the room.

When I had lost George the first time, I had felt as though I might die.

That was nothing compared to this, and...

I knew what was in his expression.

It was only one word: Goodbye.

CHAPTER 26

NOT OVER

ROSEMOND

A knock rattled the door. My hopes rose for a brief moment, but I recognized that the knock wasn't George. Then I felt horrible for being disappointed it was Ethan. After a second knock, I realized I hadn't told him to come in.

"It's unlocked," I finally murmured, crossing my robe tightly across my chest.

He opened the door slowly, his face carefully composed. "I thought you would be up."

I patted the bed beside me. "Come and wallow in my misery." He sat close enough that the bed leaned in his direction. I didn't fight it and instantly rested my head on his shoulder. He twisted and wrapped his long arm around me. In all the hours since seeing the news, I hadn't cried, but now, with Ethan next to me, I felt as if it was possible to let go. Like I didn't have to be strong every moment of every day. I sucked in a stuttering breath, and he pulled me tighter.

"Can I do anything for you?"

My nose dripped and I started to wipe at it with the back of my hand but Ethan had already pulled out a handkerchief.

"Thank you," I mumbled. I sighed, then whispered, "He won't marry me now."

"He would move all the planets and all the worlds to marry you," he reassured with a squeeze.

"One would have to displace the entire universe for him to wed me now."

"He wants to—"

"But he won't. You wouldn't would you? If you were George?"

"I...I don't know what I would do, honestly."

"Being near me has ruined George's life and probably yours. You shouldn't be comforting me right now." A sob welled up in my throat. I wasn't feeling sorry for myself. It was simply hard to understand so much kindness. I tried to pull away, but he held me tighter. "Ethan, as I told you before, you should run from me. I don't understand why you are still here."

"I am here because you need me and because you are my friend and because I love you."

And with that I was no longer able to hold back the flood of tears.

GEORGE

"How is she?" I asked, when the floorboard on the deck creaked behind me.

"How do you know I spoke with her?" Ethan replied smoothly.

I glanced back at him, and then turned my gaze towards the yard hidden in dark shadows. "Do you have a cigarette?"

Ethan eased down on the step next to me and pulled out the cigarette case from his front pocket, then patted his trousers for a light. As he regarded me curiously, he flipped open the case and offered one to me. I tapped the tip on the ground, packing the tobacco as I had seen him do a hundred times, then leaned towards the light he was offering. I took a long slow drag and sputtered a cough.

He chuckled as he lit his and blew smoke out his nostrils while he examined me.

"The world *must* be ending if you're smoking."

"*My* world has."

"So you will go on the run—you were planning to anyway. Settle on a little island and have hoards of children that will keep you up all hours of the night," he replied with a shrug.

I shook my head. "You didn't answer me. How is she?"

"Maybe you should speak with her. I never said that I did."

"One: You smelled of her perfume when you stepped outside the door. Two: You always attend to the beautiful lady first." I paused, and my heart sank when I observed a final detail. "And three: Your shoulder is damp."

Ethan absently placed his hand over his tear-stained shoulder. "How do you think she is? She is worried sick about you. She believes you are going to leave her, and she is blaming herself for everything."

"I can't speak with her until I have decided on a course of action. Seeing her, I...I can't make a logical decision."

"It seems as if you have already made one then."

I bit at the inside of my cheek and took in an uneven breath. "It isn't the decision I want to make." My voice involuntarily broke on the word want. "Did you read the papers you gathered? It says I *killed* a French dignitary while robbing the French Embassy. *And* it says I slit the throat of a bank manager when emptying a safe deposit box. He was the nephew of the *Police Chief*. I was at that bank, and that man helped me! Then there is the string of robberies all over Europe over the last five years. It is the *perfect* frame job. Every European government and the Americans all want my head on a pike. Did you see the insignia on the bottom of the Wanted poster?"

"Yes."

"Interpol—The International Police. They have been around for less than a decade but have gained significant power. The vampires that want Rosemond, they have their fingers in everything. I suspect that The Fox is one of their own. The crimes were too perfect. Too elegant...before the murder spree. The thief is a legendary cat-burglar that had never harmed a soul before this month and had stolen some of the most precious artifacts out from under the noses of their owners."

"The real Fox is a *vampire?*"

"It would make sense and this would be a convenient way to write off all of the crimes."

"It is daunting, but couldn't you hide somewhere?"

"The best way for me to protect her. To show her how much I love her, is to let her go. Even if my name is cleared, I will be famous. Someone could always recognize me. Our enemies will never stop watching me in the case that I slip and see her."

"There has to be some place on this planet..."

I waved at him to stop, already having gone in circles with myself, trying to strike some deal with God to make it all go away. "Sariel arranged for me to have a phone call with my father tomorrow. I will rely on his wisdom on this." I stabbed out the cigarette on the step. "Those things are vile."

Ethan chuckled. "I suppose so." He expertly flicked his onto the damp ground. "Are you still going to stage the accident the day after tomorrow?"

"We need to, for her sake, but I doubt I will be with her."

"You want her to do it *alone*? With all her nightmares about fire?" Ethan's voice rising in concern.

"I want to see what my father says before I make any decisions."

He nodded, but his brow was furrowed and his hands were tightly clenching his knees. "You should speak with her before you go to bed."

I looked up at the night sky and the moon peeking out between spotty clouds perforating the darkness with silver light. "Tomorrow, my brother, things will be more clear. Tomorrow." My deepest desire was to gather her in my arms and tell her everything was going to be all right. But I couldn't lie to her; therefore, I couldn't see her tonight. Swallowing despite the lump in my throat, I prayed for divine intervention.

ETHAN

Staying in bed was useless. I flung the covers off the bed and puttered into the kitchen in a sleep fog after a horrible night's rest. Rosemond's nightmares must've been contagious. The house was still fairly dark as the sun had barely crested the horizon. I was startled to see George sitting in the dark kitchen. He sipped at some coffee that must've been cold and from yesterday. I cringed at the thought. He looked almost as bad as he did the night he returned from living in the sewers. The difference was, this time, there was no hope in his expression.

George smirked up at me over his cup, elbows on the table. "You look dreadful."

Running my hand through my mop of hair, I scrubbed at my face. "I make this look good." I punched his shoulder as I walked by to perk fresh coffee. After placing the pot on the stove, I turned and plucked the cup from George's hands from which he was drinking.

"Hey!" he protested.

"You are forbidden to drink anymore of that."

"It wasn't...that unpleasant," he reasoned, squinting up at me.

I stared him down for a moment.

He wilted. "It was appalling."

"A fresh elixir will be ready in a few minutes."

A hush closed in on us as we listened to the coffee percolate. There were so many things I wanted to say to him, but there was no comfort that I could extend. I was afraid the only thing I could do to help was provide food and drink. Luckily, I'd always enjoyed the creativity of cooking.

Rummaging through the meager supplies, I placed an iron skillet on the other burner and globbed in the remainder of the fresh butter. I cubed the remnants of potatoes and ham from dinner and tossed them into the piping hot pan. Once the contents were browned I cracked the few eggs we had left, and stirred them into my savory hash. I wished there were more spices, or perhaps some toast, but it was a veritable feast considering the scant inventory from which I had to work. After spooning some onto a plate, I slid it in front of George.

"Thank you, but I don't care to eat right now."

"Don't be difficult, George. Eat. You are going to have a long day, and this will help."

He didn't reply, but he picked up the fork and started poking at the food.

I sat with my plate and consumed my portion while watching George and listening for one of the ladies. George kept glancing at the hallway. I cleared my throat and spoke in a quiet tone. "I doubt she will come for breakfast."

He pursed his lips and nodded silently, keeping his eyes locked on his eggs. "If I have to leave her. It may kill me."

"The pain won't last forever," was all I could offer.

"This from the romantic."

I put my fork down and fixed my gaze on his. "I am a romantic, but my feet are firmly planted on the earth. I don't believe that there is one soul mate out there, and that if you miss meeting her you will never be happy. If you can't be with her you will...someday...find someone else. It won't be easy, but you will. There *is* another match out there."

"I never believed in a soul mate until I met her."

"I'm not denying that she's one in a million. I'm simply saying that losing her does not mean your life is over."

George was pale and the circles under his eyes were pronounced as he tried to buy into my words. Though this was my honest belief, I couldn't imagine finding someone else who could compare to Rosemond.

He sighed. "Maybe you could bring her some food. I wouldn't want her to starve in order to avoid me."

"I don't think that it's all avoidance. But, yes, I will take her some food." I stood and my chair made a horrendous sound on the wood floor. Patting George's shoulder, I moved to the stove to fix Rosemond a plate. As I turned and headed for the hall George stopped me.

"Ethan, tell her..." he paused and looked lost. "Tell her..."

I smiled sympathetically. "I will."

When I reached the end of the hall, Sara was opening her door. She looked at me brightly. "Can you do something for me?"

I smirked suggestively. "For you, anything."

She laughed. "Accompany George to make the phone call. I think loverboy may need an extra set of eyes."

"Of course, and here I thought you were going to ask me out on a date."

She grabbed my face and squeezed my cheeks firmly. "You are lucky your face is too pretty to mark up. I have killed men for less."

Once she dropped her hand, I leaned in and whispered, "I can't help it. You warrior women are so damned attractive." I winked and added, "There is food for you on the stove."

She turned and headed down the hall. With her back to me, she teased, "You would make a good wife, Ethan."

I watched her as she rounded the corner. The truth was that she was attractive, but she also scared the hell out of me. I had no doubt that she could kill me with the flick of a finger.

When I reached Rosemond's door, I took a steadying breath, careful to control my personal emotional state before I knocked. Her voice was a croak when she granted access.

Rosemond was still in her nightclothes sitting propped up against the headboard. She may have slept in that position, if she'd slept. She had twisted a piece of lavender fabric into a figure eight, yet she was still turning it nervously in her hands.

I pointed to the fabric. "Did it offend you in some way?"

Her brow furrowed as she looked down at it and then her cheeks flushed with color. She released her grip and placed her hands over the lavender cloth as if to hide it.

"I brought some food. Figured you wouldn't risk running into Georgie."

Her breath hitched and a tear streaked down her cheek. She wiped it away instantly and gave me a strained smile. "Thank you."

Sitting on the bed, I handed her the plate. Once both her hands were occupied, I snatched the lavender fabric, which turned out to be silk and lace.

"Ethan, please don't," she cringed.

I grinned crookedly at her. Then I realized why she was embarrassed. I was holding her lingerie. Instantly, I tossed it back onto her lap and she quickly set her plate on top of it. My grin didn't fade.

"Fancy."

"I am despicable," she murmured in a self-loathing tone.

"Never believe it."

Her mouth tugged down in the corners as she took a small bite of hash; it looked as if it was an effort for her to chew. The fork clanked onto her plate. "I don't know why I am admitting this..." She bit her lip and kept her eyes focused on the food. "In the middle of the night, I had a moment of weakness and considered going to George's room...to *convince* him to stay."

"Oh," slipped through my lips before I was able to stop myself. Her hands flew to her face, covering everything but her exquisite little nose. Quickly recovering, I uttered her name suggestively, "Rosemond."

She peeked between her fingers.

Wagging my brows at her, "Well, if you would like to model for me, I'd be happy to let you know if it would've worked." I leaned back on my elbows as if waiting for her to take me up on the offer.

She let out a sort of laugh-cry and smudged away another tear. "Why is it that I admit everything to you? It is rather mortifying."

I rolled my lips inward before speaking. "Seduction was a natural thing to consider," I admitted.

"I suppose," she whispered.

"And you wouldn't be Frank without telling me everything," I paused. "I need to go. I'm escorting Georgie to make a call to his father. I'm sure there will be some resolution after we hear what he has to say." I pointed to the food. "Please finish that. Keep up your strength."

She may have said something as I shut the door, but I hurried down the hall. I had a dull pain in my chest gnawing away at me. I could feel all of this coming to an end, and I wasn't sure how I could go back to my life as it was before. It was funny how people could become such a part of you in a brief amount of time.

I rounded the corner into the kitchen and out of sheer reflex caught the motorcar keys Sara tossed at me. "You drive him, pretty boy. Romeo will navigate. See you in an hour or so."

George shot Sara a disparaging look and nodded at me. The ride to the small business was gripped in silence. George walked in ahead of me and was guided immediately back to a glass phone booth with lavish wood paneling and a padded bench seat inside. He nodded at me, his shoulders heavy, and closed the door.

The tightness in my chest returned—there was nothing I could do for him. I sat on one of the stools, far enough to give him space, yet where I could watch his reactions as he spoke to his father.

The call was long, and truthfully, George did very little speaking. After hanging up, he sat in the booth like he was made of granite or marble or something immovable. I let him sit for a quarter hour and digest whatever his father had said before interrupting his reverie.

I knocked, he didn't move.

So I opened the door, but he still didn't budge. Sighing, I slid my hand beneath his arm and urged him to his feet. He complied without resistance. I led him to the motorcar and drove in a serpentine route home making sure we weren't followed.

He never spoke a word; he didn't need to.

Grief stuck to him like paint to a canvas.

As he had said before, he was ruined—this was the calm before the storm.

CHAPTER 27

LAST

ROSEMOND

I sprinted to the front window when I heard the sound of an approaching vehicle, my heels clicking loudly on the hardwood. Anxiously, I peeped through the heavy velvet curtains. The boys came to a halt in the drive and sat there. Ethan was speaking, but George didn't move.

After a short while, Ethan dragged himself out of the motorcar and made his way towards the house. He massaged the back of his neck as he walked through the door. I stood in the entryway, a statue, ready to read the expression on his face. He startled slightly when he saw me, but said nothing.

"How did it go?" I asked.

He shook his head. "Honestly, I don't know. He hasn't said a word."

"Then I *have* lost him."

Ethan instantly stepped forward, opening his arms wide. I flew to him so quickly that I crashed into his chest, wrapped my arms tightly around him, and rested my head over his heart. The even beat of it was calming. He slowly rubbed my back until I released him several minutes later.

He met my gaze for a long moment, then his expression clouded. He abruptly cleared his throat, stepping back. His body language becoming awkward. "I should check in with Sara."

"Of course." I moved out of the way and allowed him to pass down the narrow hall.

Returning to the window, I watched George. He was as lonely as the moon. I supposed he was much like the moon and all its faces. There was something mysterious about his solitary nature as evidenced in our first weeks together. And of course Ethan's stories of the past only solidified that impression, although, I had to admit, he never really hid anything from me. There was an indefinable intensity that drew me to him. I loved the way he loved me, wholly and completely, like he could hold me on this planet with his gravitational pull. Just as the moon had the power to change the tides, he had power over me.

I glanced down the hallway hearing the muted voices of Sara and Ethan. Being alone hadn't seemed a bad thing before. Now, I felt as if my universe would be plunged into darkness because of it. And I wouldn't even have the moon to light my way.

GEORGE

I was sure my insides had been shredded, not literally, of course, but they might as well have been. I had known exactly what my father would say. He already had a team of assistants gathering papers to prove my whereabouts during each of the robberies that The Fox had committed. He, too, thought the thief was a vampire, most likely from the French coven. They said the thief probably had an association with Gareth and Cadeyn.

He didn't think the battle would be easy, but he was determined to take it to the courts, but more than this, he told me I had to leave Rosemond for her protection. There would be no such thing as anonymous for me. They'd found Wanted posters as far as Northern Africa in just three days' time. Not even the Congo was safe.

I felt guiltier with each passing moment that I didn't speak with Rosemond. But the thought of saying the actual words and breaking my promise of marriage to her felt like the most savage betrayal. Especially after our night together. I glanced at the house and noticed a tiny shift of the curtains. Squeezing my eyes shut, I sucked in a breath. It was time to talk.

FROM THE LOOK ON MY FACE WHEN I CLOSED THE PARLOR door, she knew. Without my saying one word, she knew.

Still, I told her everything. She engaged me clear-eyed. When my voice broke, she held my hand. She didn't blame or get cross with me, she simply listened.

It reminded me of the night that we had heard confirmation of her mother's death. The way she bore it amazed me, it was as if she were made of steel, yet at the same time, her pale eyes were fraught with innocence and vulnerability.

I was no longer able to endure her silence any longer, "Please, say something."

She sighed, and her eyes swept the room. The look of strength melted into despair, and she finally met my eyes. "Kiss me," she whispered. "Please."

I took her hands in mine, running my thumbs over the soft skin on the back of them. "Leaving you may be the end of me."

Then I felt the warmth of a tear hit my wrist and was surprised that it was mine. The word *ruined* echoed in my head once again. When the next tear sped down my cheek, she wiped it away as she pulled me to her lips.

She brushed hers softly against mine, a whisper. My hands went to her back as her hand looped around my neck and then found its way to my hair. Each kiss growing more fervent. Comfort, though temporary, stamped out the fear, pain, sorrow, and loss. Rosemond let out a soft moan that was part sob.

Leaning back, she looked at me half-dazed, lips pink and swollen from kissing. I would have taken another bullet for her, endured another knife wound, anything to stop the pain in her eyes. *This was to have been our wedding day.*

Fumbling to remove the contents of my pocket, I pulled out a small, black velvet drawstring bag. "I want you to have this. Maybe, after this is all over you can think on me kindly sometimes."

She took the bag and pulled out the silver Claddagh ring that was nestled inside. She released a sad, soft laugh. "I have always liked this design."

"It was to be your wedding ring. At least, temporarily. I couldn't even shop for it. Ethan had to purchase it." I pushed out a slow and steady breath. "I wanted to give you the world."

"I know," she replied as she slid it onto her finger in the position that indicated "engaged."

Tapping the ring, I opened my mouth to tell her what the position meant, but she put her fingers over my mouth.

"I know what it means. I am yours for as long as I can be."

I nodded and pulled her to me, kissing her for as long as possible.

ETHAN

It'd been twenty-four hours since the phone call to London, and we were packing the few things we had to in order to leave the borrowed home in the same condition in which we'd arrived.

Most of my midnight hours had been spent wrestling with some decisions. I hadn't been myself this morning. My mood had seemed more like that of George's intense determination. When we only had a quarter hour before departing, I beckoned George to the front parlor and closed the door.

George cocked his head to the side and inquired, "Is everything all right?"

"No." I cringed and scowled at my scuffed brown shoes for a moment. He would see right through me. "Is Rosemond still determined to crash the car and escape through the sewers by herself?"

"Yes. There is a Watcher who volunteered to take my place, but Rosemond hasn't consented. I won't force her, but..."

"It terrifies you," I finished.

"Yes," George replied matter-of-factly.

I sat down, but my nervousness bubbled up in the form of bouncing knees. Pressing my palms down on my legs, I took a calming breath. "I want to go with her...in the car."

Reflexively, he argued, "But Ethan, you will never be able to go back to your life. If you did, they would know that Rosemond was alive too."

"You already moved most of my money to off-shore accounts for me, yes?"

"Yes, as you asked."

"I don't want her to be alone. She's had nightmares every night about the fire. She can't be alone." There was a pleading in my voice that was more than pleading, despite my attempt to keep my tone level.

George froze in place and took a long look at me. It seemed as if his knees weakened, and he sat down on the couch next to me. "You bastard," he said softly.

I swallowed, yet didn't reply.

"You fell in love with her."

I didn't argue.

"You realize this makes me both want to bow at your feet and thank you for going with her. And to murder you. Slowly."

"I would have never, never interfered. Never."

"You never did." George rubbed at his jaw. "That explains the punch."

"I'm still not sorry." I raised my eyebrow.

"You shouldn't be." He dropped his head into his hands and massaged his temples with his thumbs. "She has no idea, does she?"

"No."

George raised his head from his hands and peered at me. "I have no time to adjust to this information or grow to accept it. This is all happening now. After tonight, I may only be able to see the both of you one last time." He swallowed hard and his voice became thick. "If I was to choose someone else for her, it would be you. You are as close to a brother as I will ever have," his voice faltered. "I know that no one would treat her better."

"This may be presumptuous. She may never return my affection."

He let out a sharp laugh with a sort of bitter edge. "No woman would ever deny you, Ethan. And she already loves you. Your friendship is the perfect basis for something else." He shook his head. "That is all I can say on the subject." He rubbed at his chest as if his heart was actually shattering to pieces.

"I love you, Georgie. In the manliest sort of way, of course." My humor didn't cloak the raw feeling. "I wish. I wish..."

George stood and squeezed my shoulder. "I know, my brother. I know."

I drove the hour to the outskirts of New York where we were to meet with Sara and some of her men. This allowed George and Rosemond to sit in their huddled grief together in the backseat. Rosemond had agreed to let me accompany her in the car after only a few mild protests, proving once again, how terrified she was beneath her composure.

When it was consented, she had clung to me in an embrace and whispered her thanks. The pained expression on George's face, watching us together, was almost more than I could withstand.

A half-block ahead, Sara leaned against the driver's side door of a motorcar. Her blonde hair shone brightly in the last bit of the golden light of sunset. I pulled up behind her. She walked to our vehicle and quickly spread a map out on the hood as three men exited the other motorcar and congregated around us. There was no greeting; she was all business.

"Smith and Henderson, you will be in the follow car and park here." She pointed to the map. "Mills, you will ride with us and stay in the motorcar with me after we drop the three of them at the café. We will circle and park here." She marked the next location.

Sara continued, "I already have four other men at the café. The getaway car is parked half a block down, here. You will be in the café for thirty minutes. At precisely 8:15 PM our informant will have them on this rooftop, here. This will give them a clear view of you exiting, parting ways, and walking to the vehicle.

"Rosemond, as you get in, you need to find them on the rooftop and point. We know they will give chase. At that point, use the straps we installed to belt yourselves in and crash into this pole." She pulled out the photograph she had shown us earlier and tapped it. "Ethan, you have the map to the sewers?"

I nodded.

"Do you need me to go over any of the plans again? What to do after you crash?" She looked at Rosemond and then me.

"Got it," I answered, my voice strong. I was ready. I'd gone over the tactics, strategies, and maps until I could speed through them backwards.

We returned to our motorcars, but this time Sara took the driver's seat of our vehicle, with the one called Mills in the passenger seat. He was a nondescript, dark-haired soldier-type. I crawled in the back behind Sara, sandwiching Rosemond between George and me.

Once we pulled out onto the road, Rosemond took both of our hands and squeezed them nervously. Her fingers were icy cold.

Feeling George's stare, I patted her hand with my free one and released it, leaning forward to retie my shoelace. When I sat back up, she was holding his left with both her hands to my relief.

It was now thirty minutes past sunset, but it seemed much darker now that we were between the tall buildings of New York. Like midnight was visiting. I recognized the streets' names from the map I'd studied and realized we were very near the café.

Suddenly, headlights flashed, and the whine of an engine roared in the last second before the grill of a motorcar impacted my door. The horrific sound of twisting metal, squealing tires, and human shrieks struck us. Darkness started to close in around the edges of my vision.

I glanced at the motorcar that'd hit us, only to see the large vampire who'd pulled me out of the car in the alley weeks ago. Gareth?

With effort, I rolled my head to see Rosemond and George. She'd been thrown against the door and on top of him. My heart raced; he wasn't moving. She moaned, thank God.

But someone was pulling her out of the broken window. I tried to grasp at her ankle, but my movements were delayed. The last thing I saw before losing consciousness was a mammoth of a man with glowing yellow eyes carrying her into an alleyway.

CHAPTER 28

NO CHOICE

ROSEMOND

My head felt like it was splitting open, and I became aware that I was being carried. My lids felt too heavy to open. My thoughts fragmented. Slowly, my hand drifted to the lapel of the person who was carrying me...not George...not Ethan... well-muscled...large...When the scent of his familiar cologne registered, fear shot through me.

"I won't harm you," Cadeyn purred.

I hadn't so much as flinched, but he knew. Then it occurred to me—the blood bond. He could feel any strong emotion. I didn't fight him, knowing it would be useless. I rested and tried to recover, wondering how long I'd been unconscious. It didn't feel like long. Bits of the accident started emerging. Headlights. Ethan's sharp intake of breath. George throwing his arms around me. Ethan so close to the impact...then darkness.

A wave of fear and dread washed over me, and I felt as if the blood had frozen in my veins. When fear had turned to anger and anger had turned to rage I finally managed to get my mouth to work.

"What did you do to my friends?" I struggled in his arms.

It took him a split-second longer to answer than it should have. "I did nothing."

"And your brother or your people?" I charged.

He didn't answer.

I drew in a breath in order to shout for help, but he clasped his hand over my mouth faster than humanly possible. I cursed his preternatural reflexes and started to fight him, not wanting him touching me.

"Stop," he hissed. "You're injured."

Focusing on his face, I realized that I must be bleeding since his eyes were glowing. My eyes drifted from his face trying to assess our location when he shifted and sat me upright onto a counter of some sort. We were in some type of abandoned store. Newspapers were over the front windows, and the shelves were empty. I started to sway to the side, so Cadeyn propped me up. Apparently, running would be out of the question at the moment.

The counter was high enough that I was looking at him almost eye-to-eye, despite his towering stature. His square jaw flexed as he clenched and unclenched his teeth while he probed my head with his fingertips. He leaned in closer, parting my legs. My heart started hammering in my chest, and I tried to control my breathing.

He took my chin in his hand. "I am not planning on harming you," he cooed for the second time.

"Then let me go," I whispered.

"That, I cannot do." Cadeyn raised the hand with which he held my face, and it was painted red. He leaned in closer. Fearful, I bristled barely able to contain a whimper. He stopped. "If you allow me to help, your injuries will pose no danger. You are losing much blood. You feel light headed, no?" His accent that had been flawlessly American slipped; now bits of French were evident. His phrasing sounded like that of my language tutor.

"Yes." Then I perceived the sensation of blood running down my neck and found that it was soaking the front of my dress. Raising my hand to the right side of my face, I explored gashes on my temple, on my cheekbone, and across the lower part of my jaw. They were deep enough that they would scar. As I dropped my hand in my lap, I detected a laceration on my wrist.

"I'm going to heal them." He leaned in again, this time giving me a lingering kiss on my neck. Then I felt his tongue move across the deep rent on my cheek.

I whimpered and my heart raced even more.

His eyes returned to mine. "Relax." I watched as his eyes briefly flashed red and the yellow seemed to give way to the blackness of his pupils. "You want to be here. You want to be with me." He said in a silky tone.

I managed a half-hearted grin. "You can't compel me or glamour me or whatever it is that *you* call it."

Instead of disappointment, his face registered a challenge. "I recall something you weren't impervious to."

Faster than I could blink, he had sunk his teeth into my throat. There were no heavy pulls draining me. On the contrary, I suddenly felt utter bliss, and the memory of his bite came back as he flooded me with whatever it is that vampires have the ability to excrete. My head no longer hurt, and all I wanted was to feel this way a little longer, like an addict in an opium den.

He leaned back and took a long look at me, a hint of my blood on his lips. "You have been busy since last I saw you." I couldn't understand the comment or the look on his face.

My desire was to make a witty retort about plotting the demise of his coven, but no noise escaped my lips. Then I witnessed a shadow slip from the backroom and hide behind a shelving unit. It took my sluggish mind a moment to comprehend; when it did, I desperately tried to level out my emotions. I needed to keep Cadeyn occupied.

ETHAN

I fought to control my shaking hands for a moment while crouching behind an aisle to listen to Rosemond and her captor. She sounded both drunk and worried. "What are you planning on doing with me? Will you turn me over to your queen?"

He didn't answer straight away. When he did, his voice was leisurely and I swore I could hear him touching her. "I plan to keep you for myself for a while or longer." But there was something else in his voice, something predatory.

I found a tiny gap between some shelves and peered through it. A hulking beast, who must've been Cadeyn, was rubbing his hands up and down Rosemond's waist like he couldn't touch her enough. Like he wanted to eat her up. I grasped my leg and dug my thumb into my thigh trying to keep a clear head. My only chance against that monster was surprise.

"Won't that get you in trouble with management?" she asked

"It will be our secret."

A hint of fear crept into her voice. "If you care anything for me, please let me go."

He leaned in close again and ran his nose up the side of her face, breathing her in. Then stopped to kiss each of the cuts on her face. Each kiss was more sensual than the first. I could swear that I saw his tongue linger on her skin after each.

"I have never tasted anything like you," he murmured, not answering her request.

He ran his hands on the outside of her thighs, kneading them. His breath becoming more ragged. Rage battered my insides as I tried to keep myself in place.

A soft thump in the back room drew his attention, and I wondered if I had bumped something on my way inside. Cadeyn seemed to snap into sharp focus. He cocked his head towards the back and listened.

Then, sounds of gunfire shattered the quiet close enough to the front of the store that the flash from the gun barrel was visible. One of the bullets broke through the glass and ricocheted inside the store. I silently dropped to a knee and prayed that he wouldn't walk towards the front of the building. I was barely breathing as it was.

More sounds disturbed the momentary silence outside. Rosemond's eyes kept fastening on the very spot where I was hiding as she looked over his shoulder. I decided to show myself to her. When it was obvious that Cadeyn was again wholly focused with putting his hands all over her, I looked around the end of the aisle cap. She immediately saw me and relief flashed on her face, followed by something unreadable.

"My wrist," she uttered hoarsely.

His hands stopped in mid-caress and slid to her arm. He took her hand in his and examined it. I could see her blood-soaked sleeve from here. When he raised it to his mouth, I thought my blood would boil out of my body. I couldn't tell what he was doing to her, but she leaned forward and rested against him.

Rosemond stared at my location fiercely. I leaned out once more. This time, there was no relief on her face; she glared and mouthed two words: "No...Go."

I shook my head, indicating negative, and held up one of the Watcher's special daggers that I'd snapped up before pursuing Cadeyn and Rosemond into the building. Reaching behind me, I felt the three throwing blades tucked into my belt reassuring myself they were still there.

Her nostrils flared, and despite myself, I couldn't help but think how adorable she was when she was angry. She squeezed her eyes shut and spoke to him.

ROSEMOND

"Where will you take me?" I asked, forcing some sweetness into my tone.

He looped my arm over his shoulder, and then observed me for a moment. My lids felt heavy from the new bite. He slowly ran his hands up my body, beginning with my calves he continued upwards caressing every inch of me not stopping until he reached my collarbone. He answered after a long pause. "Once the activity outside has run its course. Anywhere you want."

I let out an uneven breath to give him the illusion he was wooing me. There was more gunfire outside, and I wondered if the police were involved at this point. I glanced over his shoulder as Cadeyn kissed down my neck. Ethan peered over a shelf and started to take a step closer. I gave him a warning look. Cadeyn would have to be much more distracted.

A body thudded against one of the front windows. Cadeyn turned and started to pull away from me to move toward the storefront.

Fear shot through me that Ethan might be discovered. Cadeyn looked at me, and I whispered in a trembling voice, "Please don't leave me alone." He froze for a moment, but was still leaning away from me. His body language said he was going to survey the front.

Choking down my revulsion, I hooked his waist with my leg, herding him closer. He turned his attention back to me, distraction being replaced by hunger. I placed my hands on his broad chest and rasped, "Please," while projecting vulnerability and fear.

ETHAN

George had said the worst hour of his life had been watching her at the club, powerless to do anything. I cringed and squeezed the handle of the knife. Then she whispered something in his ear.

The monster whispered something in hers in return. It was apparent he actually wanted her to desire him.

He straightened up for a brief moment, tilting his head to the side, then whispered something to her once again. I watched as her eyes flew open, and the look of utter shock seized her features.

"I..." she finally sputtered.

"There is no mistaking," he replied warmly.

I couldn't make sense of the bits I was hearing. Her eyes

ran over my location, never lingering to give away my position. She still seemed shaken when she asked, "And you would keep me safe? You swear it. On the life of your brother?"

I wondered for a moment if she was being wooed by his promises, whatever they were. He spoke into her ear once again. She looked over his shoulder and gave me another warning look, though she couldn't see me. She mouthed the word: "Go" once more.

I leaned over enough so she could see me shake my head no.

She got a pained look and squeezed her eyes shut, running her hands over his back. She looked at me again and seemed to make some sort of decision. She mouthed one word: "heart." Then her hands stopped moving for a moment. She carefully pointed with her index fingers on both hands to a single spot on his back.

I stared for a second and nodded. She wanted me to stab him in the back and through his heart. The place she indicated was a little higher than I would have thought. But then again, vampire slaying wasn't exactly part of my education plan.

Then she did something *horrible*.

ROSEMOND

I pulled him closer, his back was fully towards Ethan. I was going to give him the only chance I could. I closed my eyes and thought of George—his lips, his hands, his everything.

Desire unfurled inside me as I pulled Cadeyn to my lips. I ran my hands into his hair and down to his ears murmuring against his mouth, anything to distract him further and muffle Ethan's impending approach.

Cadeyn reacted instantly...and hungrily.

ETHAN

Any hesitation about impaling Cadeyn fled the moment Mr. Handsy moaned in pleasure. With six silent steps and one thrust of the dagger, Cadeyn fell paralyzed to the floor, dragging Rosemond down with him. I was shocked by my success but didn't stop to revel in it.

Hauling Rosemond to her feet and pinning her to my side, I half-dragged her towards the back exit before she could get her footing. We spilled into the alley, the wintery air assailing us.

She still seemed unsteady, so I held her upper arm tightly as I towed her towards the street, then stopped short, pushing her behind me. Her forehead pressed into my mid-back.

A man stood in wait, twenty paces ahead, blocking our passage. He had a revolver aimed straight at us. Judging from the slight shake in his hand, he was human. He cocked the weapon, and I felt Rosemond grab my belt and move from behind me. Two seconds later, the man shrieked and dropped the pistol. It clattered to the ground and went off.

I grabbed her arm again, and we were at a dead run as we passed the man groaning in agony. The hand that had held the gun was split wide open.

We crouched behind a motorcar. "Good shot," I breathed.

"No, I was aiming for his heart. We left him alive." Rosemond glanced back towards the alley. "He's gone. He may have found Cadeyn already."

Both the thought of her missing and that beast chasing us jarred me. "Are you okay?"

There was a flash of pain on her face. "I'll be fine once the bite wears off. What happened to George?"

"We woke at the same time. Two men tried to stop us from entering the alley to go after you." I shook my head. "He was fighting them and yelled at me to find you." I swallowed. "I left him."

Rosemond nodded. There was no judgment or blame on her face. She pressed the sides of her head with her palms. "We can still make this work if there are witnesses and we can make it to the motorcar. Do you have the keys?"

"Yes." I glanced down the street in the direction of the vehicle and caught a tiny bit of movement—George and Sara. I could see from this distance that Sara was wounded. George was holding bloody rags to her stomach. One of the Watchers in the other car was dead in the street not far from the store we were just inside. He must've been the one fighting in front. My eyes slid back to Rosemond, her eyes trained on the roofline. Nudging her, I pointed out George.

She expelled a relieved breath.

"Should we go to him?" I asked.

She cringed. "We have to go straight to the motorcar or we won't make it."

I was about to inquire as to why, when she pointed at a shadowy figure on the roof—Gareth. I felt as if I'd swallowed cement. "Do you think we can make it? Are you okay to move that quickly?"

"It doesn't look like we have a choice. We need to draw them away from George and Sara...and let them see us die." She grabbed my arm and looked at me with desperation. "Just don't let go of me."

"Never."

CHAPTER 29

HELPLESS

ROSEMOND

We decided to wait until Gareth was looking in the other direction before sprinting to the getaway car. I looked down at my T-bar shoes. They would stay on my feet if I ran, but they could be heard a mile away. I debated on whether it was better to risk cutting my feet running or making noise while sprinting. The street looked fairly clean, as long as we avoided the glass from the broken storefront window, which wouldn't be difficult.

I drew away from Ethan and carefully removed my heels. He questioned me with his eyes, and I signed my answer. Ethan nodded and held my upper arm again once I was settled. Sitting on my haunches, I clutched my shoes with one hand and the bumper of the motorcar we were using as cover with the other. The ground was terribly cold and raised gooseflesh along my legs. Cadeyn's bite still had my head woozy; the only benefit was that I felt rather pain-free at the moment.

Ethan whispered, his lips on my ear. "Gareth has moved to the far end of the roof and is looking the other direction."

I patted his knee, and with that, we exploded from our hiding spot running straight for the getaway vehicle. I ran as quickly as my legs could carry me, my thighs burning from my long strides. Ethan kept his hand on my upper arm keeping me stable and on track as he ran smoothly next to me. I never let my eyes settle on George's location as we approached; he marked the halfway point.

The pathway was clear one second and then it wasn't. Breton dropped from a roof and stood in our way barehanded. He tipped his grey hat at me and grinned.

Ethan jerked to a stop faster than I could and tried to shove me behind him. I complied just long enough to slide a throwing knife from his belt. I threw the blade with deadly force towards Breton's heart.

Breton caught the knife, plucking it from the air as if I'd thrown it in slow motion. He propped his hat farther back on his head and stood toying with it in his hand, smiling at me as if he knew a secret I didn't.

My mouth went dry as I tried to swallow. He was an old vampire, that much was apparent, maybe older than Gareth and Cadeyn from the way he moved. I glanced back to locate Gareth; he was still watching from afar.

A female voice broke the stare down. "If you want to play, I might be a little more exciting."

Breton didn't turn. "I believe a wounded Slayer is no more than a broken toy, Sariel."

Sara had moved to the opposite side of the street from George. I hadn't seen nor heard her move. "It was just a scratch." Instantly, he turned from us and engaged her, there was a clash of steel and a spray of sparks.

We didn't wait. We ran towards the motorcar. We were eighty-percent of the way there when gunfire broke out. I risked a look over my shoulder, letting Ethan guide my path. George was standing in the middle of the road, unloading his revolver into Cadeyn, who fell to his knees looking furious. It wouldn't take Cadeyn but a minute to recover from the barrage of bullets.

We reached the Studebaker, and Ethan threw open the driver's side door and pushed me in, following behind me as he cranked the engine. It fired up, and he put it into gear as quickly as possible, the tires skidding as we lurched to a start.

We got up to speed and were almost halfway to the crash site when something landed on the roof, leaving a large dent. Throwing my upper body over the seat to the back, I grabbed a pistol from the escape bag, and then unloaded it into the roof. An exclamation of pain shrieked above us, and Ethan proceeded to swerve back and forth. We watched as a body rolled off of the roof and lay still in the street behind us.

"How long until it's after us again?" Ethan yelled.

"Depends where I hit him. Seconds? A minute?"

Ethan glanced in the rearview and said: "Oh hell, he's already up," as he floored the gas pedal. "Strap in. We are going to hit harder than we planned."

Gasping a panicked sound, I fiddled with the leather straps, trying to close the belt around Ethan. Once he was secure, I fastened the belt around myself the same moment the pole we were to ram came into view.

ETHAN

Holding the steering wheel tight with one hand, I threw my other arm in front of Rosemond as we impacted. The collision was so great I couldn't keep her forehead from connecting with the dash, though I managed to soften the blow.

The way her body drooped, it was obvious she was dazed as she fumbled for the matches, involuntary tears staining her cheeks. I ripped the lighter from my pocket and lit my side of the car to obscure the view into the vehicle as quickly as possible. I turned, and Rosemond had already lit her side.

I reached over the seat and pulled out the bottle of her blood that had been extracted this morning. "Take care of this. I'll open the escape hatch."

She broke the panel of glass that had already been scored to break and poured some of her blood on the outside of the motorcar to simulate deep cuts while trying to get out. Then she turned to douse the female body in the back, while I worked on getting the hatch in the bottom open. The heat was almost unbearable, but it was working. The chemical on the windows was burning intensely with no sign of stopping.

I jerked at the door to the escape hatch, but it wouldn't budge. Fear flooded my system. *It must have been damaged when we hit.* Smoke was starting to fill the interior. *We don't have long.*

Rosemond finished her job, and I could feel her eyes on me as she started to cough from the smoke.

I braced myself and pulled with every fiber of my being and stopped when she yelped. Her sleeve was on fire. I grabbed her arm and put out the remaining flames with my hands. This was the last she could handle; I could see her unraveling in front of my eyes. Weeks of dreams of dying by fire, and now we were stuck. I took her face in my hands. "I will get this open. This is not where we are going to die."

She sucked in a breath and nodded, seeming to calm, but in the action of taking in that breath, she took in more smoke. Her cough grew worse.

With a new surge of desperation, I yanked and the plate gave way. Punching the release button for the panels, they shifted into place. We would be concealed under the vehicle. I dislodged the panel and dropped my feet onto the pavement with the pry bar in hand. After wrenching open the manhole cover, I stepped onto the first rung. I stuck my head in the car and called to Rosemond but she didn't respond. Then I realized that she hadn't coughed in over a minute.

I stepped back up and pulled her through the opening, holding her to me as I replaced the escape hatch cover and fixed it into place with my free hand. She was completely limp against me. Carefully easing us onto the ladder, I repositioned the manhole cover. My legs were shaking and wouldn't be able to hold us this way much longer. Breathless, I leveraged her against the ladder and took a step down to heave her over my shoulder. Once she was in position, we descended the ladder quickly.

A lantern had been put in place a couple of hours before by one of Sara's men. Grateful for the light, I put Rosemond down in a sitting position against the wall.

I cupped her face. "Frank, we made it. Speak to me."

Then, everything stopped. She wasn't breathing.

GEORGE

Cadeyn screamed in fury when he had reached the motorcar. I wasn't far behind. Henderson jumped in front of me and pushed me back as I stupidly kept plowing towards the wreck, despite Cadeyn's presence. My shoulder ached where Cadeyn had thrown me to the side as he had charged past me to the vehicle.

When he reached the motorcar, he ripped the backdoor off and bellowed. Gareth was suddenly there and pulled his brother away.

Cadeyn and I were mirror images for a moment. Genuine panic on our faces—something was terribly wrong, and we could both feel it.

Clutching his burnt hand, Cadeyn stared at the burning bodies in the vehicle.

Gareth's gruff voice broke through the turmoil. "Can you sense her?"

Cadeyn pushed towards the motorcar again and Gareth yanked him back once more, shoving him to the ground.

"Can you sense her?" he asked again more urgently.

"No...nothing," Cadeyn howled, sounding more distressed than I thought a vampire could.

Gareth stalked around the motorcar and disappeared on the other side for a brief second. When he returned to his brother he was sniffing something dark on his hand. He knelt on one knee and shoved it under Cadeyn's nose.

Cadeyn eyes sparked and glowed, then he roared in response.

Breaking away from Henderson and running towards the

motorcar, I screamed. "No!! Rosemond! Ethan!" I made it three steps before he tackled me to the ground.

Cadeyn fixed his eyes on me, then crawled to his feet, looking like a stalking lion. His yellow eyes cut through the darkness. He was going to come for me, and I didn't care.

I struggled to my knees just as he flashed in my direction, a blur of movement. Right before impact a wall of muscle stepped in front of me—Gareth.

Cadeyn reached out his arm over his brother's shoulder, the tips of his fingers not a quarter meter away. "Leave him. Let him suffer." Gareth pushed his brother back a few times, increasing the space between us. "We must away."

Gareth looked over his shoulder at me one last time and smiled. His grin was malevolent and conspiratorial. It said he was behind the frame job. Gareth whistled through his teeth. "Breton," he barked.

At that moment I realized two things: Sariel was still fighting Breton, and sirens were drawing close. I blinked my eyes, and all of the vampires were gone. Then Sariel dropped to her knees beside me. "You can't be picked up by the police."

I nodded in agreement. Henderson offered his hand to help me up. Tiredly, I allowed him tug me to my feet. It was obvious Sariel wasn't in good shape; in fact, I wasn't certain how she was upright. Henderson and I each took an arm, and then the three of us disappeared into the night.

ETHAN

Pressing my ear to her chest, I listened. But the only discernible sounds were drips of water in the background and my own ragged breath. I held my breath and listened one more time.

"You will not do this to me, Rosemond." My throat was clenched with emotion. I didn't know what to do. "Think, damn you!" I shouted, chastising myself.

Then, bits of schooling filtered back to my consciousness. Amsterdam...the symposium on sudden death. She hadn't drowned in a canal, but...I tried to think through the steps they had discussed on our school trip. She didn't need to be warmed, and water didn't need to be aspirated. I racked my brain trying to dig up the memory, knowing there was little time.

"Head lower than body," I murmured to myself and swiveled her to the ground. "Manual pressure on the abdomen." At this point I would do anything. The next step came more quickly; they had used bellows to force air into the lungs and had said mouth-to-mouth respirations could work without proper equipment.

Opening her mouth, I tried to breathe life back into her—praying harder with each passing moment. One breath...two breaths...three breaths...four breaths. My hope started to fail. "Please," I implored.

Then there was a flicker, the faintest hint of movement. I thought perhaps my eyes were playing tricks on me, her eyes flew open, and she struggled to suck in some air. I rolled her on her side and patted her back, feeling rather helpless. The instant she was breathing normally, I pulled her onto my lap and held her against my chest.

"I thought I'd lost you." I repeated the sentiment over and over again while rocking her.

She didn't reply, but I could feel the warmth of her tears

seeping through my shirt. She nuzzled in under my chin, smelling of smoke and blood.

"Never do that again," I murmured, my voice still horribly uneven.

"Not for at least a week," she finally answered.

Tears flowed down my cheeks in relief to hear her voice. She was alive, and she was whole. I needed to hold her a few more minutes before I worried that the map of the sewers, along with the getaway bag, had burned in the car...just a few more minutes...

CHAPTER 30

WANTED

GEORGE

"How many bodies were there in the wreckage?" I asked Henderson the moment he had breached the threshold.

His eyes bulged, and he scoured at his face with his meaty hands. "I couldn't get behind the police lines, and they weren't talking to reporters." He tossed his fake credentials on the counter as if to emphasize his point.

My gaze turned to Sariel, "I thought you had people on the force who could check."

Sariel sighed and patiently answered, "Not in that district. It was a war zone. The vamps lost all six of their familiars, we lost four Watchers, not to mention the bodies in the motorcar. The police are tight-lipped. In their eyes, it was a massacre on the streets—open warfare."

I began to pace.

"George, sit. I have a man waiting at the rendezvous location in the sewers. It has only been a few hours. They could simply be lost."

My voice was hopeless. "Sariel, you saw Cadeyn's reaction. The blood bond was broken. You know what that means." *Rosemond's heart stopped.*

"It could mean that he couldn't sense her once she was underground."

My insides were churning, and there was nowhere to focus this tempest of emotion. I strode over and punched the wall, and then cried out in agony as chips of plaster flaked on the floor; the pain in my hand gave me something tangible to focus on.

I cocked my arm back, ready for a second strike, and Sariel caught my fist before I connected. She twisted between me and the wall, her eyes furious. She spoke in rough, hushed tones. "You will get yourself together. Both Ethan and Rosemond were dead to you the moment those Wanted posters went up. Their physical well-being has nothing to do with what you have to do. I will *not* fail your father. You will be on that ship."

I was barely able to push the words out, "I have to—"

"No. You don't. I have known you since you were a small boy. It does pain me to see you like this, but it changes nothing. Bathe. Get some sleep. We smuggle you out on that steamer at daybreak. I promise to get you word if she is well."

"Sariel," I whispered.

"I will send more men to explore the sewers. There's nothing else we can do."

ETHAN

"We should rest again." Despite the lamplight Rosemond looked deathly pale. Even though it had been hours, I still had to hold her arm to keep her from losing balance.

"I'm fine," she answered. "If any Cadeyn's coven decide explore, we need far away."

I cringed. The harder we pushed physically, the more words she seemed to drop when speaking. And what made me fear the most was that she didn't notice. "Rosemond, we are nowhere near the crash site. Aren't you supposed to rest after hitting your head?"

She looked at me, and I could see the wheels turning— slowly. She blinked, her eyes finally lighting like there was some understanding in there. "Maybe few minute."

"Thank you." We reached a junction with a few stairs and I helped her sit down. Plopping on the step below her, I stifled a groan. My body was increasingly stiff after the initial car accident. My ribs were most likely bruised judging from the agony I experienced when carrying Rosemond down the ladder. But nothing felt broken. I leaned back, but quickly leaned forward again, jarred by a stabbing sensation.

Rosemond gasped and touched my back. "Bleeding," she whispered and tugged my shirt up. I glanced over my shoulder at the strain on her face.

"Oh, Ethan." She lightly touched my left side; it was all I could do to not jump out of my skin. "Glass...nothing to clean." Fabric tearing filled the air, and I swiveled to see what she was up to. She was ripping the collar from her dress. She huffed, "Clean as gets." She pushed me back around, and I sat waiting.

It was difficult to suppress a scream as she extracted something from my flesh. I felt her arm rest on my shoulder as she extended the bloodied two inch shard for me to see. It was flat and clear like the glass from the car. Rosemond continued to pluck out tiny pieces for another minute but they were comparatively insignificant.

"We need to out of here. Need clean." She paused and groaned.

"Are you okay?"

"My head." She pressed the cloth to my lower back from where she'd removed the larger piece of glass and leaned forward, resting her head on my shoulder.

"Should we go up at the next access point?"

She sighed again, and I felt her warm breath on my neck. "No. Still dark...to risk. Could come up coven." She rested more weight on my shoulder as she continued putting pressure on the open wound.

"Rosemond, you..." I bit my tongue.

"Be okay after rest."

"I couldn't bear it if you weren't," I whispered. My concern couldn't be hidden, there was no joking about our situation. I felt as though there was nothing left. The pressure she was putting on my back eased, and I feared that if she fell asleep, she would be gone forever.

"Rosemond," I said. When she didn't respond, I repeated her name loudly trying to jolt her awake, but she didn't move and her hand slid from my back.

I twisted around and caught her just as she slumped sideways. Holding her, my ribs ached, but I didn't care. I shook her.

"Wake up, Rosemond. You will not leave me! You hear me. You will not."

Her eyes fluttered open.

I pressed my lips into a hard line. "We need to keep moving."

She looked at me confused, as if wondering how she got in this position. "Of course," she slurred in a pleasant tone, but her exhaustion was clear.

Helping her up, I clinched my teeth, not sure if my physical pain or my worry was worse. We walked on into the tunnels. All the while, I prayed that my memory was taking us in the right direction.

GEORGE

I didn't want to get out of bed. I knew if they had heard from Rosemond or Ethan, I would have been woken. Slowly, I sat up and slid my legs over the side of the bed, hating that I had slept in comfort while they were either dead or lost somewhere underground. I prayed for the latter.

Someone knocked at the door. "George?"

"Come," I answered.

Sariel stayed in the doorway. She was dressed like a dock-worker, with her hair carefully pin-curled to her head, and a fake mustache in her palm. "It is almost sunrise. We depart in ten."

I nodded, and then studied my bare feet on the dark wood floor. My voice not much more than a whisper, "Did..." I stopped myself.

"No," she whispered. "Ten minutes."

I absently dressed and choked down the bread, cheese, and

coffee that Henderson offered. He watched me with dark eyes and never uttered a word. I wondered how disappointed he was after meeting someone from 'the illustrious Yates family.'

We loaded into the Model T in silence and threaded our way towards the docks. Once there, we parked on the outskirts and slowly trudged through a few warehouses. All of us were battered and bruised, and consequently, not moving very quickly.

When we reached the water, the smell of the salt air and the screech of seagulls seemed lonely, making me feel even more isolated. I pulled the knit cap farther down on my head and flipped up the collar of the pea coat to shield me from the wind sweeping in from the ocean. I glanced at Sariel ahead of me.

The weather never seemed to bother her, though she was hunched a little forward since she was recovering from the knife wound in her belly. Slayer's healing abilities were to be admired. If she had been fully human, she would be dead.

The three of us walked on the sidewalk parallel to the ocean. I ran my fingers over the pistol in my pocket. A motorcar was idling up behind us, and my ears pricked with caution.

Henderson was suddenly very close behind me. "Sara," he whispered.

Sariel casually stopped and tightened the lace on her boot. I stood with my back to the approaching vehicle, though my mind screamed for me to look. I needed to keep my face hidden. I blew on my hands to warm them and pressed at my fake mustache, making sure it was secure. It was the darker version of what Sariel was wearing.

The motorcar stopped next to us. I put my hand in my

pocket and closed my fingers around the pistol, placing my thumb on the hammer, ready to cock it. There was no speaking, but I could see Sariel motioning in my peripheral.

Readying myself to battle, I was startled when Sariel clamped her hand down on my shoulder. Trying to read her expression, I glanced at her face, but it was cool and composed. She pushed me towards the back of what turned out to be a delivery truck.

Henderson opened the back doors. A few boxes were piled in front of a heavy curtain. Sariel shoved at me to climb in. I complied, and the doors instantly closed behind me. If it was anyone but Sariel, I would have refused.

I stepped forward, about to pull aside the curtain, just as the truck accelerated forward. I had to hold fast to the side. We rolled to a stop a few moments later, after making a few turns, and the engine cut off.

A gruff voice said, "That should do it."

Then I heard the most wonderful sound. Ethan softly uttered, "Rosemond, you need to stay awake."

"I'm trying," she said so faintly I could barely make it out. I finally reached the curtain and shoved it aside. Ethan sat shirtless on a crate in the middle of the space while one of Sariel's medics secured a bandage on his lower back. Rosemond was curled on her side resting on a shelf. He held one of her hands in both of his.

I cried out, involuntarily, tears springing from my eyes. I reached Ethan first, throwing my arms around him as he turned towards me. "I thought you dead, my brother."

Ethan squeezed me hard. "I was worried about us, too." He patted me on my back, then released me.

I dropped to my knees in front of Rosemond. She was smiling up at me, but hadn't attempted to move. She reached out, and when I took her hands, she latched onto me and pulled herself up. I felt like a schoolboy the way tears were tumbling down my cheeks. I was so sure she'd been dead, I hadn't realized the weight of it.

"She hit her head pretty hard." Ethan informed me.

I pinned her face between my shaking hands, wanting to cover her with kisses. "Are you all right?"

"Will be," she murmured.

The medic chimed in. "I believe she may have a contusion on her brain. We will keep her from deep sleep until the swelling goes down. All indicators are that she will be fine after a few days' rest."

Looking into her eyes, I ran my thumb over her lips and leaned in, pressing my cheek to hers. She smelled like the sewers and rubbing alcohol, but it didn't matter.

There was whispering behind me, and then the backdoor opened. I turned, just as Ethan finished buttoning up his shirt. He had a hat and work vest in his hand. "We will give you two a few minutes alone."

I gave Ethan a long look, then mouthed: "Thank you."

He patted my shoulder, and pulled the hat down on his head and put the vest on as he climbed out. I turned back to Rosemond, and before I could do anything she had pulled me to her lips. All I had dreamt about was holding her in my arms again. I attempted to be gentle, as we were both injured, but couldn't help but draw her closer as our mouths moved together. Her breath was as uneven as mine.

I leaned away when I remembered Cadeyn's reaction to the

accident. "The blood bond was broken." It came out a statement rather than a question.

She gave me a pained look, and it was obvious she wanted to look away, as was her habit when telling me something I didn't want to hear. "The escape hatch jammed, Ethan, he..." she paused and took a breath. "All the smoke or the bump on the head. I lost consciousness. My heart stopped. Ethan revived me. He saved my life."

I kissed her again, grabbing handfuls of her hair, burying my face in the hollow. "I wanted to spend all of my days and all my nights and all of my everything with you." I murmured.

"And I with you."

Someone knocked on the back door. I cringed knowing these were my last moments with her. Taking both of her hands she met my gaze. My throat was so clenched, it was hard to speak.

"Live a full life. Love. Let..." I hesitated. "*Someone* love you. Move on. I want you to be happy."

"I don't—" she started to protest.

I placed my hand over her lips. "Ethan, he..." I stopped and simply stated, "Be happy." The backdoor opened. I kissed her one last time and turned to leave.

"George, I need to tell you someth..." her voice sounded desperate, but it trailed off.

I turned back and looked at her expectantly.

The heartrending look on her face seemed to shift from urgent to something indescribable as she hesitated. "You will always be part of me."

Sariel was standing a few meters away and motioned to me. I shoved my hands into my pockets and reluctantly walked towards her.

I glanced over my shoulder one last time. She had moved to the front of the delivery truck and had her hands pressed against the driver's side window, looking at me with tear-stained cheeks, her expression so tragically beautiful that it took my breath away. This last image was forever to be burned in my memory, as it was the last time that I ever saw her.

CHAPTER 31

ANOTHER WAY

ETHAN

I carefully poured steaming water into the teapot to steep the tea for a few minutes. Nerves twisted in my belly as I peeked out the kitchen window. Rosemond was nestled in a wicker chair, looking out at the ocean, her gaze fixed somewhere on the horizon. I placed some biscuits on the tray, readying it for our afternoon tea.

This had become my favorite part of the day, though this afternoon was different. I scrutinized the calendar one last time; the date was still the same as it was this morning, much to my dismay. Somehow, three weeks had passed, and Sara would be back tomorrow.

She'd parked us out here for three weeks for two reasons. One: so that she could see if there were any suspicions that we were alive. And two: if it was safe, to make sure we were completely healed before striking out on our own.

I patted the pocket that contained the letter I'd written,

folded an extra blanket over my arm, and picked up the tray of tea. When I appeared next to Rosemond, she smiled up at me. It was a special smile she reserved for only a few people.

"And how will you take your tea this afternoon, milady?"

She laughed. I think it was for the first time since the showdown in New York. She pushed the blanket off of her shoulders and scooted to the front of her chair. "Well, sir, I think it might be time I served you."

I reached for the pot, and she playfully batted my hand away. Sitting, I watched her pour. The afternoon light coming off the water made her eyes look the palest shade of blue, accented by her flushed cheeks from the chilly wind.

I swallowed hard and felt my nerves rise up again. "Rosemond, Sara will be back tomorrow."

"Oh, my. You sound serious." She had a light tone, but her voice trembled ever so slightly.

I exhaled and chickened out. "Me? Serious? How could you ever accuse me of such things?" I grinned at her and leaned back with my tea, watching the steam disappear into the salty air. "You, on the other hand, have something heavy on your mind."

She closed her eyes and didn't deny it. She drew in a stuttering breath, her emotion so thick it made the blood in my veins slow. I feared whatever she was keeping from me. After an excruciatingly long minute, she opened her eyes and looked at me. "I don't know how I will do this alone. For the first time in my life, I don't know what to do."

"You don't need to do anything on your own," I replied gently.

"I have spent my life being the good girl—always following directions. Sometimes I felt caged. I see why it was necessary now," she paused. "But I've had a good life. Though I've made such a mess of things. Actions have consequences." There was a weight in her voice, it sounded as if she was quoting something she'd heard often.

"Consequences?" I whispered.

She sucked in a breath and bit her bottom lip. "I'm pregnant, Ethan."

I looked at her blankly and blinked a few times as I processed the bombshell she had dropped. I almost asked if she was sure, but she wouldn't have said so if she wasn't. Then, I was struck with a flash of memory. Cadeyn holding her and commenting that she had "been busy." I'd never thought about the fact that he'd his hand on her belly when he said it.

"Please, say something."

I put down my cup, no longer chicken. "Marry me."

A morbid laugh escaped her lips. "No."

I felt as though I'd taken a blow to the gut. "I see." I looked down and started to stand.

"Ethan, wait. I'm sorry. I didn't mean it like that. Please stay." She clenched her fists. "I can't allow you to sacrifice yourself like that. My action. My consequence."

A flicker of hope came back, but there was obvious hurt in my voice. I couldn't hide it from her. "You don't think I care about you that way."

"I don't." Her voice was soft this time. "You take care of people; it is part of who you are. It's only natural for you to want to help me."

"I don't know whether to be insulted or complimented."

Her eyes bulged slightly. "Complimented, of course. I—"

I held up my hand, and she stopped. "I have never lied to you, Rosemond. Every time I told you that I loved you. I didn't mean it in friendship as you always took it, but you were in love with my best friend, and I would never have gotten in the way of that. But he is gone, and I miss him too. This is what *is* now. I came out here to propose to you. Baby or no baby. It makes no difference to me. I love you, Rosemond." I sank down in front of her. "Please be my wife."

"But there is a baby."

"And who better to help you raise it than me? George was as close to a brother as could be." I paused, debating on whether to say the next part. "He knew how I felt about you."

Obvious shock registered on her face. "He did?"

"Yes. He said he wanted to murder me." A smile played at the corner of her lips. "He also...gave me his blessing."

ROSEMOND

Ethan stared at me with his clear, blue eyes, so earnest. I didn't want to doubt him, but how could I not? He had tirelessly given to everyone else, time and time again. Then I thought of George in the truck. He started to say something about Ethan and had stopped. Then he told me to let *"someone* love me." *Had he meant Ethan?*

I put down my teacup and started to say, "I think..." and a look of frustration passed over his face.

"Then tell me this." He abruptly leaned forward looping his arm around my waist and sliding me forward. Before I could ask what he was doing, he kissed me. I was startled, but I didn't push away.

His lips moved urgently for a moment, and then turned into a slow, methodical sizzle.

Goosebumps rose up and down my spine, and I felt lightheaded. My lips parted, and I returned his kisses as he wrapped his other arm around me.

Somehow, without giving myself permission, my hands ran up his strong, lean arms and encircled his neck.

This boy could kiss.

He eased his head back a couple of inches. "Do you believe me now?"

"I..."

He gave me one small kiss and said, "I have wanted to kiss you since the beginning. Please believe me."

I did.

And as if a veil had been lifted, I could see all the times he'd told me how he felt. I had somehow *chosen* not to see it.

"Marry me, and we will head west. We will find some place to have the simple life you said you wanted. We can put down roots and have as many babies as you want. I will raise this child like my own. You know I will."

I started to answer, and he interrupted.

"Wait." He fiddled with his pocket and pulled out a folded piece of paper that looked like it had been riding around in many pockets for many days. "I wrote this letter to you the day we left for New York. Read it, and then..."

He stood and wrapped the blanket around me, then disappeared into the house. I sat, stunned for a moment, and then unfolded the cream colored paper.

ROSEMOND,

When I first saw you on my doorstep, you reminded me of a cat. You were wet and covered in dirt, with your large lavender eyes shining up at me. I remember thinking, "Please don't be with George." And when I greeted you flirtatiously, I knew him well enough to see he was completely crazy about you. I was shocked that any woman could breach the stone walls of our George, but you aren't just any woman, are you?

Very soon, I realized you were not a household feline, but rather a lioness. You were intelligent, fierce, and loyal. In the beginning, you didn't know George that well, yet you tirelessly stayed at his bedside. When you finally allowed yourself to weep over what would have destroyed many people, you permitted me to hold you.

It was at that moment, I realized I was done for. It was obvious that you hated for anyone to see you in a weakened condition, but you trusted me enough to let your walls down. Honestly, I was attracted to you from the beginning, but that night—I fell.

Your feelings for George were obvious, and I vowed not to get in the way. I was happy to be your friend, truly, though I did hope for something else. But never would I have wished this on George. Ever.

But here we are, nowhere near where any of us thought we would be a couple of months ago, and one thing has not changed. I love you. I love all of you, and I don't care about anything that has been done in the past. I care about the future, something I hope you can see spending with me.

Here you have teased me a dozen times that I was overconfident, but I don't feel that way now. I feel as if I could sweep any woman off her feet—but you. You. I know you love me, but I guess this is my question: Could you grow to love me in another way?

ETERNALLY YOURS,
    Ethan

CHAPTER 32

EPILOGUE—PERFECT

March 11, 1931

GEORGE

A soft knock at the door caught my attention before it opened. "Package for you, sir."

I nodded and indicated the desk. "Thank you, Bennet."

He placed the package on my father's desk and retreated from the room. My trial had ended a month ago, and I still felt like my body had been worn thin, like I had been locked up for 100 years. After being denied bail, I spent 726 days of my life in the media circus of my trial until being found "not guilty."

Taking in a slow breath, I picked up the package and examined it. It had been sent from an art gallery in San Francisco. Curious, I removed the brown paper from the box and carefully freed the canvas inside.

There was no note enclosed, save the name of the painting on a card glued to the rear. I glanced at the front, and then spun it in my hands and looked at the back more closely. There were four sentences, one written on each piece of wood stretching the canvas. Instantly, I recognized Ethan's handwriting.

The notes read:

I married her.

We are happy.

And for the other thing, I thought you should know.

She is perfect.

Examining the words, I was confused for a long moment. He had married Rosemond, and they were happy. I was glad of it, though the ache in my chest almost incapacitated me. Turning the canvas again, I reread the last two sentences, bewildered as to their meaning.

I flipped the canvas and scrutinized the painting. It was of a woman turned three-quarters away, only the line of her cheek visible. Dark hair fell in waves over her shoulders as she held a small child. When I noticed the small freckle on her neck just below her right ear, I knew it to be Rosemond. The little girl she held was angelic, with her dark hair and lively eyes—hazel with dark lashes. The nose and mouth had Rosemond's delicate beauty.

My heart quickened when I noted the name of the painting. "Woman with 18 month old: A Study (Helen)." Realization dawned as I counted the months and looked at the little girl again. The eyes weren't Rosemond's. And they certainly weren't Ethan's—they were mine.

For countless minutes, I stared at the image of what I knew to be my daughter. They named her after my mother. Somehow, I knew they had argued about whether to tell me.

Ethan had to have won; Rosemond would have been in favor of keeping it from me to protect me.

I thought kindly on Ethan for a long while. Perhaps someday, if I had a family of my own, I would return the honor and name a child after him, my friend, my brother: Sebastian Ethan Kendrick.

He was right, I preferred to know.

CHAPTER 33

THE UNINTENDED: THE END IS A NEW BEGINNING

A SPECIAL SNEAK PEEK OF BOOK ONE

FOLLOW THE ADVENTURES OF ROSEMOND'S GREAT-GRANDDAUGHTER, ALERIA HAYES.

The drive home from school had done little to calm me down. Entering my room, I flicked on my stereo and fell back onto my bed. The music was a perfect blend of yearning and contempt to fit my mood.

I gingerly probed my cheekbone. It hurt enough that I decided to drag myself from bed to inspect it in the mirror. Only a faint pink mark remained. Thankfully, it didn't look like it would bruise.

Anger surfaced when I pictured Mark's stupid face after he'd slammed my locker shut, hitting me in the cheek. He hadn't meant to physically hurt me, but his behavior since I'd broken up with his best friend, Robert, was inexcusable.

It was bad enough having my last class with Robert every day and facing the constant can-you-see-how-much-you-hurt-me eyes. I should've waited a few more weeks until school was over to break it off, but it felt like I was living a lie. I just couldn't fake it. He wasn't a bad guy, but he *was* smothering me —and more recently, pressuring me.

I plopped back on the bed, staring blankly at my bag full of homework on the floor. It seemed to be mocking me. I looked away, and my eyes settled on the framed prom photo on my dresser. Then I glanced around the room at every other reminder of Robert. I grabbed a plastic bin from my closet and decided that it was time to box anything that had to do with him. Within five minutes, I had over two and half years' worth of memories shoved under the bed. It made me feel better, but there was still a weird sense of unease that made me tense, like something bad was going to happen.

One thing was apparent: there was no way I could concentrate in my room. I heard my mom in the kitchen, so I bounded down the stairs.

Before I could open my mouth, she asked, "Do you know what your plans are for tonight?"

"The girls are carpooling to a movie from Campbell Perk. I thought I could hang out with them for a bit, then stay behind to get caught up on homework."

She raised her brow while she contemplated my answer. I was in *huge* trouble for letting my grades slip after the breakup.

When she still hadn't answered, I added, "I promise I'm gonna ace my unit tests on Monday. There won't be a C on my report card."

"Then you can go. You think you'll be out past dark?" She had that pinched, worried look.

"Um hmmm, but they have to pick up their cars afterwards. I'll see if they'll meet me for dessert after the movie so we can walk to our cars together." I tried to look convincing so she wouldn't insist on driving me there and picking me up. That would be entirely too humiliating.

"Check with them. If you go as a group to your cars, it's okay."

"K. I'll check." I started a group text as I went back upstairs. I had my answer in under a minute. "Mom!" I yelled downstairs. "They said they can walk me back to my car."

"Okay, sweetie. Do you want me to pack you some food?"

"That would be awesome, thanks."

I started throwing supplies in my bag. The groan of the garage door opening made me realize it had to be close to 5:30 —my dad was home. I darted into the bathroom to touch up a little and headed downstairs.

My dad was already seated on a barstool at the granite counter, chatting with my mom as she cooked. They were both giggling about something that had happened at my dad's work, but I wasn't curious enough to ask.

Mom handed me my food as I gave my dad a huge hug from behind. We chatted for thirty seconds before he stopped to call my younger brother from his comics to set the table. I wanted to get to the café, so I said my goodbyes and mussed my brother's hair on my way out.

It was a short drive to the café. I pulled into the free parking garage two blocks from my destination and walked the remainder of the distance. A little extra studying, and I would be back on track.

I strolled into Campbell Perk Coffee Roasting Company and was pleased to find my favorite overstuffed leather chair in the corner available. I dumped my stuff on the table next to it to reserve it for my friends while there were still plenty of vacant tables. The café was laid out in a long L shape, with mustard-colored walls and a huge fireplace. Large mismatched rugs kept the sound from echoing as mellow music mingled with the aroma of coffee and sweet cream.

I looked around to see whether it was safe to leave my stuff unattended while I ordered; it was. When I got to the counter, my favorite barista was working. Becca already had my zebra mocha ready for me.

"I saw you come in," she greeted, grinning.

"I guess I'm that predictable, huh?"

"It's not a bad thing to be predictable."

"Yeah, I guess not. It's kind of fun to be able to order the usual. Not that anyone besides you would know what that is."

"Miles would," she whispered, glancing over her shoulder. "Pretty sure he has a crush on you."

I rolled my eyes. "Don't let him get his hopes up," I grumbled. *Soooo not ready for boys with crushes right now.*

"He's a nice guy." She shrugged.

"I'm sure he is. I mean, he seems nice. I just don't know him."

"Okay, no pressure. But, I haven't seen you in here with your boyfriend in a while. I think Miles has noticed too."

"Yeah, that. Hmmm. You probably won't see him much anymore," I added, not wanting to go into any more detail. I didn't think my local coffee shop employees needed to know all the details of my messed up love life.

"You okay?" She frowned.

"Yeah, things are good. I gotta get to studying though," I said, then went back the get the studying over with.

Sitting down, I curled my legs underneath me and scanned my to-do list. I decided to finish the last chapters of *The Great*

Gatsby. Afterwards, I wasn't exactly happy with the tragic ending, so I contemplated my mixed emotions.

I liked Gatsby's ability to hope, and I couldn't help but like Gatsby. His purity of love for Daisy was earth-moving. Too bad he had wasted it on her—she wasn't worthy of that type of love. I still had a hard time with the fact that he went after her when she was married. I wondered how it would feel to have someone love you so much and have it be illicit?

I closed the book and sipped what was left of my mocha. The girls would be arriving any moment now. While I waited, I picked at the food my mom had sent with me.

As I debated whether to start my next project, I leaned my head back and closed my eyes for a moment, smelling the leather chair and espresso. When I had cleared my head enough to pick up the next project, I heard Breanna laughing outside through the thick, plate glass windows. Her laugh was better than a homing beacon.

The bell on the glass door jingled as two girls entered, and Breanna practically bounced across the room, her straight, dark blonde hair swooshing back and forth with each move-ment. Her denim shorts were a little too short, and her t-shirt strained across her chest I moved my bag to the chair I was in and slipped into a seat at the table to join my friends.

"How's it going, sexy?" April purred, lifting her brows suggestively.

"Good. I finally completed *Gatsby*. I only need to finish reading a play and do some review."

"So, what are the chances that you will go to the movie with us?" she asked hopefully.

"Sorry, I promised my mom I would get caught up. *Believe me*. I would rather be with you guys. I promise I'll hang out more after finals. So much, you'll be sick of me." I winked. "We're doing a study session tomorrow, right?"

"Yes, and you better," she threatened.

Just as I was about to add more, Marie and Kaela strolled in. They were my two closest friends in our group. Marie was about to open her mouth and ask me something when April interrupted.

"Nope, already asked her."

"Just dessert later tonight then," Marie confirmed.

I nodded.

"Okay, but you better be here after the movie. Don't you *dare* walk to your car alone. Did you see that another girl went missing in the North Bay two days ago?" Kaela said, driving home the point.

I swallowed. "No, I hadn't. Where?"

Marie answered, "Pacifica. We are serious. No walking to your car alone. I'm blonde, so *I'm* totally fine. But *you* ain't so lucky." She flicked her waves comically. She was joking, but at the same time, totally serious. That was the fourth girl in the in the Bay Area to go missing. All of them were average height, fair skinned, light eyed, brunette, and between the ages of sixteen to twenty. *So* not good for me.

Both Kaela and April were brunettes, but Kaela was just five feet tall. April had olive skin and huge brown eyes, so I was the only one who fit the profile.

Marie pushed my shoulder. "And, by the way, we are splitting lava cake later."

I saluted Marie, and with pursed lips, she dismissed me in a return salute. Since the breakup, I had become a hermit. Marie was leading our group in my absence, even though she hated it. I was grateful, and as soon as school was out, I was sure I would be ready to take over again and things would get back to normal.

The five of us bantered back and forth for the next forty-five minutes. The girls ordered their coffees to go and gleefully left to watch the movie, promising to see me in a little over two hours.

I decided to stay at the table and cleared my stuff from the leather chair. Flipping open *The Tempest*, I let Shakespeare's words saturate my brain, getting lost in the vocabulary and wishing we spoke as articulately today. My vocabulary was larger than normal; consequently, my friends were always teasing me about my word choices.

I stretched and glanced up at the counter just as Miles shot a jealous look towards the door. Confused, I peeked over at the entering customers. Robert, Peter, Tyler, and Mark were weaving their way to the counter.

Furious didn't begin to explain how I felt. This was *my* hangout, *my* safe place, and Robert knew that. Was he checking up on me? Why would he choose to come here? It wasn't like it was anywhere near his home. I tried to keep calm, hoping that they would get their drinks and leave, but I wasn't that lucky.

They settled in two tables away. Tyler looked at me contemptuously every so often. I could see the veins running over his lean muscles, his skin already glowing with a fresh tan. He would have been good looking if it wasn't for his personality. I growled internally. He was wicked smart, but he always used it to manipulate others. I was sure he'd been talking trash about me to Robert every moment he could. And Mark was easily swayed by Tyler's negativity. Mark was the reason people stereotype jocks.

Peter was my only ally in the group. I missed him more than any of the others, but I understood that he couldn't be my friend anymore. He couldn't bear being split in two; he was my oddly charismatic, yet introverted poet friend.

Peter stood at a few of inches shy of six-feet tall and was a water polo player at our school, his light brown hair perennially sun-bleached, even in winter, and his skin always golden. His eyes were like dark-chocolate and always seemed to shine, like they were a beacon showing his kind soul. He loved me, but his loyalty was to Robert, and I could never begrudge him that. He had apologized profusely to me, but he couldn't handle hanging out with both of us.

After a while, Robert stood up and disappeared into the restroom. Mark and Tyler took advantage of his absence. Mark started tossing bits of a pastry at me, crumbs scattering all over my table. I tried to ignore them, staring intently at my book, gritting my teeth. My jaw started to throb, so I relaxed my mouth.

A larger chunk landed on my shoulder and debris went into my hair and down my dark button-down shirt. I still tried to maintain my cool, but shot them a disgusted glance. I could see that Peter was trying to dissuade them, but Tyler was prodding Mark.

Tyler hissed "slut" through his teeth, and I saw Peter smack him on the shoulder. This only encouraged Tyler, and a whole string of derogatory comments meant for me slid through his teeth.

Cussing was never my thing, but some expletives were definitely coming to mind. I sat, deciding whether to fight or to flee—wavering back and forth. They were acting like I had committed some unspeakable crime, like I had cheated or purposely tried to hurt Robert. I was not guilty of either crime, yet I still felt guilt the size of a small planet.

I didn't know if it was worse to be the dumper or dump-ee. I had never said anything bad about Robert, nor was I planning on it, but his friends were making my patience wear thin.

I slipped the books I wasn't using into my bag and looked at the clock on my phone. The girls wouldn't be back for at least a half hour, and it was now very dark outside. I could have called my parents, but I didn't want to bother them. I was sure I would be safe for two blocks by myself, even though warning bells were going off in my head.

Or, I could just walk over and punch Mark in the face and return the favor from earlier today. My anger started growing, and I clenched my fists until my nails began biting into my palms and my knuckles turned white.

Mark laughed at me goadingly, his ruddy face infuriating.

Robert returned, and the boys seemed to settle down a little bit, but it was too late. Mark was going down. All four of them looked at me as I stood up. My chair popped back loudly from behind me. But at that exact moment, I felt a light touch on my elbow and an unfamiliar voice charmingly said, "Hey, honey, are you ready to go?"

I looked up, bewildered, my adrenaline pumping and ready for confrontation. And then I felt even more baffled, as I had no clue who this guy was, but he was...*beautiful*.

ACKNOWLEDGMENTS

Of course, I need to begin with my ever patient husband, who faithfully supports me in all of my endeavors. You are still my rock.

Beth, an overwhelming amount of appreciation for faithfully trudging through the first draft. Your ability to both tear things apart and still be reassuring is amazing. You are definitely my number one fan in the 25-40 category. ;)

Alexis, you once again dazzle me with your mad skills. Thanks for all the hours amidst your hectic schedule. And thank you for loving this book so much.

Rachel, thanks for the constant encouragement and for listening when I need to think out loud. I appreciate you tracking all the threads and pointing out all of the "funky syntax."

Rachel (trudreamr), I appreciate all that you do on the fan site and for helping with last minute edits. Your enthusiasm helps spur me on. You are definitely my biggest fan in the 16-25 bracket. See how I solved that? Xoxo.

James, thanks for helping me streamline some of the chapters. And to Tamar, thanks for pouring through proofs in search of errors.

And yes, there are still others: thanks to Lisa K., Rebecca K., Micaela G., Kristina D., Judi H., Jessie L., Amy A., Shanda

A., and Roy for giving me both feedback and encouragement. Laura S., you are a good sport; maybe someday I'll write about that practical joke. I'm sure I missed someone. Thanks to everyone for all of the support.

Vera Walker, You continue to amaze me with your graphic design wizardry. You achieved epic status on this one.

Chronological Order

For ultimate suspense, read
the prequel after book two.

Extras can be
read along
with the books

The Watcher Series

The Unintended: Book One

The Nexus: Book Two

The Sacrifice: Book Three

The Fallen: Part One: Book Four

The Fallen: Part Two: Book Five

Allure: A Watcher Series Prequel

Light & Shadow: The Watcher Series Shorts & Extras

Storm and Solace: A Beauty & the Beast Retelling

In this *Beauty & the Beast* role-swapping mashup, Saxa is stripped of her powers and cursed by her two sisters. She has twelve weeks to change her ways or lose everything—including her life.

Brandr, shipwrecked after a terrible storm, is swept into the world of gods and goddesses. When he trades his life for his brother's, he sentences himself to a world he knows nothing about.

When their paths collide, nothing is as it seems. Who will survive this game of immortals?

ALSO BY ROBIN WOODS

Creative & Fiction Writing Books

For Larger Projects

Prompt Me Novel: Fiction Writing Workbook & Journal

General Inspiration

Prompt Me: Creative Writing Workbook & Journal

Prompt Me More: Workbook & Journal

Prompt Me Again: Workbook & Journal

Genre Specific

Prompt Me Sci-Fi & Fantasy: Workbook & Journal

Prompt Me Romance: Workbook & Journal

Prompt Me Horror & Thriller: Workbook & Journal

Prompt Me Mystery & Suspense: Workbook & Journal

Reading Log

Prompt Me Reading Log & Analysis: Workbook & Journal

ABOUT THE AUTHOR

Robin Woods is a former high school and university instructor with two and a half decades of experience teaching English, literature, and writing. She earned a BA in English and an MA in Education.

In addition to teaching, she has published six novels, eight creative writing books (and counting), and has multiple projects in the works.

When Ms. Woods isn't chasing her two elementary school kids around, she's spending time with her ever-patient husband, or sitting in a coffee shop wondering how vampires like their lattes.

For more information, an extended bio, free writing resources, links to social media, and free extra scenes, visit her website at www.robinwoodsfiction.com

Thank you for reading. If you enjoyed this novel, please take a moment to write a review. It is the best way to help authors you love. Blessings!